MEANT FOR HER

Christopher

I came from the biggest hockey family in the NHL.

Records were set by my grandfather, my father, and now my brother.

I was taught to love the game, but more than that, I learned early on the men you play with are your family.

You get on the ice every night and protect them, celebrate the wins, and pick each other up when you fall.

So when we lost Benji, I stepped in to help his wife and kids, but this pull I feel when it comes to them is something more than I can even understand.

Dakota

My life was perfect until six months ago.

Gone was the husband I thought I knew and in his place was a stranger.

I saw him change before my eyes.

Then he was gone, leaving me and our girls alone.

I wanted nothing to do with anyone or anything that took him away from me.

But no matter how many times I've told his best friend I don't need help,

he's there doing things for us, and the worst part is I want him to.

BOOKS BY NATASHA MADISON

Southern Wedding Series
Mine To Kiss
Mine To Have
Mine To Cherish
Mine to Love
Mine To Take
Mine To Promise
Mine to Honor
Mine to Keep

The Only One Series
Only One Kiss
Only One Chance
Only One Night
Only One Touch
Only One Regret
Only One Mistake
Only One Love
Only One Forever

Southern Series
Southern Chance
Southern Comfort
Southern Storm
Southern Sunrise
Southern Heart
Southern Heat
Southern Secrets
Southern Sunshine

This Is
This is Crazy
This Is Wild
This Is Love
This Is Forever

Hollywood Royalty
Hollywood Playboy
Hollywood Princess
Hollywood Prince

Something So Series
Something Series
Something So Right
Something So Perfect
Something So Irresistible
Something So Unscripted
Something So BOX SET

Tempt Series
Tempt The Boss
Tempt The Playboy
Tempt The Ex
Tempt The Hookup
Heaven & Hell Series
Hell And Back
Pieces Of Heaven

Love Series
Perfect Love Story
Unexpected Love Story
Broken Love Story

Faux Pas
Mixed Up Love
Until Brandon

STONE FAMILY TREE
SOMETHING SO, THIS IS ONLY ONE & MADE FOR FAMILY TREE!

SOMETHING SO SERIES
Something So Right
Parker & Cooper Stone
Matthew Grant (Something So Perfect)
Allison Grant (Something So Irresistible)
Zara Stone (This Is Crazy)
Zoe Stone (This Is Wild)
Justin Stone (This Is Forever)

Something So Perfect
Matthew Grant & Karrie Cooley
Cooper Grant (Only One Regret)
Frances Grant (Only One Love)
Vivienne Grant (Made For You)
Chase Grant (Made For Me)

Something So Irresistible
Allison Grant & Max Horton
Michael Horton (Only One Mistake)
Alexandria Horton (Only One Forever)
Something So Unscripted
Denise Horton & Zack Morrow
Jack Morrow
Joshua Morrow
Elizabeth Morrow

THIS IS SERIES
This Is Crazy
Zara Stone & Evan Richards
Zoey Richards
Stone Richards (Meant For Stone)

This Is Wild
Zoe Stone & Viktor Petrov
Matthew Petrov (Mine To Take)
Zara Petrov

This Is Love
Vivienne Paradis & Mark Dimitris
Karrie Dimitris
Stefano Dimitris (Mine to Promise)
Angelica Dimitris
Zoe Stone & Viktor Petrov
Matthew Petrov
Zara Petrov
This Is Forever
Caroline Woods & Justin Stone
Dylan Stone (Formally Woods)
Christopher Stone
Gabriella Stone
Abigail Stone
ONLY ONE SERIES
Only One Kiss
Candace Richards & Ralph Weber
Ariella Weber
Brookes Weber
Only One Chance
Layla Paterson & Miller Adams
Clarke Adams
Only One Night
Evelyn & Manning Stevenson
Jaxon Stevenson
Victoria Stevenson
Only One Touch
Becca & Nico Harrison
Phoenix Harrison
Dallas Harrison

Only One Regret
Erika & Cooper Grant

Emma Grant

Mia Grant

Parker Grant

Matthew Grant

Only One Mistake
Jillian & Michael Horton

Jamieson Horton

Only One Love
Frances Grant & Brad Wilson

Stella Wilson

Only One Forever
Dylan Stone & Alex Horton

Maddox Stone

Maya Stone

Maverick Stone

MADE FOR SERIES

Made For Me
Julia & Chase Grant

Made For You
Vivienne Grant & Xavier Montgomery

Made For Us
Abigail Stone & Tristan Weise

Penelope

Payton

Made For Romeo
Romeo Beckett & Gabriella Stone

Meant For Stone
Stone Richards & Ryleigh Beckett

Meant For Her
Christopher Stone & Dakota

Luna

Rain

Southern Wedding Family Tree

Mine To Have

Travis & Harlow

Charlotte

Theo

Mine To Hold

Shelby & Ace

Arya

Mine To Cherish

Clarabella & Luke

Zander

Mine To Love

Presley & Bennett

Cadence

Charleigh

Mine To Take

Sofia and Matty Petrov

Mine To Promise

Stefano Dimitris & Addison

Avery

Mine To Honor

Levi & Eva

Cici

Mine To Keep

Grace & Caine

Meadow

SOUTHERN TREE

Southern Family tree

Billy and Charlotte
(Mother and father to Kallie and Casey)

Southern Chance

Kallie & Jacob McIntyre

Ethan McIntyre (Savannah Son)

Amelia (Southern Secrets)

Travis

Southern Comfort

Olivia & Casey Barnes

Quinn (Southern Heat)

Reed (Southern Sunshine)

Harlow (Mine to Have)

Southern Storm

Savannah & Beau Huntington

Ethan McIntyre (Jacob's son)

Chelsea (Southern Heart)

Toby

Keith

Southern Sunrise

Emily & Ethan McIntyre

Gabriel

Aubrey

Southern Heart

Chelsea Huntington & Mayson Carey

Tucker

Southern Heat

Willow & Quinn Barnes

Grace (Mine To Keep)

Charlie

Southern Secrets
Amelia McIntyre & Asher
JB Normand
Southern Sunshine
Hazel & Reed Barnes
Sofia (Mine To Take)
Kaine
Denver

Copyright © 2024 Natasha Madison. E-Book and Print Edition
All rights reserved. No part of this book may be reproduced or transmitted in any form or by any means, electronic or mechanical, including photocopying, recording, or by any information storage and retrieval system, without permission in writing.

This is a work of fiction. Names, characters, places and incidents are the product of the author's imagination or are used factiously, and any resemblance to any actual persons or living or dead, events or locals are entirely coincidental.

The author acknowledges the trademark status and trademark owners of various products referenced in this work of fiction, which have been used without permission. The publication/ Use of these trademarks is not authorized, associated with, or sponsored by the trademark owner.

All rights reserved

Cover Design: Jay Aheer

Photo by Wander Aguiar Photography

Editing done by Karen Hrdicka Barren Acres Editing

Editing done by Jenny Sims Editing4Indies

Proofing Julie Deaton by Deaton Author Services

Proofing by Judy'sProofreading

Formatting by Christina Parker Smith

meant for HER

NATASHA MADISON

ONE

KODA

THE BED DIPS beside me as I slowly open my eyes. The sunlight streams in from the side curtains as I wait to see who's climbing into bed. Soft movement behind me has me guessing it's one of my girls. I smile and wait for it, then I feel it. The knee in the back as they try to crawl on the bed, then the hand on my shoulder. "Mommy," Luna says, trying not to speak loud but not knowing how to whisper. "Mommy, I awake." She leans over me, shoving her face into mine. Her soft brown hair falls around her face and lands on mine, tickling me.

I try not to laugh when I roll over and wrap my arms around her, bringing her to me. "Happy birthday, my little one." I turn, cuddling her in my arms as I kiss her neck four times. "Four birthday kisses," I say, kissing her again three times, this time as she giggles in my ear. "So what does the birthday girl want for breakfast?"

She releases a huge sigh as if she's deciding the future of the world. "I want pancakes." She turns to me. "No, no." She holds out her index finger. "Waffles." Her eyes go big and the smile even bigger. "Wait, no." She gets on her knees. "French toast." I wait for it, knowing that she'll change her mind again. "Mommy." She claps her hands. "Breakfast taco!" She folds her hands together. "Like Uncle Chrissy." I throw the cover off me as I slide my feet into my pink Ugg slippers. "Pancake with scrappled eggs."

"Scrambled," I correct her, and she nods.

"And sausage." She holds both her hands outstretched. "With maple syrup."

"That's a big breakfast," I tell her. "Don't forget, we have your birthday party this afternoon."

"I'm hungry." She stands in the middle of my bed in her pink nightgown. "Like a hungry, hungry hippo."

I chuckle and look at the side table where my phone is, touching the screen to see that it's just after 6:00 a.m., giving me enough time to make her the breakfast tacos, and she will still be okay for her birthday party.

"Okay, I'm going to brush my teeth, and you should do the same." I move my hand in front of my nose. "You almost killed me with your morning breath."

She bounces from her feet to her bum, then scoots off the bed. "Your breath smells gooey."

She runs out of my room. "Don't wake your sister up," I warn softly. She looks over her shoulder and smirks at me when she gets to my door, just like her father.

I stand here for a minute, looking at the side of the bed that has again gone unslept in. I look down at my feet before walking toward my bathroom.

The white floors shine in the sunlight. The four windows brighten the room so much you don't have to turn on any lights during the day. I use the toilet, then walk over to the double sink, grabbing my pink toothbrush from the middle cabinet. As I brush my teeth, I ignore looking over at Benji's side of the bathroom. His side still has stuff out from last night when he used it before he went out to meet some friends, instead of staying in with me and watching a movie or just staying with the kids.

I put my toothbrush back before I wipe my hands on the white hand towel. Then I grab my phone and walk toward the double doors. Rain's door is still closed, which means she's still sleeping. She's six going on thirteen, but I think she's seeing a lot of things kids shouldn't see. Walking down the winding staircase, I see Benji's keys on the table at the door. "At least he's home," I mumble as I walk past the formal dining room we hardly use.

I make my way to the back of the house, where we spend most of our time. When I walk into the kitchen, I look over to the family room and see Benji sleeping on the couch, one foot on the floor, one on the couch. His pants are unbuckled, and his shirt is lifted on one side. His collar is stained with what looks like red lipstick. Nine months ago, this would have cut me off at my knees. Now, it's just like a kick in the stomach. I walk closer to him, his head turned to the side where he has the same color of stain on the side of his neck. His scruff from not shaving for the past two weeks is getting thicker, but that's what you get when you're on summer vacation. I notice a small plastic bag with two white pills in it on the coffee table.

My blood boils when I hear footsteps on the stairs. I bend down and grab the bag in my hand before turning around and bending to knock his hand. He mumbles in his sleep before he turns his head to the side. The footsteps sound closer, so this time, I bend down and push his shoulder, making his eyes snap open. "Huh?" He looks at me, trying to get his eyes to focus. "What?"

"Luna is up and coming down the stairs," I tell him, "and you stink like a skank. She even left her mark on you this time." I point at his neck, and he rolls his eyes right before he turns over.

"Stop busting my balls," he mumbles, "it was a friend."

"Trust me, the last thing I want is to get anywhere near your balls," I hiss at him. "Now get the fuck up, your daughter is coming."

I kick the couch before turning away and walking into the kitchen. "Daddy!" Luna shouts his name as she runs into the room and jumps on the couch. I toss the contents of the plastic bag into the garbage disposal before turning on the water and starting it, hoping that it makes more noise than it should.

"Daddy, Daddy," Luna calls out again. This time sitting next to him as his face is turned away from her, his arm now wrapped around her bottom to make sure she doesn't fall. "Daddy, it's my birthday," she announces to him proudly.

"Yeah," he slurs. "Happy…" His eyes close.

I grit my teeth. "Luna, why don't you come and help me make the pancakes." I smile at her, hoping she comes without asking any questions. "Benji!" I shout his name, and he lifts his head. "Go lie down upstairs in the playroom."

He sits up, kissing Luna on the top of the head, before stumbling to his feet and walking out of the room. I watch him walk out before turning back to see Luna on the couch watching her father walk away. "Do you want to do the eggs for the pancake tacos?" I ask, trying to redirect her attention. It doesn't take much since she's only four.

She comes running into the kitchen, standing beside the big gray marble island, hopping on the chair I have at the side. "I want to do the eggs," she informs me, and I walk over to start the pod in the coffee machine first before walking over to the industrial, double-doored, stainless-steel fridge. Opening it, I grab the clear basket that holds the eggs. I put it in the middle of the island before bending down to grab a plastic mixing bowl.

"Here you go." I put the bowl in front of her and grab two eggs. "Start with this." She smiles at me as I walk to grab my coffee.

"Mom," Rain says when she walks into the kitchen, rubbing the sleep from her eyes, "Dad came into my bedroom and fell on my bed." She walks around the island to come to me. I open my arms for her as she hugs me around my waist. "And he stinks."

"He needs to brush his teeth," Luna states, cracking the egg on the counter and then smashing it in her hands and into the bowl, shells and all.

"I'm making breakfast tacos for Luna's birthday," I say. She smiles at me, then walks over to Luna.

"Happy birthday, Luna." She gets on her stool with her.

"Why don't you two go watch television, and I can cook breakfast?" I urge them as Rain steps off the stool and holds her hand out for her. Luna steps down and puts her hand in her sister's as they walk to the family room.

Five hours later, my in-laws are ringing the doorbell and entering the house. "Where is the birthday girl?" my father-in-law, Eddie, says.

"It's me! It's me!" Luna runs out of my bedroom toward the stairs. "I'm the birthday girl."

"Be careful!" I shout as I hear her walking down the stairs before sliding my feet into my black sling-back shoes.

"You grew overnight," my mother-in-law, Gretchen, says to her.

"Hey," Benji mumbles before entering our bedroom. "What the fuck are my parents doing here so early?"

"It's almost noon, and the guests will be here for your daughter's birthday party in an hour," I remind him. "You know, the thing we've discussed all week."

He runs his hands through his black hair. "Yeah, I know. I just thought it was earlier than noon."

"Well, when you walk into the house at five thirty, noon feels like six o'clock, I guess."

"Are you keeping tabs on me?" He puts his hands on his hips.

"You think I have time to keep tabs on you?" I shake my head. "I have two kids to keep up with. The last person I have time to keep tabs on is a grown-ass adult."

"Sounded like you were keeping track of when I was coming and going." He takes his shirt off, and I see the bite mark right next to his nipple. He's not even trying to hide anything these days. I blink away the tears fighting to come out.

"Not that you can comprehend anything when you are like this"—I walk over to grab my phone and put it in the back pocket of my white jeans—"but we have a Ring cam that alerts me when someone is at the door." I look over at him as he pulls down his pants, leaving him in just his boxers. "That's the only reason I know what time you came home."

"Don't be a pain in the ass." He tosses his pants toward his closet. "I have the biggest headache."

"I bet," I mumble. "For today, we can pretend it's all shits and giggles," I say to his retreating back as he walks into the bathroom, "but I'd like to have a conversation with you."

"About?" he asks over his shoulder. "I really have to focus on my training." He mentions his off-ice training that he should be doing but isn't putting effort into it.

"Well, I'm sure you can spare me a couple of minutes," I throw over my shoulder, walking out of the bedroom and closing the door.

Walking down to the kitchen, I find the caterer setting up. "Hi," I say as I make my way to the backyard, where it's being transformed into a carnival-themed birthday party. They are setting up the blow-up bouncy houses next to the popcorn stand.

"Mommy," Luna says, running to me, "they brought a pony." When she tells me, my eyes go big, and I smile.

"Grandma says I get a turn first because it's my special day." She jumps up and down, and all I can do is smile at her. *Nothing is going to ruin her day*.

Benji comes out thirty minutes later, wearing shorts and a T-shirt, his hair still wet from the shower. His bloodshot eyes are now clear thanks to either his eye drops or who knows what else. He stops beside me for a second. "Hey," he says, kissing my cheek as if nothing was just said before. As if he didn't come home after God knows what. "This is nice. Where is the birthday girl?" He looks around and walks away from me in Luna's direction.

"He looks good, right?" I look to my right, where my father-in-law watches Benji tickle a squealing Luna.

"Yeah, keep telling yourself that," I say before being called inside about something. I don't get a chance to say anything else because guests start arriving.

For the whole afternoon, we both pretend that our life isn't falling apart. Or at least I'm pretending. I'll do what I need to do to make sure my girl has the best birthday.

Even when the cake comes out, and we stand behind it with the girls in front of us, we pose for pictures like we've done a thousand times before. His hand is around my waist, but I put one hand on each girl's shoulder instead of around him.

Guests stay way after the kids' bedtime. When I

finally walk upstairs with Luna sleeping on my shoulder, Rain trails me. "Go put your pj's on," I tell her as I walk into Luna's room, taking off her shoes. I just let her sleep in the shorts and T-shirt she changed into when she got soaking wet after accidentally turning on the hose to help the pony get a drink of water.

Closing Luna's door softly behind me and walking into Rain's room, I see Benji walking into the house at the same time. "I'm going to go for a drive." He looks up at me and walks out the front door, closing it softly behind him.

I tuck Rain in before walking back to my bedroom and getting ready for bed. I'm so tired I fall asleep within a couple of minutes.

I'm the first to wake up the following morning, seeing it's just a bit after seven. I slide my slippers on and go to make myself a coffee before everyone wakes up. Seeing Benji on the couch again, I roll my eyes, going over to him. His skin looks so pale, and when I get closer to him, I know something is wrong. I bend down and shake him, but his body feels stiff and cold to the touch. "Benji!" I shout his name while the back of my neck feels like it's on fire. Even the follicles on my head are hot and tingly. "Benji!" I yell again, my voice more frantic as I try to nudge his shoulder. "Oh my God. Oh my God." I put my hand to my mouth at the same time I hear footsteps on the stairs. My fear turns to panic as I run out of the room and meet Luna at the bottom of the stairs. "Go upstairs," I urge her, and she just whines.

"I'm hungry." I don't wait to answer her before I pick

her up and run up the stairs. On the way to my bedroom, I see Rain come out of hers. "Don't go downstairs!" I shriek. "Come in my bedroom, now." I don't wait for her to come to me. Instead, I walk to her and grab her hand by the wrist and drag her with us into my room. The tears are now freely running down my face. I put Luna down on her feet, closing the bedroom door behind me and standing in front of it. "Go get me my phone." I point at my bedside table, the girls looking at me with fear. "Rain," I say to her, "please go and get me my phone right now."

She runs to my bedside table, bringing the phone back to me, and I dial my father-in-law, Eddie, who answers after one ring. "Hello."

"Eddie," I say his name as the sob rips through me, "you need to come over here. Benji—" My knees give out on me as I sink to the floor, knowing my life will never again be the same from this day forward.

TWO

CHRISTOPHER

"WHY ARE THERE so many people here?" I look over at my brother, Dylan, who is sitting on one of the daybeds in the middle of the beach. "And why the fuck is it so loud?" Kids running and adults laughing and talking combine with the DJ who is set up, and it is noise overload.

"You can blame Zoey and Gabriella for that." He mentions my cousin Zoey and our sister, Gabriella, as he looks out at everyone around us. "They mocked Uncle Matthew yesterday, saying his vacations were becoming boring with a capital B. I thought his head would explode. His eyes started to twitch." He laughs, remembering the conversation from yesterday. It's our annual summer vacation, where we are finally all off and together. Since most of the guys play hockey and are in the league, their only free time is after playoffs. So we started doing the family vacation, but Matty's wife's family has also joined us this year, so it's close to over two hundred people. We bitch and complain about this family vacation all year round, but once we're here, everyone remembers why we come. It's the best time of the year, and I wouldn't trade it for anything in the world.

"I'm hungry," I state, looking around and finally seeing my cousin Stone walking to the beach with his girlfriend, Ryleigh, beside him. The two of them met at Gabriella and Romeo's house party, Ryleigh being Romeo's sister.

"Look at those two." I point at them, and Dylan laughs as Ryleigh squints at the noise. "She looks like she's going to barf." He gets up. "I'm going to look for my wife."

"You think of barfing and automatically think of your wife," I joke. He flips me the bird as I also get up off the daybed.

I shake my head as I make my way through the throngs of people. I spot my grandfather, Cooper, sitting with my uncles Matthew and Max. "Hey," I greet, walking over to him and kissing him on his cheek.

"Are you staying out of trouble?" he asks, leaning back to look at me with a smile. He's at the top of most of the boards, even after retiring so long ago. He's the one you're always competing to beat his records. My brother, Dylan, has beat a couple of them, but he still holds most of them and happily points it out every single time.

"Me?" I point at my chest. "I'm never trouble."

"Please," my uncle Matthew says, "didn't you leave with the server?"

I scoff at him, putting my hand in the middle of my

chest as if he hurt my feelings. "Uncle Matthew, you think I would sleep with a server who will be around for a whole week? That would be a rookie mistake. She'd follow me all week and cockblock me for everyone else." I wink at him.

"I don't know if I should be proud of what he just said or smack him upside the head," my uncle Max ponders while my grandfather laughs.

"Well, either way, I win." I look over to see Stone coming to grab some food. "I'm going to get some food." I look over at the buffet. "Talk later."

I walk a couple of steps to catch up with Stone. "You look tired as shit," he says to me once he's standing behind me at the buffet line, holding two plates in his hand.

"Yeah, I woke up being kicked in the balls by Payton, who thought it was a good idea." I mention my nephew, who snuck into my room through the back door that I didn't lock. I will never make that mistake again.

I load up my plate and start having lunch with my father and mother, and then thirty of us end up at the table. I get up when Dylan calls me to go with him in the water with his son, Maddox.

We're walking on the hot sand when we spot Stone and Ryleigh in the water hugging. "I hope they aren't banging in the water," Maddox states, making me laugh. Stone looks over at us, and then he and Ryleigh walk out of the water.

"I have to put my phone down," I tell my brother, who nods and continues into the water. I'm halfway to the chairs when I spot Stone, "Did you guys bang in the ocean?" I tease them. "No one wanted to send the kids in."

Stone just gawks at me when the phone in my hand rings. "Why the fuck is Coach calling me?" I press the green button and put it to my ear, hoping like fuck I'll hear him with all the background noise. "Hey, Coach." I smile, putting one finger in the other ear.

"Christopher." His voice cracks, and I see my uncles Matthew and Max rushing to get to me. I feel like the ground is spinning when I hear his next words. "I don't know how to tell you this, but it's Benji." The bile rises from my stomach. "He's gone." The phone drops from my hand into the sand.

My hand goes to my mouth as the blood drains from my body. "Benji's dead."

Stone looks at me, his face going as white as mine feels. "What do you mean?" he asks, reaching down for the phone. "Hello," he says into the phone, "it's Stone Richards."

I hear the commotion around me, but all I can hear is the echo of my heart beating in my ears. I feel like the beach spins all around me. "I got him," someone says, and I feel arms around me as I'm being carried off the beach. I look over and see some of the women with tears streaming down their faces. I don't even know how I make it to my room, but I'm sitting in a chair while my sisters Gabriella and Abigail run around my room packing stuff.

"I think he's in shock," my father says beside me. I

look over at Uncle Matthew, who types on his phone while Max talks on his. Stone stands in the back next to his father and the rest of my uncles, waiting in the wings for me to ask them to do something.

"What can we do to help?" Casey, Sofia's grandfather, asks when he comes into my room.

"We're getting him on a plane now," Max tells Casey.

"The girls." The words finally come out of my mouth, as I think of Koda and their girls. "How are the girls?" It's the stupidest question I think I've asked in my life. How are the girls? How do you think the girls are? His girls are probably fucking devastated.

"From what I got"—Matthew comes to me and squats down in front of me—"Koda found him this morning unresponsive."

I shake my head. "I spoke to him yesterday," I say, trying to make sense of this. "It was Luna's fourth birthday. He called to tell me thanks for the Barbie Jeep I bought her." I look over when Abigail sobs, and Gabriella rushes over to her, putting her arm around her shoulders. My hands go to the top of my head. "This can't be happening."

I don't know how I get dressed, but I'm walking up the steps to the plane forty-five minutes later. "I need to call Koda." I look over at Stone, who hasn't left my side since all of this happened. I reach into the back pocket of my jeans and pat it, but it's empty. "My phone?" I say, looking around in a panic.

"I got it," Stone assures me, handing it to me as Ryleigh boards the plane and sits in front of me.

"You guys don't have to come with me," I tell them. I pull up Koda's name and see the last time we texted was right before the season ended when I asked her about stuff for the kids. I originally texted Benji, but he just brushed it off and said to ask Koda.

"What the fuck do I even say?" I look up at both of them.

"How about you just ask how she's doing?" Stone suggests. "Or if she needs anything."

"I can tell you right now how she's doing. She's probably devastated and in shock." I look down at the screen.

"I don't think you should text or call her," Ryleigh says softly. "I think she's going to be overwhelmed right now, and her main focus will be the girls. I think you get home and tomorrow morning you show up at her house."

"That isn't the worst idea," I say, my foot moving up and down with nerves as the door closes.

"Uncle Matthew is meeting us there for the funeral," my father shares. "It took everything in him not to jump on this plane." There was no fucking way my father would have let me get on this plane without him. Even if I told him not to come, he would be on another plane right behind me.

I look out the window, listening to the two of them talk, my head swimming with all kinds of questions. My phone is blowing up in my hand with texts from teammates and other players in the league who knew how tight Benji and I were.

We got drafted in the same year and have been on

the same team since. Fuck, I was the best man at his wedding. I was there for it all. Rain and Luna are like my nieces, and every game they would come to, I would throw pucks over the glass. Five hours in the air feels like a blur. When we land, an SUV waits to take us to my house. "Are you going to answer your phone?" Ryleigh asks when we get into the SUV. I was so lost in memories I didn't even hear it ring.

I look down and see it's Eddie, Benji's dad, calling me. "Hello." I answer the phone, my voice cracking, my heart breaking as I think of what he's going through.

"Hey, son," he says, his voice heavy, "I just got your message."

I look down at my phone and pull up my messages, seeing I sent him a message to call me right away. A message I must have sent to him when everything was happening. "Eddie," I start, my voice thick as I feel the tears on my face, "I'm so sorry." The words are not enough. "What can I do to help?"

"We just left the funeral home…" He tries to hide his sobs. "I just left Koda at home."

I put my head back on the headrest, closing my eyes. "How is she doing?"

"She's a fucking rock—" he says, but then his voice goes lower. "I think she's in shock."

"I wanted to go see her and the girls." I look out the window at the streetlights passing me by in a blur. "I'm on my way home now, but it'll be after eleven."

"She just took something to try to sleep. The girls are in bed with her," he relays softly, "but it would be good if you came tomorrow."

"I'll be there as soon as you tell me I can be there," I tell him. Fuck, I would sleep outside the house if I had to.

"Come around nine. We should all be at her house by then. I know Coach and a couple of the other guys will be coming in the afternoon."

"Okay." I inhale. "I'll see you then." I disconnect the line and look over at Ryleigh, who has her head on Stone's shoulder. My father sits next to me, watching me more than anything else.

We pull up in my driveway, and I feel like I'm a robot just going through the motions. I dump my bags in the closet and take a shower. The whole night, I don't sleep, not one wink, the guilt starting to sink in.

At six o'clock, I finally get out of bed and make my way downstairs to make coffee. "Having trouble sleeping?" my father asks three minutes after I've gone to the kitchen. I just nod. "Do you want me to come with you?" The lump in my throat feels like it's clogging my breathing. All I can do is shake my head. "I'll drive you, wait for you in the car."

"I got it, Dad," I assure him, and all he does is look at me. He looks like he hasn't slept a wink all night. I go upstairs and get ready. Stone and Ryleigh haven't woken up by the time I leave at eight thirty to make my way to Benji's house.

My eyes feel like little pieces of sand are stuck under my eyelids as I walk up the four steps to the brown front door. I reach out, pressing the bell, hearing footsteps running to the door. "It's Uncle Christopher!" Rain shouts from inside the house. "I saw out the window." The door unlocks, and she swings it open.

"There is the prettiest six-year-old I've ever seen." I put a smile on my face, and all she does is smirk at me before I bend down and take her in my arms. I close my eyes, trying to fight the tears. "How are you doing?"

"I'm sad," she admits softly, and I don't have a chance to say anything else as Luna comes running to the door.

"It's Uncle Chrissy," she says, jumping up and down, excited to see me. I'm really hoping she doesn't remember the next couple of days.

"There is the birthday girl." I open my arm for her to run into the other side of me before I pick them both up and walk into the house. You can feel the tightness, and the tension fills the rooms. Even with the curtains all open and the sun coming in, you feel the sadness through the walls.

"You guys are getting heavy." I kiss their heads, walking from the front door to the family room. Eddie is there, his eyes bloodshot and puffy, no doubt from crying all night.

I put the girls down on their feet before walking over and hugging Eddie. "Thanks for coming," he says, and I look around for Koda.

"Where's Koda?" I ask.

"She's in the basement going through pictures to give to the…" He doesn't finish the sentence. "You can go down there with her. I'm going to take the girls out to my house for a bit. Change of scenery."

I nod at him, turning and walking to the basement

stairs. Benji used to call it his man cave. I put one foot in front of the other but don't race to get down there. My heart rises to my throat as I make it to the bottom step. The room has his jerseys hung in glass boxes from the whole time he's played. Hockey pucks are also on display from different points in his career. Pictures of him with different family members throughout the years, and then the one of him and me at the Winter Classic from two seasons ago. We froze our fucking asses off, and you can see our ears and noses are bright red.

I look around the room and don't see Koda anywhere. Then I hear the door open from the side, and she steps out. Her brown hair is piled on top of her head; she's wearing leggings with a white shirt. She stops mid step when she sees me, her eyes wet from crying, her nose also pink. "Hey," I say, not sure if I should go to her or not. "Eddie said you were down here." She comes into the room and stands facing me. "I'm sorry I wasn't here before."

"You're sorry," she practically hisses at me, and I can feel her anger. "I bet you're fucking sorry." Her chest rises and falls so much it's almost as if she ran a marathon. "Good to fucking know."

Her words shock me. "Koda," I say softly, "what can I do to help?"

"What can you do to help?" She laughs, but it comes out in a sob. She holds up her hand when I step toward her, stopping me in my tracks.

"I don't know, what can you do to help?" She shakes her head. "How about getting him some help?" She hisses out the words. "Don't tell me you didn't know something was wrong with him." The words slice me right into the chest, and it feels like someone is twisting my heart and squeezing it all at the same time. "I bet the whole fucking team knew that something was wrong with him, but what did you guys do?" Her voice is low. "Not a fucking thing. You just ignored all the fucking signs. You guys had to have known." She tilts her head to the side, her body shaking in anger and grief. "I mean, you spent more time with him than I did, and I fucking knew."

"It wasn't like—" I have no words left in me because she's not fucking wrong. We knew there was something wrong with him. I knew he was off. I even tried to talk to him about it, but he blew it off. I should have persisted and made him listen to me. I should have done a lot of things.

"I found him," she snaps. "I was the one who woke up and found him dead on my fucking couch while our girls slept upstairs!" She's furiously wiping the tears away from her face as fast as she can, but they are coming out too fast. "Can you imagine if they saw him like that?" I try to take a step toward her, but she takes a step back. "Yeah, when you go to bed at night in your perfect little fucking world, you think of that."

"Koda," I whisper, begging to go to her and hold her. To let her know I'm sorry I didn't do anything.

"You were his best friend." She uses her fingers to do quotation marks. "You were there when we got married. When we had the girls, you were supposed to look out for him." She shakes her head. "Get the fuck out of here, Christopher."

THREE

CHRISTOPHER

I SLIP THE black jacket over my white shirt, pulling out the cuffs. The pressure in the middle of my chest is tighter than it's ever been in my life. My eyes burn since I've only slept maybe four hours in the past three days. Each time they blinked, it took all my energy to open them back up.

Stepping out of my closet, I find my father sitting on my bed, dressed in a suit similar to mine. His hand outstretched by his side, his eyes watch me as I tighten my tie, making it feel like it's choking me. "Hey," he mumbles, "how are you doing?"

"Does it matter?" I answer honestly. "I'm not the one who is going to bury my husband, father, or son today." It's been two days since the showdown with Koda, two days since she told me to get the fuck out of her house. Two days since we've said anything to each other. I've been in contact with Eddie, who filled me in on the plans for the funeral.

"No, but you are burying someone you called a brother," he reminds me, and all I can do is stare at him. *You knew, and you did nothing.* Koda's words repeatedly played in my head for the past two days. She was not wrong. I knew he was up to no good. Knew he was not himself. I knew, but did I do anything? No. I went away on vacation with my family as he died on his fucking couch, leaving his wife to find him. Anger creeps up, and I wish he was still alive so I could beat his fucking ass.

"I'll be fine." I ignore the way he's looking at me. "We have to be at the funeral home soon." I turn away from him to walk out of my bedroom. When I get downstairs, I find my house full of my family. All my uncles and aunts have descended to come and stand with me, and most of my cousins are here. Stone stands by the front door next to Dylan. "You guys don't have to all come." I look around at all the eyes looking at me. My mother stands in the hallway, wearing a black dress and holding a white tissue. Gabriella and Abigail are beside her, and a few of my aunts behind her.

"We're going with you," my father declares, looking around the room and getting a chin nod from Uncle Matthew. "If you need us."

"I'm not the one who needs anything." My voice goes higher than I want it to go, and my fists ball at my sides. "His wife and kids, who have to live without him, need…" I shake my head. "I'm going to take my own car."

"I'll drive," Stone says quickly, blocking the door, and I don't even bother answering him. Instead, I just walk out into the warm, sunny day and look at the sky, wishing today to be over.

We arrive at the funeral home at the same time as a black sedan with tinted windows pulls up. The media has already lined up across the street, making my hands ball into fists. "Can they do that?" I ask my uncle Matthew, who stands behind me. "Like, can't they respect privacy?"

"Them standing across the street is them respecting their privacy," he states. "Like it or not, it's a public street. Anyone can stand wherever they want."

I shake my head and look over at the SUV. Koda gets out wearing a black skirt with a matching jacket and black shades cover her eyes. Her hair is pulled back in a ponytail as she holds Rain's and Luna's hands, both of them dressed in black. Rain looks down at her feet while Luna smiles at Koda. My heart, or whatever is left of my heart, in that second is gone.

"I think you should go." My father slaps a hand on my shoulder. "The team is lining up." He motions with his chin to my teammates lining up on the side of the open doors.

I take a deep breath. "Here," Stone says, taking off his black sunglasses and handing them to me, "take these."

My hand shakes as I reach up and take them out of his hand. I put them on and walk over to the team. Hugs are exchanged, and a couple of words are also expressed before Eddie walks over to us. I don't know what he says because I block out everything as I look into the funeral home and see Koda sitting in a chair with Rain next to her and Luna on her lap. Her hand holds one of Rain's while she has one on Luna's leg. With her glasses on, I can't see her eyes, but I see the tears streaked down her face. I can see the tip of her nose is pink, and I can see her trying not to shake while crying.

We get in line as we walk into the funeral home to give our condolences. Eddie stands next to his wife, right next to Rain, who stands next to Luna, who is glued to her mother's side. Koda's parents are on her other side. "Uncle Chrissy," Luna says the minute she sees me. "You have a candy?" She leans in and whispers. After every game, Benji and I used to walk out of the locker room together, and I always had candy in my pocket for her. "In there." She points at the right pocket where I always kept them.

"Yeah, girlie." I smile at her through the tears running down my face but that are hidden behind the glasses I'm thankful I'm wearing. I reach into the pocket and take out two. "You share with your sister," I tell her, and she grabs both of them from my palm.

Rain smiles at me as she takes one from her sister, and I look at Koda, neither of us saying anything before I reach out and hug her. Her body is stiff as she lifts a hand to my back. "Thank you for coming," she says through her tears, and all I can do is nod. She doesn't want me here. I know this, but I'm thankful she doesn't make it known to everyone around me.

Today is one of the worst days of my life, carrying his coffin out of the funeral home to the hearse that will take him to the cemetery, all while hating him for what he did. The knot in my stomach just gets bigger and bigger.

The tightness in my chest makes it harder and harder to breathe.

With my head hanging down and my hand going to my neck to loosen the tie, I walk to my car with Stone, my father, Dylan, and my uncles Matthew and Max. Everyone else is probably at my house. "Are you going to the house?" Stone asks softly.

"I don't know," I tell him, looking over to see Koda getting into the SUV with the girls. "There's not much more to say."

"You don't have to say anything," my father says. "You just have to be there. He would do it for you."

"I guess he would," I mumble instead of shouting "I wouldn't fucking put my family through that."

"We'll drop you off and then just text me when you're ready," Stone says. "Your own personal Uber driver." I chuckle at his joke, getting into the car.

"How long before this day is over?" I ask softly as we drive toward Benji's house.

"Just a few more hours to go," he replies just as soft. "Tomorrow will be better."

"Tomorrow will be better," I repeat the words, "or it can be a whole lot worse."

We pull up to the house, where cars are lined up and down the street. People walk in all dressed in black with their heads down. "Do you want me to come in with you?" All I can do is shake my head. "Okay, well, you let me know if you need me, and I'll be right over."

My hand reaches out to grab the door handle. "Thank you." My voice is thick.

"No need to thank me." He slaps my shoulder. "It's what we do."

I open the door, stepping out and closing it before anything else is said. Walking up the path, I spot a couple of the teammates with their wives, who just nod at me. Everyone is probably waiting until they can get the fuck out of here. Walking into the house, I have to zigzag through people. It's jam-packed, people chatting with each other like we just didn't bury Benji.

I look around before I step outside, seeing the kids running around. I spot Rain and Luna being chased by two older boys, who, from what I remember, are Koda's nephews. They come to the games a couple of times a year. I pull out a chair and sit outside, my eyes on the girls, making sure they are all right. I don't know how long we stay out here. All I know is they went from playing tag to hide-and-seek to racing to playing in the tree house. The sun is starting to go down, the sky turning a bright orange before it turns purple.

Eddie walks out, then pulls out the chair beside me. "The kids should be getting ready for bed." I don't know what to say to that. "Everyone is almost gone."

"Do you need me to do anything?" I look over at him, and the anguish is written all over his face. He buried a son today, and he has to keep it together to help his daughter-in-law and grandkids.

"Nah," he says, "caterers are clearing up as we speak."

"Where is Koda?" I ask, not even sure why I'm asking. The last time I was here, she was telling me to get the fuck out.

"I think she went downstairs," he replies. "She said she needed a minute." He gets to his feet then. "Okay, kids, time for a bath." He claps his hands together as the kids moan about not being tired. They follow him inside, and I get to my feet, pushing the chair under the table before heading inside.

The caterers are in the kitchen cleaning up, with some service people drying things. I'm about to take my phone out of my pocket and text Stone, but instead, my feet move toward the closed basement door.

Turning the handle and quietly closing the door behind me, I walk down the stairs. The lights are on, and as I get to the last step, I see her. Koda. This time, she's sitting on the couch with her head back, looking at the ceiling. One hand is on her lap, the other on the armrest as she holds a glass with amber liquid inside. I don't say anything to her, but she must sense she isn't alone because she looks over at me. "I was—" I start to say but then stop when the tears pour down her face.

"Is everyone gone?" she asks, and I nod. "He had this big fanfare." She laughs bitterly. "The headlines are all saying how horrible and tragic it is that he's gone. Someone even wrote he had an aneurysm. Wait until they find out he died of a fucking overdose." I look at her. "He was cheating on me," she whispers, the words draining everything from my body. "I mean, I don't know if you call it cheating since I don't think it was really him." My feet feel like they are superglued to the floor, as she brings the glass up to her mouth and takes a sip. "I kept sitting here trying to pinpoint the day it all started to change." She looks at me, shaking her head.

"For the past two days, I've been racking my brain, wondering when it fucking changed, and I can't for the life of me figure out the exact date. He started acting differently at first. It should have been my first clue. Falling asleep at the table, in the middle of the meal. Then he would be irritated at times. I thought it was his knee acting up and he was trying to pretend it was okay. Thought he was pushing himself too much at training. Told him that his body would heal on its own, and the more he pushed, the longer it would take." The tears fall over her eyelids and she looks like she's in another world as she tells me this story.

"Then I started finding little plastic baggies here and there. In his pants pockets, in his luggage. I thought, *well, that's strange, if the doctor gave him a prescription, shouldn't it be in a bottle?* As the weeks went on, he changed more and more. When he was on the road, the phone calls would be few and far between." She shrugs. "Then when he was home, he started hanging around with these people I'd never seen before in my life. They'd come over unexpectedly, and he would leave and return a couple of hours later. It would take fifteen minutes before he was out, and nothing I could do would wake him up. He fell asleep once while Luna was in the bath, and he was supposed to be watching her. Fuck, she was in the bath." She shakes her head, the tears flowing nonstop.

"We fought that night when he finally woke up, still on the bathroom floor. It was after three o'clock in the morning. He was passed out for nine fucking hours while I waited for him to wake up." The knots in my stomach now feel like they're tearing through. "He said he was sorry and it wouldn't happen again. He was fine for four days." She spins the glass in her hand. "Then he came home one Saturday night, shirt on backward. When he took it off, he had marks on his chest. Marks I did not leave. Marks someone else made." I was wrong before. If I thought today was hard, I was wrong. This right here, this listening to the hell she has been living, this has to be something that will forever be engraved on my soul. "Told me to lay off him. Everyone does it. I was a cold stuck-up bitch." She looks at me then, the pain written on her face.

"Koda." I take a step toward her. "He loved you more than life," I tell her. "You know he did. You and the girls were his life."

"Maybe once he did," she says calmly. "After that day, he didn't even try to hide he was with other women. He would be okay for a couple of hours during the day. The rest were him off doing whatever it was that he fucking did." She inhales. "He would wake up and stumble around the fucking house until he went to the bathroom, and about forty minutes later, he was in tip-top shape until he was so tired he had to nap again." She leans forward, putting the glass on the table in front of her. "I should have left." Her voice quivers. "What kind of mother lets her kids stay around a drug addict?"

My feet move without my head knowing what is going to happen. I sit next to her, putting my hand around her shoulder. "Don't you fucking say another word."

"The day before he died, I found pills again on the coffee table. At this point, they were literally all over the fucking place. At least when he was on the road—" Her body shakes in my arms. "I picked them up and put them in the garbage disposal. What the fuck would have happened if Luna or Rain thought they were candy?" She looks up at me. "I was giving him until this weekend, and then I was going to leave him." She shocks the shit out of me. "I was going to tell his father everything. I was going to fucking tell everyone everything." She looks at me. "But you guys all knew, and no one did anything to save him." The minute she says those words, I think I'm going to throw up.

"You guys just watched him kill himself." She closes her eyes and sobs in my arms. I lean back on the couch, her tears seeping through my jacket and then through my shirt. So many fucking tears. I never knew someone could cry that much. As the sobs start to drift off, her body gets heavier next to me, and when I look down, I see she's sleeping. I put my cheek on the top of her head, my own tears running down my face. I don't move from the couch for what feels like an eternity. When I hear footsteps coming down the steps, I look over to see Eddie there. I hold my finger to my mouth to tell him to keep quiet.

"You should bring her upstairs," he whispers. "She's probably out."

I move as gently as I can, tucking my arm under her legs and getting up. Holding her in my arms, I walk up the steps softly, going to her bedroom and laying her down in her bed. I kiss her on her forehead before turning and leaving the room.

I don't say anything to anyone. Instead, I walk out the front door, closing it softly behind me. *You guys watched him kill himself.* Her words hit me in the stomach. I take a couple of steps before two things happen to me at the same time. My stomach lets go of everything it was holding in and I throw up all over the side of the driveway. Then my knees buckle, and I crash to the ground. Car doors being slammed shut make me look up, and there I see it. My family waits for me. "I've got him," my father says, walking to me, but he's never alone because my uncles are two steps behind him. Stone waits at the car for me. "Let's get you home."

FOUR

Dakota

Three weeks later

"MORNING, EDDIE," I greet him as he walks into the kitchen a little after nine.

"Morning, Koda," he says, smiling at me. "Where are the girls?" He looks around the kitchen as I was just about to clean up the breakfast dishes.

"They're upstairs getting dressed," I reply, looking over to the hallway to make sure Rain or Luna aren't there. "I was going to talk to you." He pulls out a stool and sits down, putting his hands down on the island in front of him. "You know we love having you here," I say, my voice trembling a bit, my hand shaking, "but it's time to get back to normal." The sting of tears comes to my eyes, and I blink them away furiously. "Or better yet, back to our new normal."

"Koda," he says softly, "are you sure this is the right time? I mean—"

"Yes," I state, trying to make my voice firm. It's been over two weeks I've been planning on talking to him about this, and today, I finally got the courage to bring it up. "It's not that we don't love having you here. But if Benji was here, you wouldn't be here all the time. Hell, you'd probably be preparing to go down to your Florida condo for the winter." He looks down at his hands.

"Benji would want…"

"It doesn't matter what Benji would want." I swallow down the lump in my throat. "He's not coming back, and it's time for us to find our routine."

"You're right," he concedes. "I just worry."

"And I love you for it. I really do." I smile at him. "But for everyone's sake, this needs to happen. My parents went back home after two weeks, and now it's time for us to get into our groove."

"What do we tell the girls?" He looks over at me. "What if they think I'm going to abandon them?" He wipes the tears from his eyes.

"We aren't going to tell them anything," I tell him. "If they ask, you are busy. It's not like you aren't going to see them, or I'm blocking you from seeing them. It'll just be like before when they see you on Saturday."

"Koda…" He looks at his hands, his bottom lip quivering. "I just want you to know…"

I hold up my hand. "I know," I deflect, not really knowing what he has to say but also afraid of what he might say.

He just nods. "Why don't I get out of here?" He pushes away from the island. "Maybe go play a round of golf?"

"That sounds like fun." I try to sound chipper. He pushes the stool in, taking one more look around. "You call me if you need anything."

"I will," I assure him, trying not to sound like I'm as scared as he is about leaving me with just the girls. I hold up my hand, willing to be strong and watch through blurry eyes as he slowly walks back out the front door. The door closing feels like the finality of something. I stretch my hands in front of me on the island and place my forehead against the cold marble countertop. "You can do this." I'm trying to give myself a pep talk. "It'll just be like he's on the road." I sigh deeply, the lone tear running down my face when my head reminds me that he's gone and not coming back.

When I hear the sound of the girls walking down the steps, I stand straight and spin around. I turn on the water in the sink and pretend I've been cleaning, and not telling their grandfather he had to go and second-guessing myself.

"Hey." I look over my shoulder when they walk into the kitchen as I place a plate in the dishwasher. "Did you guys put away your pj's?"

"Yes," Luna and Rain answer at the same time.

"Brush your teeth?" They both nod in answer. "You guys get thirty minutes of iPad time." I look over at the clock to see the time. "I'm going to finish doing the dishes and cleaning up, and then we'll go do some back-to-school shopping."

"Where is Grandpa?" Rain asks, looking around. "Did he leave?"

"Yeah." I turn back to look at the running water, not sure I can take it if there is fear on their faces. The past three weeks have been a learning curve for all of us. They also still sleep in bed with me like they did the night Benji died. *Baby steps,* I keep telling myself, *one thing at a time*. Step one was getting Eddie not to come over every day. Step two will be sleeping in our own beds. "He forgot he had a golf game. So it's just us."

"Okay," they both say as they sit on the couch, each of them with their iPad. I quickly finish up the dishes, controlling my breathing in and out so I don't have a panic attack.

"I'm going to get dressed," I tell them, jogging up the stairs to my bedroom. I make the bed and keep the kids' pillows on it even though it doesn't go with my bedding set, then make my way into the bathroom to brush my teeth. I look over to the other sink. I haven't touched it since the day of the birthday party. From the day before he died.

His razor is on the side, his toothbrush tossed in front of the sink. His aftershave is down on the other side. I spit out the toothpaste and rinse my mouth before placing my toothbrush in the cabinet, ignoring the way I want to go over to his side and throw all his shit out.

Instead, I move over to my closet, grabbing a pair of light blue jeans off the hanger and sliding into them. They used to be skintight on me, but in the past three weeks, I've lost about fifteen pounds. I grab a white T-shirt that also fits looser than it did a couple of weeks ago. Slipping my feet into flip-flops, I walk out, turning off the closet light and looking into the dark closet in front of me.

My heart speeds up before I can even stop my feet from moving to his closet. My hand reaches out to turn on the light, but before I do it, someone asks, "Mom, is it thirty minutes?" My hand drops before I switch on the light.

"Time to go." The hand slaps my thigh. I look at the dark closet once more before walking out of the room.

We spend the whole day at the mall, going from store to store. The entire time, I'm keeping a brave face up. The whole time trying not to think this is going to be the first year when Benji doesn't take the kids to school in the morning. Before he started not being himself, he was the most amazing father. When he wasn't on the road, he would drive the kids to daycare before heading to the rink.

"Do we want to grab something to eat?" I ask them when we walk out of the mall, my hands full of bags.

"Can we have pizza?" Luna asks as she steps into the SUV and buckles herself into her booster seat.

"Sure," I say, putting all the bags into the trunk before pressing the button to close it and making our way home.

I'm almost done unloading the SUV when a car pulls up behind me. Looking over my shoulder, I see it's Brittany. She's married to Cole, a player who played with Benji. "Hey." She kicks open her driver's door before reaching over and grabbing what looks to be a baking dish from beside her. "I knew I should have called before I came over." She gets out and closes the door with her hip. "I just thought…"

I smile at her. We have hung around together since our husbands played on the same team. Her two girls are each a year older than my girls, so they are always together when we go to the games. "This is a nice surprise."

"I'm sorry I haven't come by," she says, and my stomach gets tight. Will there ever be a day when people don't apologize to me? "But it's summer break, so we went up to the cottage for a couple of weeks."

"That's okay," I respond. "Do you want to come in?"

"I'd love to but my parents are down, so I have to get back." She laughs. "There is only so much of my parents Cole can deal with."

We walk up the steps to the house, and both girls are excited when they see her. She walks in like she always does and places the food down on the island. "We're having pizza," Luna informs her.

"Sorry." I look over at Brittany.

"Oh, please." Brittany shoos away with her hand. "This can freeze, and you can eat it when you want."

We talk for a couple of minutes before her phone rings. "Sorry, I have to go." She frowns. "But I'll call you sometime next week to catch up."

We walk her to the door, and once she leaves, I look at the bags. "Okay, grab your stuff and take it to your room," I tell the girls. "I'll order the pizza."

The girls and I sit side by side at the island as we eat pizza, and when it's time to take showers, they head in together. I walk back downstairs, grabbing three black garbage bags, and head upstairs to the closets. I throw them in Benji's closet, turning and going to make sure the girls are okay.

I wrap them both in towels. "Get your pj's on, and we'll put a movie on," I tell them, knowing they will probably fall asleep midway through. It takes thirty-five minutes before the girls are out, and I'm a pack of nerves the whole time.

I sneak out of the room; my only thought is getting through this mission. "I will not waste away," I whisper once I'm in front of the closet. Standing here, my whole body practically trembling, I lift my hand and flick on the light. I didn't even come in here when the funeral home needed a suit. Eddie did. I inhale, smelling him. At the same time, my heart comes up to my throat, and I think I'm going to be sick.

I quickly put my hands on my knees, trying not to hyperventilate but failing miserably. "You can do this." I close my eyes and take a deep breath before I look over, ignoring the wetness on my face. I walk over to the suits hanging on the side. So many suits, but they all look the same to me. I reach my hand up to touch the sleeve, slowly slipping it off the hanger. The silk inside the jacket slides through my hand and lands on the floor on my feet. The little plastic bag slips out from the inside pocket, right where his name is embroidered. Two white pills. My hands shake like a leaf on a tree in the middle of a windstorm. I pick it up, holding it in my hands.

"You chose this over your girls," I say out loud, the sadness I felt not too long ago turning into anger. So much fucking anger, I walk over to another suit and rip it off its hanger, the hanger swinging back and forth as I search the pockets finding it empty, tossing it onto the floor with the first one. I move from one suit to the next until all his suit jackets puddle around my feet, and I hold twenty-seven little plastic baggies. I move from the suits, walking over to the T-shirts. Throwing them all on the floor, I look for more. His jeans are the next to go, finding more fucking bags, but this time with cocaine in them. Every single piece of clothing he had in that closet is now on the floor.

My knees then give out on me. Luckily, the jackets on the floor don't mess up my knees as much as they should, or maybe I'm just numb. Looking at the baggies in my hand, all I can do is sob until it becomes too much. Even staying on my knees is a feat, and I'm on my side in a daze, my body limp, but my hand holding tight around the baggies I found. Blinking and looking up at the empty closet, all that remains is the hangers, some still moving from when I ripped the clothing off them. The emptiness of it all puts pressure on my chest. I don't know how long I lie here surrounded by his clothes. I don't know how I get the energy to get up to my knees and then to my feet. I hold the walls as I walk out of his closet and toward the bedroom door. The whole way down to the kitchen, I have to make sure I'm holding on to something so I don't fall on my face.

Standing at the kitchen sink, I look over to the couch I found him lying dead on. The memory of his white face looks back at me. Holding out my hand, which is holding on tight as a vise to the drugs that took my husband away from me, I turn the water on. As the baggies fall into the drain, a couple of them miss, so I have to shovel them in there. When nothing is left in the sink, I turn on the garbage disposal, my eyes blurred from the tears. I softly tune it out and then turn the water off. I take one more look at the couch before I make a mental note to get rid of it.

I walk back upstairs to his closet, get back on my knees, and fold everything to place in the garbage bags. I have to go back down for three more bags, and by the time I'm done, they're filled and placed in the middle of the room. I put my hands on my hips before making my way out of the room. Stopping one more time, I take one more look at the room before turning off the light.

FIVE

Christopher

I TURN INTO the parking garage, taking off my pass before scanning it, and the white barriers go up as the black garage door slowly opens. Moving down the slated underground parking garage, I make my way over to my parking spot.

I toss the pass on the passenger seat before I turn the truck off. I grab my keys and phone, then step out. As I look around, the garage is half empty, but my eyes automatically go to Benji's spot behind mine. It sits empty, though the nameplate on the concrete wall with his name and number is still mounted there. I exhale the deep breath I didn't know I was holding before turning and walking toward the silver door.

Stepping into the arena, I hear people talking and look into the offices that have their doors open. "Hey," I say to a couple of the office staff.

It's been my home for the past eleven years. Drafted second overall when I was eighteen, I thought I was the king of the world. Until I realized we were a club that was on a rebuild. Not going to lie, it fucking sucked in the beginning. We sucked. Period. We finished at the bottom of the standings every year for three years straight. It was all the new up-and-coming kids. The few veterans didn't give a shit about anything since they had a contract and were going to retire. We were a bunch of rookies who looked amazing on paper, but when put together, we each wanted to be the hero. It took a while to see that in order for one of us to be the hero of the game, we had to play like a team.

The pictures lining the hallway toward the locker room show the last seven years of learning how you find success working as a team. Pictures of different game moments through the years. My eyes almost want to avoid the picture of Benji and me during our rookie year. It's the night we both got our names on the score sheet. Me for my first goal, and Benji for the assist on the goal. I stop in the hallway as if I just walked into a wall. My eyes are on the picture; both of us have the same picture in our house. But this one is blown up to the size of the whole wall.

It's me about four feet off the ice, jumping to celebrate the goal with Benji skating to me. You can barely see my face, and all you see of Benji is his back. But that moment is a moment we'll never forget. It's when Benji and I bonded. We were line mates and roommates. We shared an apartment and even hotel rooms until we could get our own.

"How are you doing?" someone says, and I look over

at Cole who walks toward me. He's wearing the same thing I'm wearing. Black gym shorts with the matching T-shirt. Only difference is I have my baseball hat on—backward of course.

"I'm good." I lie to him because what the fuck can I say to him. "You?"

"I'm still in fucking shock," he admits, looking at the picture. "Fucking asshole." He shakes his head. Looking down, he slaps my shoulder, then moves on to the locker room.

"Yeah," I whisper, putting my head down and following him toward our locker room.

When I walk into the locker room, the black carpet looks freshly washed, the team logo of a factory, buildings with a bridge over it in the middle in white, black, and gold. The same logo on the ceiling lights up. "Hey." I look around the room and see a couple of the rookies already here. The wooden bench sits in a half circle around the room. Each cubby has our jersey hanging there, with our name in gold on the shelf on top with our number. Another shelf on top of that has our helmet with our number on it, and then above that is a picture of us. Four words go around the top of all the pictures—accountability, passion, one goal.

"Yo," a couple of them call to me as I make my way over to my stall.

I place my phone and keys on the top next to my gloves. "I can't believe summer is over already," Andreas, our goalie, whines. "It was gone in a blink of an eye."

"Did you go home?" Connor, a defenseman, asks.

Andreas came from Sweden and was drafted a little over five years ago.

"For a bit," he says, "then came back." He looks over at me and then looks down. The whole team came back for the funeral. There wasn't one player, one coach, one member of the team who wasn't there for the funeral.

I sit here almost like I'm not here, which is the weirdest thing I've ever done. Usually, I'd be in here, undressed and ready to hit the ice in fifteen minutes. A couple of minutes of chitchatting but my ass would be on the ice. But now it's like I am stuck to this seat and have no motivation to get the fuck up.

It's been over a month since Benji died. Thirty-seven days, to be exact. Thirty-fucking-seven days I've been in this daze. Thirty-seven fucking days of nothing but questions that can't be answered. "You going to work out before getting on the ice?" Cole asks as he shakes his pre-workout drink in a plastic bottle.

"Might get on the bike." I tap the bench under me. "Maybe hit the weights." He stands there like he's waiting for me. "I'll meet you there."

It takes me about five minutes to move my ass, take off my baseball hat, run my hands through my hair—which is longer than I usually keep it—before I walk over to the gym. I train with Cole, side by side. Neither of us says anything, and instead, we get lost in our own thoughts. I wonder if he is thinking that it feels fucking weird without Benji here working out with us. I wonder if he's thinking we should have fucking done something. I wonder if he's thinking maybe I could have changed it.

The only time I shut off my brain is when we are on the ice. It was instilled in me when I was a kid that whatever happens out there, happens out there. When you get on the ice, you focus on the game. Focus on helping everyone around you. Focus on the play. I'm one of the last ones on the ice after Andreas, who was working with the goalie coach in the corner.

Practically no one is left here once I get out of the shower. I get dressed, sliding my hat back on my head before picking up my phone and keys. I walk out with my head down, avoiding the picture on the wall.

The tightness in my chest starts as soon as I sit in the truck and back out, looking over to his spot. I'm driving out of the parking garage when my phone rings. Looking at the center console screen, I see Dad calling.

Reaching over, I press the green button. "Hey," I say once it's connected.

"Hey yourself." He chuckles. "What's up?"

"Not much, just left first day of practice," I tell him even though I know he knows because we spoke last night before I went to bed. After the funeral, it took a week for everyone to stop watching me. It took Stone two weeks to get back to his life, and he only left because Ryleigh had to get back to work. It took three weeks for my father to leave, begrudgingly, because he had to attend his hockey camp for underprivileged players. Even though he said I wasn't going, I got on the plane with him. I stayed at home for a couple of weeks and then came back alone.

"How was that?" he asks softly.

"Fucking horrible," I admit. "They still have Benji's parking spot and locker."

"And you're pissed about this?" I don't know if he's asking me a question. "How pissed would you be if you got there and his stuff was cleaned out?" Now I know he's asking me the question, and the minute I think about it, my throat almost closes up. When I don't say anything for a full minute, he continues, "That's what I thought. What about Koda? Have you spoken to her?"

The minute he mentions her name, my hands grip the steering wheel so hard I feel like if I wasn't driving, I would be able to break it off. The last time I spoke to her, she cried in my fucking arms, her tears soaked into two layers of clothing to penetrate my skin, telling me how bad it really fucking was. If Benji was alive, there is no doubt in my mind I would have beat the shit out of him. I would have hit him over and over until my knuckles broke. That is how furious I was at him. I carried her up to her bed, tucked her in, and walked out of her house, where my family carried me home. "Nope," I say, my tone angry.

"Did you call her?" he asks, making the irritation now come out.

"Every day," I reply. "She hasn't answered one of my phone calls."

"Have you tried to text her?" His voice is soft. "Sometimes it's easier to talk to someone when you don't have to talk." He sighs. "If that makes sense."

"I have not tried to text her. I figured if she needed me, she would have called. Considering I left her twenty-five voicemails." Did I call her every single day since he died? Yes. Did I leave a message every single time? No, I stopped after the first twenty-five. I was sure she blocked me on her phone anyway since it went straight to voicemail.

"Have you thought about what I said?"

I try to chuckle. "I don't know, Dad. You've said a lot of things."

"About you talking to someone." His voice goes really low as I pull into my driveway, hitting the button to open the garage door and driving in.

"There is no need," I huff. "I'm fine."

"Well, I don't think you're fine," he snaps. "In fact, I know you're not fine. So you have two choices." Suddenly, I feel like I'm back in high school, and I'm about to get punished for something. "You can either call your uncle Viktor." He mentions my uncle who is a recovering addict. He's been sober and clean for over thirty years and makes no secret about it. "Or I call him, and he pays you a visit."

"Pays me a visit?" I try to joke about it. "You've been hanging around too much with Uncle Matthew if you are starting to talk to me like you know people who can pay me a visit." Even that joke makes him laugh.

"I actually do know people." His laughter is loud now. "And one of those is your uncle. So you decide, Christopher, what is it going to be?"

"Fine." I sigh. "I'll call him."

"Good. I'll let you go so you can get on with it." I'm about to hang up on him. "Oh, and if you think you said that just so I would get off your back, you're wrong. I'm also going to call him." I don't have a chance to hang up on him because he hangs up on me.

"Fuck," I grumble, getting out of my truck with my phone in my hand and jogging up the five stairs in the garage that lead to the mudroom. "Fuck, fuck, fuck."

I walk into the kitchen and head straight to my living room. The room with the ninety-eight-inch television mounted on the bare white wall where I spend most of my time.

I know I have to call my uncle, but before I call him, I pull up Koda's text thread.

Me: Hey, just checking to make sure everything is okay with the girls and to see if you guys need anything.

I hit send as I fall into the couch before I pull up my uncle's name and then press the phone button. "Please don't answer," I mumble, as I move my leg up and down with nerves. "Please don't answer."

"Well, look who it is," my uncle Viktor says instead of saying hello. "Was wondering when I was going to hear from you."

"My father thinks I should talk to you." I don't beat around the bush because in a family like ours, he's probably already spoken to my father.

"So you don't think you should talk to me, but your father does." His voice is rich and warm. "How are you doing?"

"Fine," I cut out right away.

"I don't know how you can be fine." His words shock

me. "You lost one of your best friends unexpectedly." My stomach sinks. "I don't know about you, but I would not be fine." He doesn't give me a chance to say anything. "Fuck, I would be beside myself with grief."

"What difference does it make?" I put my head back on the couch and slouch down, looking at the white ceiling. "What fucking difference does it matter if I am beside myself with grief? Who the fuck cares? I'm not the one people need to be worrying about. People should be worrying about his wife and his two girls." My voice goes higher and higher. "That's who people should be worried about."

"People should most definitely be worried about them. But people should also be worried about those who loved him." I close my eyes. "Just because you think people should be worrying about Koda and the girls doesn't mean we shouldn't worry about you, Christopher." He says my name softly, and a tear escapes from the corner of my eye, rolling down to my hair. "You have every right not to be fine. You have a right to be sad or even angry."

"Oh, I'm fucking pissed," I admit. "As much as I love him, Uncle Viktor, I fucking hate him." The minute I say the words, guilt washes over me.

"What do you hate him for?"

"For being stupid. For fucking doing the shit he was doing."

"Did you know he was an addict?"

"Yes and no," I answer honestly. "I knew he was on something. Knew it in my gut, saw some signs, but that he would have overdosed? Fuck no. Never in my wildest dreams did I think it would get there."

"As someone who has come back from an overdose," he says, his voice never changing, "I can say it's nothing that is done on purpose."

"God," I mutter, the tears now coming out like a dripping faucet, "why couldn't I fucking stop him?" My voice cracks. "Why the fuck didn't I have a chance to stop him?"

"Guilt," my uncle says. "Guilt is worse than living with sadness and anger. You see, guilt will eat away at you. Guilt will take over your whole life, and you won't even fucking know the most important thing."

"And what is that?"

"That you're the one still alive. That it didn't matter what you said, what I said, what his wife would have said to him. The ball was in Benji's court and no one else's." Neither of us says anything as my eyes get heavy. "Now, I'm going to call your father and tell him I spoke to you. But I'm also not going to lie to him. You need to speak to someone, son," he suggests softly. "Someone who has the tools you need to cope with it." I still don't say anything. "I want you to call me tomorrow." I'm about to say something. "If you don't, I'm calling your uncles Matthew and Max, along with Grandpa and your father, and we will start the phone chain." I smile because my family can be a lot of things and can be a lot to handle, but the one thing they do is show up when you need them.

"Fine, I'll call you tomorrow."

"I love you, Christopher," he says, the tears starting

over again, "like you're my son." He doesn't have to say it. None of them have to say it because we know. "And I'm proud of you."

"Thanks, Uncle Viktor." My voice is a whisper. "Give Auntie Zoe a kiss for me."

"Will do," he assures me, and I hang up the phone, placing it on my stomach. I lie here, looking up at the ceiling as the room gets darker. Only when it's pitch black does my phone beep on my stomach.

Picking it up, I see it's a text from Koda. My hand fumbles to unlock it, hoping she's about to give me something, anything. But there in the middle of the screen is her answer, and just like that I'm cut off at the knees again. One word and one word only.

Koda: No.

SIX

Koda

One month later

"OKAY, MY GIRLS," I announce once I walk into the kitchen, tucking my white cotton button-down shirt into my light beige cargo pants, "are we ready for school?" I clap my hands as the girls finish their breakfast. "First day of school." I shoot up my hand, wiggling my fingers like jazz hands.

"Are you done?" I ask Luna, who puts the last piece of strawberry in her mouth and nods at me. "Go brush your teeth."

"Okay, Momma," she agrees, sliding off the stool she was on and skipping over to the downstairs bathroom, where they both have extra toothbrushes for after breakfast time.

"What about you?" I look over at Rain. "You done with yours?"

"Yeah," she says softly, pushing her plate with three

strawberries toward me. "I'm going to go brush my teeth."

"Okay." I put the plates in the sink to deal with after drop-off. Luna comes back, skipping the whole time, a smile on her beautiful face.

I squat down in front of her. "You know how pretty you are?" I ask, and she shrugs with shyness. I kiss her nose before Rain comes back in. Her accordion uniform skirt sways left and right as she tucks in her white polo shirt.

"Ready?" I ask as she slides her white-socked feet into her blue Mary Jane shoes.

"Ready, Freddy," Luna chirps before walking to the front door, where I usher the kids out of the house. Grabbing each of them, I slide their backpacks onto their shoulders, and Rain picks up her lunchbox.

We walk down the steps toward the white Range Rover. "Oh, girls," I say, stopping as I'm opening the back door of the SUV, "we need to send Grandpa a picture of the three of us."

I squat down between them and smile at the camera. "Say hip, hip hooray for school." I extend my arm in front of me and snap a picture of the three of us smiling. I was very good with my makeup today; you can barely see the black circles under my eyes from sleeping three to five hours a night.

I open my text and hurriedly text Eddie before I get Luna in the car, helping her buckle her seat belt, while Rain does hers. "It's going to be a good day." I slam the back door closed and then open the driver's side door.

The kids and I listen to music on the way to drop off Rain first. Driving is the time I kind of hate the most because I let my mind wander. It's been almost three months since Benji died. Our new normal has been a learning curve for all of us. After I packed away his clothes and had Eddie take them out, I thought it would be easier, but it's been harder than ever. I sometimes find Rain crying and saying she misses her dad. Luna is a little less often because I don't think she gets the full picture.

I pull into the parking lot, seeing a couple of familiar faces from last year. I also see a couple of the wives huddled together, talking and laughing. I get out of the SUV, opening the back door to let Luna out before helping Rain get down.

"Have everything?" I ask, looking down at her. I avoid looking up because I can feel that all eyes are on us. I know people are watching, wondering how we are doing. Wondering if we are coping. Wondering how the fuck I'm going to do it. Or maybe it's all in my head, and my paranoia is cutting in.

I hold the girls' hands as we walk into the schoolyard. "Are we going to have the best day?" I ask them, and they both nod at me. I finally look up at everyone and see a couple of people quickly look away, afraid of getting caught staring at us, while a couple of the wives hold their hands up and wave.

I stop by the brown door where the teacher waits for everyone. "Okay, Rain." I squat down in front of her, blinking away the tears that are itching to come out.

"Give me a hug."

She wraps her arms around my neck. "You'll be here to pick me up, right?" she whispers.

"You betcha," I assure her. "Then we'll go and get Luna together," I whisper in her ear before kissing her cheek. "I love you, baby girl."

"Love you too, Mom," she replies and then turns around, walking into the brown door. I stand back up and watch her walk down the hall with another little girl. My heart feels like it's going to pound right through my chest. I wait until I can't see her anymore and quickly wipe away the lone tear from the corner of my eye.

"Shall we go drop you off?" I look over at Luna, who's standing beside me, holding my hand.

I walk toward the gate to leave the schoolyard but have to move more to the side when the school bus gets here. About seventy kids all rush to get into the school. I come face-to-face with the wives, who are all hanging out chatting. "Hey," Paulette says to me, a smile on her face, "how are you?" She comes to kiss me on my cheek.

"Hi, guys." I put on a fake smile, going to the four of them and kissing their cheeks. The team has been really good about bringing food for us periodically. At first, it was every single day, sometimes twice a day. The calls were nonstop, but now they are slowing down, which is something I knew would happen.

"Hey," Brittany reminds me, "don't forget Friday night." I look at her confused about what Friday night is. "Remember, I called you last week?" She laughs. "It's the big family skate day right before the preseason starts." It's something the team has been doing for the past ten years. It was a night when everyone had the best time. Back from summer break, right before heading back to the reality of being on the road and starting the season. It was one of the girls' favorite times, so I said yes because I thought they would love it, but deep down, I don't think it's a good idea.

I swallow down the big golf ball. "Yeah, I think we're still good to go," I say, put on the spot, knowing I can't lie with Luna here. Because one thing I've learned about lying with kids is that they will out you each time. "I'll let you know." I look down at Luna, who is waving like crazy to a couple of girls who have come over for playdates. "You ladies have a great day," I say as quickly as I can to get the fuck out of here.

Drop-off for Luna is a little less awkward but still the same. The teachers look at us like they all feel sorry for us, and I have to fight not to tell them all to fuck off, which is the stupidest thing. Luna quickly waves her hand before rushing to play with her friends.

With my head down, I walk out of the daycare to the car. The phone beeps in my hand, and I see it's a text from Christopher.

Christopher: Happy first day back at school and daycare.

My heart hammers faster and faster seeing the sentence. When the phone pings again, this time the back of my neck is burning.

Christopher: I'd like to come by and see the kids, maybe take you guys out for dinner? Let me know.

"What the fuck," I mumble. Opening up the text app, I see that instead of sending the picture to Eddie, I sent it to Christopher. "Fuck, fuck, fuck," I curse, pulling open the driver's side door and getting in. Christopher is the only one who has been calling daily. Every single day, he calls, and every single time, I decline the call. I don't even know why I decline the call; I just do. But lately, he's been texting me also. Every single day, he asks me if I need anything. I answered him once and never again, but the texts still come. He tries to word the sentences different each time, but in the end, it's the same. Are you and the girls okay? Bottom line—we are not.

I toss my phone aside, starting the car and driving to go get myself a coffee before I make my way over to my appointment.

The phone feels like it weighs a million pounds as I pull open the glass door before taking the elevator up to the seventh floor. "Hi," I greet as soon as I step off the elevator. "How are you, Melanie?" I say to the receptionist.

"I'm great, Dakota." She smiles, using my full name. "She is waiting for you. You can go ahead."

I nod at her, walking toward the open brown door in the corner, stepping in, and closing it behind me. "Hello, Koda," Dr. Mendes says to me, her face beaming with a smile. "How are you doing?" She walks around her desk to greet me. "Please, have a seat wherever you want." She points at the couch she has in the corner or the single chair beside it.

"Hi," I reply softly, going to the couch and sitting

down, "I'm doing…" I take a breath and let the tears come. This is my safe space. "Just dropped the kids off at school."

"It's a big day," she notes softly, going to sit in another single chair that faces the couch. "First day of school is emotional on a whole other level."

I nod at her. "It really is." I wipe the tears away. "I know them being in school is going to be good. I know they need it, but I'm…" I try to think of the words. "I think I'm feeling lost."

"Well, you've had a roller coaster the last three months," she points out. "It's like you are constantly on the go to make sure the kids don't feel like they are missing out on anything, and now it's slowed down, and they have gotten off, but you are still on there waiting."

During one of my insomnia nights in the beginning, I spent a long time on the internet searching for things about how to go on after losing your loved one. The most mentioned was seeking help, so I called the top name and came to Dr. Mendes. We had a phone call before anything to see if we meshed well, and I loved her from the get-go. The first meeting with her was a rough one because all I did was sob. Literally sobbed for a whole hour. I think maybe I got out five words, but she just sat there knowing this was what I needed, and in the end, I really did. Especially since I never shed a tear in front of the kids, being free to do this with her, knowing no one was going to catch me, was freeing in a way. "Yeah," I say, sitting back and playing with the white paper coffee cup in my hand.

"What else is on your mind?" she asks, looking from me to my hands nervously trying to stay busy.

"There is this big event this Friday with Benji's team," I admit to her.

"And are you going?" She looks at me, and I take a deep breath.

"I don't know if I should," I say softly.

"And why shouldn't you?" she asks.

"Because I'm still furious with them," I snap. "I'm so fucking pissed that they helped him lead the life he did."

"Did they really help him?" Her voice never goes up or down.

"I mean, they didn't put a stop to it." I shrug. "Then again, neither did I." The guilt of not speaking up before he died is always the last thing I think about before I drift off to sleep and the first thing I think about when I wake up. If I have a minute to spare during the day, it's there like a nagging thought. *What did you do to help him?* It's the loaded question that runs through my mind. It also guilts me that I have no answer to that question. Or better yet, the answer to that question is nothing. I did nothing to help him, just like they did.

"Benji is the only one who was responsible for what happened. Not you, his teammates, his father, or your girls. He was the one who made the decision each time he took those drugs." She's one thousand percent right. No one could have helped Benji if he didn't want it.

"It's a disease," I try to defend him, but even I know.

"Yes, it is. And people get help every single day." She leans forward. "When they want to."

"It's going to be fucking awkward," I finally say. "Like everyone is going to be there with their family, and then it's the sad widow and his kids."

"Have they treated you differently?" I shake my head at the question. "And if Benji was still here, would you go?"

"Well, I'm not sure." I stop there. "I mean, I'm sure the kids would go with him, but I'm not sure I would. The kids would love it."

"This is your new normal," she reminds me. "You can either stay home and wallow in the grief or—"

"Or?" I respond right away. "Whatever the or is, I choose or." She laughs at me. "For the girls, I'll suck it up, and worst case"—I smirk—"it'll be a three-session week. And you'll see me every second day."

"We can work with that." She nods at me, and the rest of the hour is spent planning how I'm going to start to take back my life, or at least try.

The week flies by with school and me trying to make sure I'm busy every hour of the day the kids are gone. My house is now ready for winter even though it's only September. Most of the summer clothes are packed away, and the winter clothes are waiting to be worn.

It's Friday night, and the girls are running into my room wearing blue jeans and their team jerseys with Benji's name on them while I sit on the bed putting on my white sneakers. "I'm ready," Rain announces, smiling at me. "Did you pack my skates?"

"I did," I assure her. "I did that this morning after I dropped you off."

"Mine too?" Luna asks, and I nod at her, wondering how the fuck she is going to go on the ice without Benji. I mean, I can skate a little bit, but not enough to make sure she doesn't fall. Worst case, I'll fall and she'll fall on top of me.

"Yes, yours too," I say, hoping she gets there and decides she'd rather play in the kids' suite than go on the ice.

"Let's go." I get up, grab the light blue jean jacket, and put it on top of the white shirt I paired with my black leggings. I roll the sleeves to the jacket before walking out with the girls. Every second we get closer and closer to the arena, I feel like I'm going to throw up. I have to breathe in through my nose and out my mouth. The pressure on my chest is so tight I cough a couple of times to help with my breathing.

Pulling into the underground garage makes my hands shake when I hold up the parking pass. The door opens right away. I make my way down and turn the corner when I see Christopher getting out of his truck. His eyes automatically go to mine and his face fills with a smile as he points at what used to be Benji's parking spot. I pull into the spot, seeing they have yet to take down his name. My heart jackhammers in my chest.

I don't have a chance to even think twice about it when the girls yell his name, "Uncle Christopher!" Rain unbuckles her seat belt.

I turn off the car and unlock the doors right before he opens the back door. "Oh my goodness." His voice is like butter. "Look at these girls," he gasps, "they got so big."

"Uncle Chrissy," Luna announces, "I brought my skates." The minute she says that, I inwardly cringe, knowing I will have no choice but to embarrass myself by getting on the ice with her.

"I hope so." He grabs Rain by her waist and takes her out, kissing her cheek. "Did you bring yours?" She nods as he puts her down, closing the door and walking around the other side to do the same thing with Luna. "Someone got taller," he croons when he kisses her cheek, "you are almost the same height as me."

He puts her down as I get out of the SUV. "Hey," he greets me, wrapping his arm around my waist and kissing my cheek. "It's so good to see you." I just nod at him, taking him in. He's wearing light blue jeans with a white shirt and a black jacket on top. His black-and-white Vans finish the outfit. It's a casual outfit, but the way it fits him, it's more like he's a model than anything else. I mean, his looks make all the girls go crazy for him, but it's the way he cares about everyone and everything that makes him special. He's always the first one to help if something happens to anyone. He goes above and beyond for his friends. He showed me time and time again when it was with Benji, whether it was to help build that tree house in the yard or he had to get a Santa Claus costume because he forgot. It was always Christopher as his backup guy. He lets me go and looks at me again. "I'm so happy you guys came. If I knew you were coming, I would have come picked you up."

"We should get in there." I avoid answering his

statement and instead go to the trunk to grab the girls' bags. I'm about to grab them when I feel him behind me. He reaches past me, our hands landing on the handles of the bags at the same time.

"I got it," he says when all I can do is stare at his hand covering mine. I quickly slip my hand from under his, turning to the girls while he grabs the bags.

"Let's go," he invites, and we walk to the door. It's a walk I've made hundreds of times before, but it's so much different this time. I look over at the girls to make sure they are okay as we step into the hallway leading down to the locker room.

I don't know why I expected it to be awkward and weird, but it's nothing like that. It's like it always was when we attended a game.

The kids head into the locker room and sit down where Benji's name still hangs, which is right next to Christopher, who takes off his shoes and quickly puts on his skates. I go through the motions of getting the kids in their skates. I can hardly hear the noise around me from all the squealing kids because my heart pounds so loud and fast it's echoing. I sit down next and put my skates on, trying to tell myself it's not going to be as bad as I think it will be.

"I'm ready," Luna states, grabbing her little helmet. "Mommy, are you coming?"

"Um," I start and look at my skates. I think about how awkward it's going to be with me ending up on my ass. But I'll do it for the kids and hope for the best. I'm about to stand and pretend I'm okay when I see Christopher get up on his skates.

"How about I take them?" Christopher says. "If it's okay with you?"

"Are you sure?" I ask, and he looks at Rain and then Luna.

"Can I take you on the ice with me, and Mommy can just stay and take pictures?" he asks them, and they nod.

"I need you to hold me," Luna tells Christopher. "I don't know how to skate."

"I won't let you fall, pretty girl," he assures her softly. "Take your skates off and meet me out there." The girls wobble away from me, saying hi to everyone as they make their way to the ice.

"Are you sure about this?" I ask softly.

"Yup." He nods and then smirks, his blue eyes getting even brighter. "This way, you can't avoid me," he declares before he walks out of the room to join my girls.

SEVEN

CHRISTOPHER

"ARE YOU TWO ready?" I clap my hands as I follow them down the carpet toward the ice.

I make sure I walk next to Luna, who doesn't look like she's been on skates since last year.

"I need one of those." Luna points at the little metal skating helper some of the little kids use.

"I need one also," Rain says softly, and I tilt my head to the side.

"You know how to skate," I tell her, and she shakes her head. I know that last year Benji said he was getting them into skating lessons during the week.

"Dad stopped taking me…" She looks at me, feeling like she is telling me a secret she shouldn't be telling me. It is right then and there my hatred for Benji comes rearing back in full force. I've pushed it away for the past couple of weeks. I am talking to my uncle Viktor daily even though he doesn't have any medical training. He went through it, and I feel like I can open myself to him. My hands ball into fists by my sides. "I used it the last time."

"Okay," I concede, trying to make it seem like I don't want to take the metal skating helper and throw it across the room. "Stay here," I tell them, skating onto the ice and grabbing one before going back to them. "Rain, you are going to train with this one," I inform her, and I see Luna's face go down. "And you are going to skate with me." Her whole face lights up. "Until you are comfortable on skates, I'm going to hold you so you can see how easy it is."

"I don't want to fall," Luna tells me, and I laugh.

"I won't let you fall, princess," I assure her, holding out my hand for Rain, who squeezes mine as she moves toward the metal contraption. "I'm going to skate beside you for a bit," I tell her, "until you are ready to take off."

"Okay, Uncle Christopher," she replies. Her voice is filled with enthusiasm as I move over and grab Luna.

"You ready?" I ask, and she nods. With the helmet, her head looks bigger than her body.

I put her down on her skates, and she does what every person does. She tries to walk with them and swing her feet front to back. "Easy there." I put my hands under her armpits. "Lift one foot and then put it down," I urge her, thinking back on the way my father taught my sisters, who hated every single second of it. Luna does what I tell her, but then just tries to speed skate. "Nice and easy," I remind her, looking over to Rain, who is killing it. "Look at what Rain is doing," I tell Luna, who looks over.

"I'm doing that," she argues. I laugh and look up to see

Koda standing behind the bench with some of the other wives. She's trying to keep up with their conversation, but her eyes are on the girls. She steps away for a second, taking out her phone to snap a couple of pictures.

Rain picks up more and more confidence as she skates with a couple of the other girls who she hangs around with. I stay as close by as I can, but with Luna getting the hang of it, I can't do it for long. "Uncle Chrissy," she says, "I want water."

"Then let's skate over to the bench," I urge her and slowly lessen my hold on her, enough for her to skate by herself, but also tight enough to catch her if she were to slip.

"Mommy!" she screams when we are almost to the bench. "I can skate."

"I saw." Koda comes over to the open bench door. "You were doing so good." I keep my hands around her chest until she steps up and Koda catches her.

"Did you have fun?" Koda asks Luna while I lean against the boards. My eyes roam the ice to catch Rain, who is letting go of the metal contraption to try it on her own.

"Yeah," she huffs as she takes off her helmet and puts it beside her on the bench. Koda hands her a water bottle.

"I'm going to go with Rain," I tell Koda, who smiles and nods before I take off and meet up with Rain.

"You ready to go without the help?" I ask, and she smiles at me.

"What if I fall?" she asks softly.

"Then you get up," I encourage her, "and if you fall

again, you get back up."

"But—" she says.

"Nothing wrong with falling down, Rain," I tell her, skating backward. "It's about trying not to fall the next time, and if you fall, then you try again. Eventually, you won't fall. Or if you do?" I smirk at her. "It'll still be okay."

"Okay," she says, moving aside and keeping her hand on the helper for a second before she lets it go, "I'm going to go."

"You can do it," I assure her, skating in front of her, giving her enough space but not wanting to be too far away. In case she falls forward, I'll be there to catch her. The wobbling takes a couple of seconds to stop, but then she takes off.

I see her arms going round and round at her sides like a helicopter as she tries to steady her balance. I skate closer to her so I can catch her if she falls, but she shouts, "No, let me do it!" So I stand as close to her as I can, letting her do her thing. It takes a couple of more strides and then she falls and laughs. "I did good for a bit." Her smile fills her whole face as I hold out my hand to help her up. She takes my hand and slowly gets up, trying not to fall but doing it like a fucking champ.

"You did amazing." I smile at her, my chest tightening for a second. "You going to go again?" She nods. By the time the hour is over, she's skating faster than some of the kids who play hockey, and I feel so proud.

The bell rings, telling us the Zamboni is coming out to clean the ice, so we skate off toward the bench. I look around, searching everyone to see if I see them, but I don't see Koda or Luna. I follow Rain to the locker room, where everyone on the ice sits, taking off their skates while a couple of the kids run around. Rain sits next to me and I hand her a water bottle that was sitting on the bench. She unsnaps the bottom of her helmet on one side and then the other side before taking it off. She grabs the bottle of water and drinks three gulps before turning to me. "Can we do that again?" Her eyes light up when she asks that question, and I vow to make sure I make her eyes light up like that again.

"You bet," I tell her, bending to untie my skates. "I'll talk to your mom and see if we can get you on the ice next week."

"Okay," she says, then leans forward and mimics my movements.

"Hey." I look up and see Koda walking back into the room. "Sorry, I was…" She points over her shoulder. "Luna wanted to eat, then she wanted to go and play." She looks all flustered, and before I tell her that it's all good, Rain is calling her.

"Mommy, I skated all by myself," Rain declares, her voice full of excitement, her face full of joy. "All by myself and Uncle Christopher said we can do it again."

"Oh, wow," Koda says, bending to help Rain untie the skates, "that's amazing." Then she helps put on her sneakers.

"Can I go play?" she asks her mom, who nods at her, so she jumps up and runs out of the room with a couple of the other kids.

"Thank you," Koda murmurs softly, avoiding looking at me as she packs up the girls' stuff. "You didn't have to do it."

"Yeah," I reply, giving a couple of the guys the chin up when they turn to walk out of the room, "I know I didn't, but I wanted to." She looks up at me, and I look around to see if many people are around to take in this conversation. I see there are maybe five people left, but no one is paying attention to what is happening between us. "I've been calling you."

She's about to say something when both Luna and Rain come barreling back into the room, singing her name, "Mommy."

She looks over at them. "Can we go sleep at Noel's house?" Rain asks her.

"Please-please-please." She folds her hands together and bounces on her tippy-toes up and down.

"Yeah, please-please-please," Luna joins her.

"I don't know." Koda hesitates when Cole and Brittany come back into the room with their two girls running in front of them.

"Sorry, they ambushed us," Cole says to Koda, "I couldn't really say no. Plus, they said they will make me watch *The Little Mermaid* again." The way his lips get tight, I have to look down for him not to see me chuckle. "I have been waiting all week for this."

"I don't know," Koda starts, "I don't want to burden—"

"Burden us," Brittany pleads, "it's better when they are there because it's like they babysit themselves."

"Well," Koda replies, "I guess if it's okay." I can see

the turmoil all over her face. "I guess it's okay with me."

"Yay!" the four girls scream and jump up and down.

"Okay, give Mom a hug," Cole urges. "Might as well get this over with so we can get straight to the movie."

I watch as Koda gets on her knees to hug the girls. "You be good," she instructs them, "and if you need anything—"

"We will call you," Brittany reassures her, and she ushers the four girls out of the room. I think I even hear talk about painting nails.

I get up, then take Koda in as she tries to put on a brave face, but knowing she is probably freaking out that they are gone. I reach for the kids' bags. "Let's go," I mumble to her as she looks up at me with shock on her face.

"What?" Her voice is soft.

"We're going to go get something to eat," I tell her, ignoring how my hand is gripping the bags, knowing that she's been ignoring all my calls and texts for the last three months. "What do you feel like, burgers or sushi?" I make my way out of the room, hoping she just follows me.

"You hate sushi," she points out as we step into the parking garage.

"It's not that I hate it," I try to say, "it's a texture thing." I stop at her Range Rover.

"You don't have to do this, Christopher." She looks at me. "I'll just head on home."

"Again, I don't do things because I have to. I do things because I want to." Her eyes watch me. "Now, do you want to follow me or do you want to come with me?"

"No, I'll follow you," she replies and I hold on to the bags.

"Okay. I'm going to hold on to these bags." I hold up said bags in front of me. "Just to make sure you don't ghost me."

She throws her head back and booms out a laugh that I haven't heard in over three months. The sound even shocks her. "That made me laugh," she says, her green eyes lightening. "I'm not going to ghost you." Her face is beautiful when she laughs, and I can bet my ass she hasn't laughed in a long time.

"Well, when you park next to me, I'll hand over the bags." I don't waste time talking to her. Instead, I walk over to my truck and open the door, tossing the bags in there. "Where do you want to go?" I watch her as she walks over to her SUV. "We can hit up McCloughan's."

"Oh, they have good burgers and fish and chips." She opens her door. "I'll meet you there. Bring the bags." She laughs, getting into the SUV.

"I'll follow you!" I shout at her. I don't know if she hears me, but I wait for her to pull out of the parking spot.

I follow her and pull into the parking spot beside her. She gets out and comes over to my driver's door and waits for me to open it. "Now, can I have my bags?"

"Yes." I laugh, grabbing the bags and handing them to her. "You can." She takes the bags from me, then turns and places them in the trunk. I meet her as we walk into the bar. It's booming because it's a Friday night.

We walk up to the hostess stand. "Two," I say, and she smiles at us as she looks on her iPad before telling us to follow her. I put my hand on Koda's lower back, making her walk ahead of me. The hostess places the menus on a table in the middle of the room, but my eyes go to a table in the corner.

"Can we have that one?" I point. "It's quieter."

She nods, and I walk over with her. Koda takes her jacket off before sitting down in the chair that backs to the room. I sit in the corner facing her, shrugging off my own jacket. Koda grabs the menu, avoiding looking at me. "So." I lean back in my chair. "Are we going to get the weird stuff out of the way so it's not awkward as fuck?"

"I don't know what you mean." Even when she says the words, I know she's lying.

"Okay, well then, I'll start. I've called you"—I put my hands on the table, my index finger moving up and down—"every single day. But you know that."

"I was—" She starts to come up with an excuse, but I hold up my hand to stop her.

"Then I texted you."

"I answered you." Her voice is strong, then goes lower. "Once."

"Yup." I nod. "Got it. One whole word. No."

"Well, I didn't need anything." She puts her arms on the table, crossed in front of her. "So that was my answer."

"Did you send me the picture of the first day of school because you wanted to?" Her eyes quickly look away from mine. "Or was it a mistake?"

"It was a mistake." Wow, I thought for sure she would fight me on it. "I thought I sent it to Eddie."

"Well, I must say"—I laugh—"totally thought you would bullshit me."

"There is no reason to bullshit you, Christopher. There is also no reason for me to answer your phone calls or your texts."

"And why is that?" I know I should tread lightly, but this is also three months of building for both of us.

"Because you were calling to see how we are. We are fine." She doesn't even give me a chance to say anything before she continues, "You were also texting to ask me, and again, we are fine. If Benji was alive, you wouldn't be calling me."

"True but—"

"There is no but, Christopher, it would be awkward, and I didn't want to. That should be enough."

"I guess it will have to be for now," I say before the server comes over to interrupt us. I look down and order a burger while she orders the fish and chips with a side of onion rings and mac and cheese.

When the server leaves, I look back at her. "Rain wants to go skating more." She looks at me, grabbing the glass of water in front of her. "Can I take her?"

"Christopher," she says my name, putting the glass of water down.

"If you are going to hand me the 'you don't need to' bullshit, I'm going to start getting really pissed," I snap, and her eyes go big. "I'm sorry, I shouldn't have." I look down, and my leg shakes under the table. I was supposed to come in calm and cool and show her all I want to do is help, but instead, I just snapped at her.

"See?" She points at me. "This right there, the feeling sorry for me, is why I didn't answer your phone calls."

"Feeling sorry for you?" I repeat the words, not sure if she actually said them. Maybe I misunderstood.

"Yeah."

"I don't feel sorry for you," I tell her. "I feel a lot of things about the situation, but I don't feel sorry for you." She opens her mouth and then closes it. "I'm just doing what I hope someone would do for me if the roles were reversed." I move back when the drinks come and she just looks down and then up again.

"You can take her skating," she murmurs.

"Thank you," I say as the food comes. "I can even take Luna."

"Are you sure that won't be too much?" she asks as she takes a french fry and dunks it into ketchup.

"I think I'll be okay," I finally reply. "You can come if you want, or stay home and relax. Read a book, watch TV." She laughs again. "How was back to school for the kids?" I try to leave the conversation on neutral ground.

"The kids were happy to be back with their friends," she shares, telling me stories that happened to the girls during the week. The conversation is light and not forced. It feels weird to be sitting alone with her in a bar, the two of us, but I guess this is our new normal.

I pay the bill when she gets up to wash her hands, and when we walk out, I have to admit it's been a great night.

"So what are you going to do the rest of the night?" I ask when we get to the cars, not sure I want to call it a night yet.

"Not sure." She shrugs. "It's been a while since I've been home by myself."

"Are you going to walk around naked?" The minute I say the words, I want the earth to open and for me to be swallowed whole. Her eyes almost bug out of her head. "Oh no, not like that. I was thinking of the episode of *Friends*. When Rachel is home by herself and…" I put my hands on my face, feeling it turning beet red. "Oh my God, I am not thinking of you naked."

"Geez," she says, "thanks, I guess."

My heart sinks. "No, it's not that," I groan. "Tonight was nice." I avoid looking at her because she's probably thinking I'm a fucking creep who is picturing her dancing around her house naked. For the record, I wasn't, but now I can't help the flash of her naked in my head. "We should do it again."

"We'll see." She turns to walk to her SUV. "Have a good night." She opens her door. "I'm going to try not to walk around my house naked." I put my head back and groan, and I stop when I hear her giggle. "Night, Christopher."

"Night, Koda." I get into my truck and wait for her to leave before following her. We live about six streets apart. Actually, most of the team lives around the same area, except when she turns right, I turn left, heading to my house. I'm pulling up into the driveway when my phone rings in my pocket, pulling it out I see a number that isn't stored.

"Hello." I put the phone to my ear.

"Hi, Christopher," the female voice greets. "This is Keely, we met at the restaurant the other night."

"Oh, yeah," I say, not moving from my truck. "How are you?"

"I'm good, I'm good. I was just calling to let you know I had a lot of fun the other night." She mentions last Saturday when I went out with a couple of rookies to have dinner, and we were next to a group of girls. We started talking and exchanged numbers.

"Yeah, it really was."

"We should, I don't know, do it again?" Her voice is hopeful. "Maybe just meet up and go have a coffee."

"Yes," I agree right away, "that sounds good. Are you free next Wednesday?"

"Yes," she replies cheerfully, "I am."

"Great, how about we touch base on Tuesday?"

"That sounds amazing. Thank you." She lingers for a couple of minutes.

"See you then," I finally say, hanging up the phone and then looking at it again. My head suddenly replays the night over and over again.

Instead of going into the house, I open my text messages and scroll down until I see her name.

Me: Did you get home?

I don't know if she will answer me or not, but I'm shocked when a message comes in right away.

Koda: You literally followed me.

I laugh and turn the truck back on before backing out

and making my way over to her house. I get out of my truck and jog up her steps, ringing the doorbell. It takes her a minute before she opens the door. She's out of the clothes she wore before and is now in a baby-blue lounge set. "Hey," I say, holding up my hand.

"Hey," she replies. "Sorry, I was naked and had to get dressed."

"Funny." I point at her. "I was in the neighborhood."

"You live in the neighborhood." She crosses her arms over her chest.

I laugh. "Okay, fine, I knew it would be weird not having the kids here, so I figured you would like company."

"But how am I supposed to dance and sing naked if you're here?" She moves to let me in, closing the door behind me.

"I guess you'll have to maybe bake cookies or something," I tease her as we walk back to the family room. "You got a new couch." I take in the new couch and see she's poured herself a glass of red wine that sits on the coffee table. The big-screen television is paused on a movie.

"I did," she confirms, "it's way comfier than the last one." She walks into the room and sits down right in front of the wine. "Plus, I didn't find my dead husband on it."

"Damn." I sit beside her. "How many glasses of wine have you had?"

She laughs. "My therapist says I shouldn't hide the fact why I changed it."

"I mean, my therapist gives me the same advice," I share, and she gasps.

"You see a therapist?" She grabs the glass of wine and takes a sip.

"No, not really. I talk to my uncle Viktor," I admit. "He is a recovering addict."

"Oh, yes," she says, remembering him. "Is it helping?"

I shrug, not wanting to talk about it and ruin the night. "What are you watching?"

"*Hope Floats*," she replies, and I just stare at her. "It's Sandra Bullock."

"She was great in *Speed*," I counter.

"We can watch that one after." She grabs the remote to start it, and I have to wonder if she doesn't want to be alone or maybe this is her letting me in. Either way, I'm not going to question it. "You didn't miss much."

"I'm sure I'll catch up." I take off my jacket and toss it to the side. Forty minutes into the movie, Koda grabs a throw blanket hanging on the back of the couch and cuddles into the couch. Ten minutes after that, she's asleep. I know I should get up and take off, but instead, I lay my head back, and fifteen minutes later, I'm asleep myself.

EIGHT

Dakota

"BREAKFAST IS READY!" I shout over my shoulder, putting the plates of pancakes and fruit on the counter for the girls. "Let's go before we're late."

They come running in from the family room, getting on their respective stools. "Mom, did you call Christopher," Rain asks, picking up a blackberry and eating it, "about skating?"

"I have not," I tell her, "but I will. I'm going to go get dressed." Grabbing my cup of coffee, I walk up the stairs.

The last time I saw Christopher was four days ago when I opened my eyes and found the television on the menu and Christopher still sitting next to me, but his head was back and he was sleeping. I thought about waking him up, but instead, I fell right back asleep, only waking up at seven o'clock when his alarm on his phone started blaring. I felt him sit up next to me and opened my eyes, seeing him turn it off before rubbing his face.

He looked over at me, the sleep still in his eyes. "It's seven o'clock." His voice was thick with sleep.

I stretched my arms over my head. "I can't believe you slept all night sitting up."

"Me too. I'm surprised I don't have a kink in my neck. This couch passes the test." He chuckled before he got to his feet. "I guess I'll get out of your hair."

"Yeah, I haven't had a chance to sing naked yet." I tossed the cover off me before standing. "I really have to get on that."

"I will never live that down." He grabbed his jacket off the back of the couch and held it in his hand before he turned and started to walk out of the room.

"You didn't even take your shoes off." I followed him out of the room. His head down, looking at his shoes.

He stopped at the front door and turned to look at me. "Thank you for last night."

"I didn't do anything." My voice was lower than I wanted it to be.

"No, but you didn't tell me to fuck off." His hand reached for the handle of the door, and he opened it. "You let me come in instead of doing your own thing."

"You're welcome." I smiled at him. He gave me a quick nod before he walked out of the house to his truck. I watched him pull out of the driveway before I closed the door and went on my way.

Now here I am, four days later, and Rain has brought him up every single day, sometimes twice a day. I walk into my bedroom, going to the closet to grab an outfit for today. "What does one wear to a survivor meeting?" I ask myself as I take a sip of the hot coffee in my hand. I pull out a pair of black jeans, slipping into them before taking out a long, white button-down cotton shirt. I look over at my sweaters before I select a beige crop one that falls to my stomach, with the white button-down coming out on the bottom. "This looks clean cut." I look at myself in the mirror before sitting on my little bench and putting on a pair of white sneakers.

After I brush my teeth and hair, I am one minute ahead of schedule. We rush out of the house, and drop-off is over before I know it. The girls and I have gotten into a smooth routine. I'm even starting to get into the groove of things. I go to therapy twice a week—usually on Monday, after the weekend, and Friday, right before the weekend.

The weekends are when I think it hits me the most. It's usually family time, but our family always feels like it's missing something, so I go above and beyond to make sure the kids don't feel like they're missing anything.

I pull up to the address I plugged in my GPS, then park and get out. I grab my black crossbody purse, holding it in my hand so tight that my nails cut into my palm. I look around, seeing a couple of people standing outside the door. One of them holds a white Styrofoam cup. As soon as I get to the door, he smiles at me. "Are you here for the Nar-Anon meeting?"

"I am." I look at him.

"I'm Shawn." He extends his hand. "I'll be running the meeting today."

"I'm Dakota." I nervously shake his hand. "But

everyone calls me Koda."

"Nice to meet you, Koda," he says. "You can go in and sit anywhere you like."

"Thank you," I reply, pulling open the door and second-guessing why I'm even here. Maybe it's too early in the grieving process for this. I walk down the five steps to the open blue doors, and my knees almost give up on me with each step. The room is bare, with just white walls and wooden chairs in a circle. I look around, trying not to turn around and run back out of the room. I see a brown table in the corner with a silver coffee pot and a stack of white Styrofoam cups beside it. I stand here I don't even know how long. My mouth feels dry, like there is no liquid in my body.

The back of my neck tingles, while my stomach feels like there is a tsunami going on in it. "Hi." I look over to the side and see a woman with long blond hair. "I'm Callie," she says with a smile, "you're new."

"I am." I try not to seem as nervous as I am. "Does it show? Is there an arrow over my head flashing?"

She laughs at my stupid joke. "Yes." She points over my head. "It's red right now." I hold my purse in front of me with both hands. "We were all new once upon a time."

I think about her words when I hear clapping and look over to see Shawn walking in without his cup. "We're starting the meeting. Everyone, please grab a seat."

My feet move for me, grabbing one of the seats and sitting down. "I see some new faces," Shawn says, looking at me and another man sitting across from me.

"We'll go around the room and introduce ourselves. I'll start, my name is Shawn, and I'm a recovering addict. I've been clean for the last twelve years and four months. Four thousand five hundred and one days. I was on every single drug you can think of." His voice goes softer. "OD'd five times. The last time, it took them eight shots of Narcan to start my heart again. Left me in a coma for two months, which is why I was able to get clean. Woke up and knew I never wanted to do that again. I relapsed two months later for a week, and that was when I looked the devil in the eyes and walked away. But I'm also here because I'm not only in recovery, my wife, Callie, stayed an addict long after I got clean. The pressure to stay clean and also get her clean was an enormous monkey on my back." He smiles. "But she's here, and I am thankful every single day." Callie smiles at him. "Who's next?"

I wait until I'm the last one left to speak because listening to everyone's story makes me feel like I'm not alone. Like what I went through wasn't out of the normal for someone who is living with an addict. Like I didn't do anything to make him do what he did. There is a mother who is trying to get her grown son to go to rehab, and he's not listening. He has her sleeping on the floor because he has sold everything they have.

"My name is Koda," I start nervously, "well, Dakota, but everyone calls me Koda." I laugh but feel the tightness right above my stomach. "I'm married to an addict." I use the present tense, and then I catch it. "I was married to an addict." My palms get sweaty. "Ninety-seven days ago, my husband died of a drug overdose on our couch." The tears that I've had in my eyes for everyone else's story slide out. "The day after our daughter's fourth birthday. Luckily for me"—I look down at my hands—"or unlucky for me, I found him. I knew he was using drugs, but I didn't know what kind of drugs. I didn't know where he got them from. I didn't know how to help him." My voice trembles. "I really wish I could have helped him."

"Wasn't your place," a man named Shepard says, shocking me. "I mean, it was your place to help him, but it was his place to want the help."

I nod at him. "That's what everyone says, but how does one go on? How do I not feel guilty that I didn't try harder? How do I look my girls in the eyes when they get older and learn the truth that their mother didn't do enough?"

"No one can answer that for you," Shawn says. "Only you can do that." All I can do is nod.

The rest of the meeting is just everyone talking about how they can get the person they love help. How they've tried countless times, again and again, and have come up empty-handed. When I finally walk out of there and get in the car, I think I'm about to have my first serious nervous breakdown. I put my hands in front of my face when the sobs come, and my phone rings at the same time. The speakers in the car tell me, "Dr. Mendes calling."

"Hello," I answer, my voice breaking.

"I guess I called right on time," she replies softly.

"How did you know?"

"I knew you were going to the meeting today, and I was wondering how it went."

"It was fucking brutal. So many stories about how people got better, and the only thing I could think about is, why the fuck didn't Benji want to be better?"

"Maybe he didn't know how?" She tries to answer my question with another.

"Well, he should have. If not for me or him, then for our girls," I snap. "He chose drugs over everything." My voice goes louder. "Who does that?"

"An addict," she says softly. "You can sit down and ask the 'why me' question each time and hope he somehow answers you."

"I have to accept that my husband was sick," I admit softly. "That what he had was a sickness." I swallow. "A disease."

"I think if you are going to heal, you need to work on forgiving him before anything else."

"Yeah, easier said than done. I feel sorry for him for about two point five minutes before the sorrow turns to plain-out anger that he did what he did."

"I want you to start a list," she suggests. "A to-do list. One thing on that list should be something to do for the kids, and one thing has to be something to do for you. Not for you that includes the kids. But just for you. Like go for a bike ride for an hour or have a picnic with yourself while the girls are at school. It has to be something for you and no one else."

"I haven't done something for myself in a long time," I admit.

"Well, now is the time to start."

"Take charge of my life," I agree with her.

"We can call it whatever you want to call it. We can discuss it on Friday." I can see her smile at me.

"Sounds good. Thank you for checking up on me."

"It was my pleasure, Koda." She hangs up the phone as I pull out of the parking lot. Going to the supermarket, I pick up things for dinner before stopping to grab myself some flowers because I've never bought myself flowers, and I like how they look.

When I get the kids from school and daycare, the first thing Rain asks is if I called Christopher. I know I can't put it off for much longer. So when I've started dinner, I pick up the phone.

Pulling up the text chain of the two of us. Lately, I've answered him with a *we are all good but thanks for asking*. He still calls daily. I still don't answer him, but I've started answering his texts.

Me: Hey, I have a question for you.

I put the phone down, thinking he'll text me when he has a minute, but instead of texting me, my phone rings, and I see it's Christopher. "Hello." I put the phone to my ear while I pull out the chicken casserole I put together when we got home.

"Hey," he says, and it sounds like he's walking, "what's up?"

"You didn't have to call." I chuckle. "It could have waited."

"For you to change your mind and then say forget it?" He laughs, and I have to remember that he knows me and has known me for a really long time. "What can I help you with?"

"Do you know of any skating classes?" I ask, holding the phone with my shoulder as I put the casserole dish on the stovetop. "Rain really wants to go skating."

"What are you guys doing now?" he asks.

"We're just about to eat." I look down at the casserole dish, the steam hitting my face. "Why?"

"I can see if I can get some ice time at the rink I go practice at," he says, "but if it's too close to dinner."

"What about after?" The words come out of my mouth and shock not only Christopher but me. "See if you can get some time after. If you can, why don't you come and eat?" He stays silent. "Unless you have dinner plans with someone else."

"No, I have nothing planned. Give me five, maybe less."

"Okay," I agree, putting the phone on the counter. It takes him two minutes to call me back. "That was fast."

"He answered my call," he jokes with me. "You should try it sometime."

"Did I not answer my phone twice?"

"That you did." His voice is smooth. "Okay, he has an opening from six to seven." I look over and see that it's just a little after five. "I can be at your place in thirty-seven seconds."

"Thirty-seven?" I shake my head.

"Thirty-five if I don't have to do the last stop sign." I hear the door slam on his end. "Then we can get the girls and go skating."

"I can take them." I look over, knowing Rain will love this.

"Already in the car and halfway there," he states. "See you soon."

He hangs up before I can say anything, and he wasn't lying when he said it takes him thirty-seven seconds to get here. The doorbell rings as soon as I take the plates out of the cupboard. "Go get the door," I tell the girls, who run to the door, and then I hear the squeals from both of them.

"Uncle Chrissy!" Luna screeches at the top of her lungs. "Mommy, Uncle Chrissy is here!" She runs into the room to tell me before running back out. I smile as I plate the girls' dinner and then look over to see the three of them walking back into the room with Luna in Christopher's arms. He's wearing a black jogging suit. "Look, Mom."

"I see." I smile at him as he puts Luna down. "Go wash up for dinner," I tell them, and they run into the bathroom.

"You were not lying about thirty-seven seconds." I stay in the kitchen and watch him walk toward me.

"Smells good in here," he compliments. "Did you tell the girls yet?"

"How much do you think I can get done in thirty seconds?" I tilt my head to the side. "I didn't even have a chance to plate dinner."

"I can do a lot in thirty seconds," he states, looking at the food.

"I don't know if you should boast about something like that." I bite my lower lip to stop myself from laughing when his head whips up.

"Wow, walked right into that one." The smirk fills his face.

"That you did." I shake my head and prepare him a plate, then hand it to him.

"For the record, longer than thirty seconds," he boasts, and I can't help but giggle at him. He takes the plate. "What did you do today?" he asks, walking to the stool and taking it out.

"I attended a meeting with recovering addicts," I report, and his head flies up so fast it's shocking he doesn't give himself whiplash. He's about to ask me something when the girls run back into the room.

"Let's eat," I say, looking at the clock, "because Uncle Christopher has a surprise for you." I look over at him, and he looks at the girls.

"You have to eat all your food." He points at their plates. "Then I'll tell you." He smiles at them, his eyes lightening. He then looks at me. "You too."

"So bossy," I mumble, making the girls laugh as I look over and realize that he's the only one who really expects nothing from me. Eddie expects me not to talk bad about his son. He expects me to protect his reputation. Everyone expects me to be okay and be my old self. But Christopher doesn't expect me to be anything or say anything. He just wants to know if I need help and what he can do to help me. I then look at my flowers and put something on my list for myself.

NINE

CHRISTOPHER

"DID I DO good?" Rain asks as we get off the ice. The doors to the Zamboni open for it to take the ice, and I see a couple of kids waiting to get on the ice. "I didn't fall a lot," she says, proud of herself.

"You didn't," I agree with her. "You were born to skate," I mumble as I help Luna step up to go to the changing rooms.

"Me too?" Luna asks as she walks to where Koda sits.

"You too," I answer her.

"Mommy, I was born to skate," Luna repeats to her as she smiles at her. She sat behind the bench the whole time while we were on the ice. It took Luna about twenty minutes before she felt confident enough to release the metal bar. Then she fell four times in a row and took it back, but Rain got better every single time she got back up.

"I know," she says, getting up, "the both of you did so good."

"Next time, you could come with us," Luna invites as we walk toward the changing room.

"Umm," Koda hesitates, "I don't know."

"Can we come back," Rain asks when she takes off her helmet, "tomorrow?"

"Whenever your mom says it's okay." I throw it back to Koda, who stares at me, and it looks a little like a glare.

"Let's check our schedule," she deflects before she squats down in front of Luna, helping her untie her skates. Rain already has hers off and is drinking the Gatorade I got them as soon as I got into the rink.

We walk out of the rink with me holding the bags while Koda holds the girls' hands. When she called me on the phone and asked where to take the girls skating, I knew exactly where to take them. I called up Guy, who owns the place, and he said to come right in, but I would have to leave by seven because the ice was rented. It's the same arena I train at in the summer with my family.

"Buckle in," Koda states while I put the bags in the trunk. I slam the trunk at the same time as she closes the back door. We head back to her house, and Luna is practically sleeping by the time I unbuckle her.

"In the bath and then bed," Koda says to her, and she just mumbles as she walks into the house, heading for the stairs. "Say thank you to Uncle Christopher."

"Thank you, Uncle Chrissy," Luna mumbles, not even looking over her shoulder as she holds the railing to the stairs, lifting the other hand to say goodbye.

"Thank you, Uncle Christopher," Rain says to me,

hugging me around the waist. I bend to kiss the top of her head before she skips off.

"Thank you again," Koda adds, and I nod to her and walk out the door. I wait an hour before I text her to see if she's up.

Me: Hey, are you up? I want to ask you something.
Koda: No.

I laugh at her dry humor, and instead of texting her, I call her. I don't even know if she will answer me, and I'm more than a little surprised when she does. "Wow, she answers."

"But did I?" She laughs, and I can hear the television in the background playing from her end, and I wonder if she's watching another Sandra Bullock movie. "Maybe it's your imagination."

"Well, whatever it is, I'm not going to question it." I get up and make my way to the kitchen to grab a glass of water. "What do you think about putting Rain in hockey classes?"

"What?"

"Like, signing her up to be on a hockey team." I walk out of the kitchen, turning off the lights and heading to my bedroom. "She's really, really good, and she likes it."

"You don't think maybe she should do figure skating?"

"Wow, sexist much?" I put the glass of water down on the bedside table. "I have nieces who play hockey and are better than some of the guys."

"Yeah, but—" she says. "I don't know."

"I can ask a couple of the guys," I suggest. "Maybe call Guy and ask about a house league."

"The only problem with that is, what about Luna?"

"Put her in also," I quickly add. "It'll do them good."

"They're already in gymnastics," she counters, "and piano. I would have to see the schedule."

"Piano?" I ask.

"Yeah, they started this summer. I needed something to keep them busy, you know, after all the Benji stuff, and piano it was."

"How do they like it?" I ask, suddenly wanting to know all the details.

"I mean, it was rough at the beginning when they would practice at the same time." She laughs. "But it's getting a bit better."

"How was the meeting?" I close my eyes, hoping she doesn't shut down on me. I know I should just wait for her to tell me more instead of me just jumping in and asking her.

"It was different," she states. "We sat around and told stories about how our lives were affected by drugs."

"Did it help?"

"Yes and no." She exhales. "Like, I was happy to hear I wasn't the only one. But then I kind of felt jealous of the ones who still had their loved one there so they can try to help them."

"I know it goes without saying," I start softly, "but I never thought it was that bad." She doesn't say anything. "I knew something had to be done, but…" Neither of us says anything.

"Let me know about the skating and stuff, and I can decide," she says after three minutes of us sitting on the phone in silence.

"Will do," I confirm, hanging up the phone before I fuck up and say something else to her.

I pull up my uncle's number and put it on speakerphone. "This is a late-night phone call," he answers.

"Yeah, sorry, I took Luna and Rain skating," I word vomit. "What do you think of me attending meetings?"

"I mean, nothing wrong with going to meetings and talking." His voice is always so soft. "What brought this on?"

I could tell him about Koda, but I don't want to take what she told me and tell someone. It's hers, and she shared it with me, and I'm going to keep it close to my chest. "Just something I read online," I lie.

"I can see if there are meetings near you. Ask around."

"Thank you, I really appreciate it."

"Anytime, kiddo. Go to sleep. You have a game tomorrow night."

"Got it." I laugh and hang up on him, and then I text Guy.

Me: Hey, do you have any information about skating for a six-year-old and a four-year-old?

I'm about to put the phone away when there is a beep, and I look down and see that it's Keely.

Keely: Hey ;) just checking to see if we are still on for coffee tomorrow. My day is open, so just let me know.

I close my eyes and think about canceling it, but then I'll just have to make it another day. I might as well go and get it over with.

Me: Sorry, forgot I have work tomorrow night. But I

can do coffee at around ten.

"Please say no," I tell my phone when I see the three dots come up. "Please say no," I chant again. "Fuck," I swear when I see her response.

Keely: That works for me. Where do you want to meet?

"Nowhere," I say while my fingers type out a little coffee shop about twenty minutes away.

Keely: See you then. Have a good night, Christopher.

I'm about to toss my phone to the side when another text comes in, and this time it's from Guy.

"People are just on the ball tonight," I mumble as I read his text.

Guy: There is a local team called Pirates. The good news is they are just starting up for the season. Spoke to my contact over there, he's waiting for your call. Let me know if you need anything else. Richard 878-355-2398

Me: Thanks, man, appreciate it.

Only after I send the text do I put my phone away before going to take a shower. I get up the next day, my head feeling all over the place. I get dressed in my light gray pants and a long-sleeved waffle shirt. I grab the black Tom Ford belt before putting on my white sneakers and heading out the door.

I put the address in the GPS even though I know where it is. It's a force of habit, plus it tells me if there is traffic, and the one thing I can't do is traffic. I mean me and a million other people.

As soon as I pull out of the driveway, I hit up the

number that Guy sent me. I'm expecting to be leaving a voicemail, but the man answers after three rings. "Richard Sithal."

"Hi, Richard, my name is Christopher. I got your number from Guy at Locker Room Ice." I tap the steering wheel. "I was looking to get my girls into a hockey camp or skating, whichever one you have." The way "my girls" slips out and I don't correct myself is something I have to think about later.

"Hey, Christopher," he says, "how old are the girls?" The conversation lasts five minutes, and he gives me the information about an open skating this Saturday morning at eight o'clock at Guy's arena. After I hang up the phone with him, I immediately call Dakota.

She answers after five rings and sounds out of breath. "Hey."

"What are you doing?" I ask.

"I'm cutting the grass and planting a tree," she pants. "What's up?"

"Don't you have a lawn service?" I pull into the parking lot of the coffee shop.

"Yeah, but I canceled it." Her breathing sounds like it's getting more controlled. "Is that what you called me for?"

"No," I say, but then a million questions are coming to my head, like why the fuck isn't someone cutting her grass? And what kind of tree is she planting and why? Instead, I look over and see the girl I'm supposed to be meeting. "I'm calling because I want to know if the kids have hockey gear."

"They did," she says, "but that was last year. Why?"

"I found a skating class for them to try out this Saturday morning at eight o'clock," I tell her. "The guy said to bring them in and see if they like it. But they have to be dressed." Keely lifts her hand from beside my truck. "Can you send me their sizes, and I'll get them stuff?"

"Don't buy anything yet," she snaps. "Let me see what fits and what doesn't, and I'll go from there."

"Okay," I agree, trying to prolong the conversation but knowing I have to get off the phone. "I have to go." I look down. "Later."

She doesn't bother answering me. Instead, she just hangs up. I exhale before I turn off the truck and open the door. My heart pounds in my chest as I try to block out the conversation I just had. "Hi." I walk to her and extend my hand while she goes in for a kiss on the cheek. "Oh." I try to go left and right while she laughs. "Sorry," I say.

"No worries." She laughs it off, and her brown eyes light up. "It's nice to see you."

"Yeah," I say, "shall we go inside?" I hold out my hand for her to walk in front of me. She looks over at me, and the only thing I can think of is how long before I can leave without her thinking I'm an asshole.

I wish I could say the rest of the date went well. It didn't. Keely tried to ask me questions, but my answers were one word. I would counter, ask the same questions and just nod, not putting in a word more. Let's just say when we left there, I wanted to kick my own ass. Luckily for me, I don't have time to dwell on it because there's a preseason game tonight.

We end up winning three to one, but it doesn't count, so no one cares. When I get home, I look at my texts to see if Koda texted me, but obviously, she didn't. The only one who texted me is Keely.

Keely: Thank you for today. It was so much fun.

My eyebrows pinch together because it was not fun. Nothing about it was fun. It was like getting a root canal over and over again. Or watching wet paint dry.

Keely: Hope we can do it again.

She ends it with a smiley face, and instead of just saying *yeah, that sounds good, let me check my schedule*, my head has other ideas.

Me: Yeah, that sounds great. If you aren't busy in two weeks, how about you join me for the first game of the season?

I press send before I even think about what a stupid, stupid mistake it is. I look down and my hands shake because I did not want to do that. And now there isn't anything I can say that won't make me look like a complete and ultimate asshole. A text comes in before I can do anything and think of an excuse.

Keely: Oh my goodness, I would love that.

"What the actual fuck are you doing?" I ask myself, looking down at the phone, closing the chat before I do something else that is totally fucked up and not right.

I pull up a thread with my cousin Zoey, who is more like my sister. I go to her when I don't want my sisters to know anything or catch on to things.

Me: Question.

I wait for her to answer my text, knowing she always, and I mean always, has her phone on her. She's a PR guru, so she always waits for one of her clients to get into a scandal. Sadly, they've never had the chance, and she is always left waiting.

Zoey: I probably have an answer.

Me: If I have coffee with a girl and it's like the worst time, and then I ask her out again, is she going to think it's a date-date?

Zoey: If you had the worst time, why invite her out again?

Me: Because.

Zoey: That's a solid response.

Me: I don't know, I felt bad she thought it was the best time ever.

Zoey: Wow, good thing she didn't declare her love for you or you'd be having her baby.

I snort out laughing.

Me: It's a great thing, or I'd probably ask her to marry me.

Zoey: But seriously, did you ask her out again?

Me: I did.

Zoey: Why would you waste her time like that?

Me: If I knew, I wouldn't have texted you with the question, now would I?

Zoey: Well, you can always cancel.

Me: Then won't I be an asshole?

Zoey: You are taking her out on a date you don't want to go on.

Me: But at least I'm not canceling.

Zoey: Yes, that's much better than you not wanting to be there with her.

Me: Ugh.

Zoey: If you don't want to be an asshole, go on the date, but then you have to tell her you aren't looking for anything more than a friend.

Me: That is going to make me even more of an asshole.

Zoey: The minute you asked her out on a second date, you became an asshole. This is just you being less of an asshole. You're welcome.

Me: Fine. I'll do what you said.

Zoey: Good man, still an asshole, but good man.

I can't help but laugh at her.

Me: Good talk.

I toss my phone to the other side of the bed before I rub my hands over my face. "You are an asshole."

TEN

Dakota

"IS UNCLE CHRISTOPHER coming?" Rain asks as we walk out of the house on our way to their hockey practice. Or whatever it is that this is. All I know is we have to meet him at the rink by seven thirty on a Saturday. I mean, it's not like we sleep in, but still.

"I want Uncle Chrissy to tie my skates," Luna mumbles as she steps out of the door while I wait to close it.

"If he's not there, I will tie them," I tell her, and I don't have a chance to say anything else because the girls squeal his name.

I look over my shoulder and see him standing there, leaning against his truck. He's wearing another pair of black joggers with a hooded sweater this time. A baseball hat turned backward; he has stubble on his jaw, but all I can really focus on is him holding out his hands to the side with a huge-ass smile on his face as the girls run toward him. "Who's ready to skate?"

I walk down the stairs with the girls' bags in my hand,

making my way to them. The sleeves from my sweater fall from my elbow to over my wrist. "Let me help." Christopher walks over to me, grabbing the bags from my hand. "Open the trunk, will you, so I can put the stuff I bought in?"

"Stuff you bought?" I ask, confused. "What are you talking about?"

"Nothing much," he says, opening my trunk and then going to his and coming back with two small hockey bags. "Just like, chest protectors and elbow pads. Some shin pads, just a little bit of everything," he mumbles as he puts the bags in the trunk. The girls are already loaded in the back of the SUV.

"I didn't know you were going to be here this morning." I take a deep breath. "I would have made you coffee."

"We can get coffee after," he suggests, avoiding looking at me. "We should get going. We have to check them in. I filled out their registration papers, but things are missing."

"You filled out registration papers?" If someone had told me three months ago, or even last week, that Christopher Stone would be filling out kids' registration forms, I would have bet money against that person, knowing it would be a sure bet.

"Yeah, I don't know their medical history and all that," he states, walking around the SUV and opening the door. "Did you want me to drive?"

"Um, no," I say as I walk to the SUV and pull open the driver's side door in time to see him turn in his seat and share his excitement with the girls.

"Are we all buckled in?" I look in the rearview mirror at the girls, who are both smiling so big it feels like it's Christmas morning. I buckle myself in before I pull out and make the mistake of looking over at Christopher. "How long were you out there waiting?"

"About fifteen minutes," he answers as if it's nothing, and all I can do is pick my jaw up off the floor. I don't say another word to him because the kids ask him questions about if he'll be on the ice. What happens if they fall? Is he going to tie their skates?

We pull into the parking lot, and it looks like almost all the spots are taken. He's out of the car before I even turn it off, opening the back door and getting the kids. I join them in the back of the SUV, where Christopher hands me a manila folder. "The papers are in there," he tells me as he puts both bags over his one shoulder, then grabbing their bag with skates.

He presses the button to close the trunk before turning and walking toward the doors. The girls walk on each side of him, and I follow them. I take out my phone and snap a picture of it.

When we walk in, I'm a little taken aback by all the parents there. I look around quickly to see if there are any faces I recognize, breathing a sigh of relief when there are none. "Hi," Christopher says to the guy sitting behind a brown table. "My name is Christopher."

"Yes, you called about your girls," he says, and my eyes go wide. I immediately look down at the girls to see if they caught that, but they are much too interested in getting on the ice.

"This is Rain, and this is Luna." He smiles down at them. "That's Mom." He points over at me. "Dakota. She has the forms that need to be filled out."

"Perfect, you can go in there, and they will hand you a jersey for each girl. I got the payment already, so you're good to go," he says, pointing at the hallway we went in the last time.

"You got this?" Christopher says to me, motioning to the guy with his head, and all I can do is nod.

"Let's go, girls," he urges them, and they don't even turn around to say goodbye to me. I walk over to the desk, open the folder, and see that he filled out all their things with their names and birthdays. I go through the medical side of it and check no for everything before handing it to the man.

"Thank you." I smile at him, turning and seeing all the parents walking into the rink through the two brown doors. The cold hits you as soon as you step foot into the rink. I walk up the two steps to sit on the bleachers, looking at the side. I see a couple of the kids lining up at the door when a guy walks out wearing a black tracksuit and helmet. The kids move away to give him a chance to open the door before they get on the ice.

I sit here looking at the kids skate onto the ice. A couple of them know how to skate while a couple of them fall as soon as they get on the ice. Then the kid in back also ends up either tripping one of them or falls into one of them. It's like a chain reaction. Then I see Christopher with the girls right next to him. Luna looks like she's going to fall over with all the padding, and she says something to him, and he just laughs at her. But my eyes then go to Rain, who smirks at Christopher before she gets on the ice. I hold my breath, thinking she might fall since she's never skated with padding. But she moves side to side like Christopher taught her the last time. On the other hand, Luna skates and ends up on her bottom two seconds later. I'm about to get up and go to her when I see Christopher tell her something, and she nods and gets up. He looks over the crowd and spots me.

He comes over and sits next to me. "Fuck, it's cold in here." He chuckles, rubbing his hands together. "I don't think I've ever sat on this side before."

I shake my head. "How are they?"

"Excited AF." He looks at me, and his smile is contagious. He looks back on the ice and rubs his hands together, then blows on them.

"Are you nervous?" I ask, seeing his eyes on the girls making sure that he can have them in his sight the whole time.

"No." He pffts at me, then leans into me and looks around before he says, "But if one of those fuckers push them down."

I can't help the way his tone hits me; my head goes back, and I laugh out loud. The sound echoes in the arena, and a couple of the parents look my way. I push him with my shoulder. "What if the girls push them?"

"They probably deserved it," he states, and I roll my eyes. "What?" He shrugs.

"A couple of things," I start when I take my phone

out and snap a couple of pictures of the girls, prompting Christopher to do the same thing. "One, how much does this cost?"

"Don't worry about it," he says without even looking at me.

"What do you mean don't worry about it?" I make sure my voice is low.

"It means I took care of it." He finally looks over at me. "So what's next?"

"What?" I'm now confused.

"Well, you said a couple of things." He turns back to look at the ice. "What is the next thing?" Then he turns back to me.

I don't know if it's his blue eyes or the way his voice goes low, or the way he always turns back to make sure the girls are okay that literally takes all the words out of my vocabulary. "Um." I quickly turn away. "How many times a week is this thing?"

"It's either Saturday or Sunday, depending on what team they get put on. But I was talking to Guy, and he said I can rent out the ice a couple of times a week if I want to."

"That's a lot of hockey." I watch the ice, seeing Luna struggling, but Rain is being put in one group after another.

"I can take them." He puts his hands on the bench beside my leg. "You can, I don't know, go to Target."

I close my eyes, laughing. "What's wrong with Target?"

"Nothing, I just know when a woman goes in there,

they are gone for a while." His eyes never leave the girls. They go back and forth from one group to the next.

"You are not wrong," I agree with him. The kids stay on the ice for fifty minutes until the bell rings, and then one of the men blows the whistle for the kids to get off the ice.

Christopher is already on his feet, walking down the bleachers to the door, leaving me by myself with the rest of the other moms. I get up and walk toward the door and the waiting area.

A couple of the kids come out with their fathers, their hair wet, and then I see them. Luna walks out first, with Rain holding Christopher's hand.

"Mommy." Luna runs to me, and I bend to pick her up. "I fell," she reports happily, "but then I got up. I'm a superstar."

"Are you?" I ask, and she nods, her hair wet and stuck to her forehead.

"That's what Uncle Chrissy said." She plays with the collar of my sweater. I swallow down the lump that has suddenly risen from my stomach. "He said Rain was a superstar too."

"Mom, did you see?" Rain asks when she comes to me. "I went from group to group because I was too good."

"That's my girl," Christopher praises, holding up his fist for her to fist bump him. "Now, how about we go and eat some breakfast?"

"I'm hungry." Luna squirms in my arms to get down. "I want breakfast tacos."

"Yes," Christopher says, walking toward the door with the girls, holding it open for them. "I want extra hash browns."

"Me too," Luna agrees, walking out with Rain.

Christopher looks over his shoulder at me, holding the door open. "You okay?" he asks, and I want to tell him I'm not okay. Nothing about this is okay. Nothing about this morning should be okay. Nothing about him taking my girls to hockey should be okay. Nothing about this is okay, yet everything about this feels okay.

I look at my phone and make a note of the date and realize that for the first time in over a year, I don't hate Benji. "I'm coming."

ELEVEN

Dakota

"HAVE YOU DECIDED what you're going to do?" Dr. Mendes asks.

"That's a loaded question." I look over at her. "Have I decided what I'm going to do for dinner? Have I decided what I'm going to do when my girls go to sleep tonight?"

She laughs with me. "I meant, have you decided what you're going to do about the first game of the season?" I nod at her.

"Aha," I say, "I'm not sure. I know I should go. I know the girls are going to want to go. I know if I go, in the end, I'll have a nice evening out."

"But?" She always goes to but, and it sometimes feels like I'm having a conversation with the girls. We can have this, but would you rather this?

"But should I even be there?" I shrug. Last week, the team's general manager made it a point to call me and tell me that even though Benji isn't with us anymore, my place will always be with the association.

"It's not like you've never been to a game before." The minute she says the words, I point at her.

"That's true." I take a sip of my coffee. "But I don't know."

"So maybe do it for the girls." She smirks. "And a little for you."

"I have to be at a hockey arena tomorrow morning at seven o'clock," I snap, "on a Saturday." She throws her head back and laughs. It's been over two weeks since the girls started hockey whatever it's called. Two weeks and they thrive at it. Even Luna is getting better and better.

"I don't know, but something tells me you'll survive." I bring the cup of coffee to my lips and snort before I take another sip. I will survive.

The session ends with me deciding I should go, if just for the kids. I put "drink wine in a bubble bath" as something to do for myself after tomorrow.

The kids don't even complain when I wake them both up at six, which bothers me to no end. The soft knock on the door still surprises me, but then again, it doesn't. Christopher has been to every single practice in the past two weeks. I know with the season starting this weekend, he won't be able to make some of them.

"I made you coffee." I hand him the black thermos I prepared for him, just in case he came.

"Thank God." He holds out his hand to grab the thermos. His hand is colder than mine, and I can feel a shiver crawl up my spine. "I literally rolled out of bed five minutes ago."

"Well, it looks like it." I chuckle while he glares at

me. Practice is pretty much the same as it's been the last two weeks. The two of us sit side by side while Christopher leans over occasionally and points out kids he'll have problems with if they do one more thing to the girls. In the past two weeks, we've talked on the phone every single day when he calls to check on the girls, and sometimes, he will text me random things during the day, which I usually answer with a thumbs-up or down.

"See you tonight," he says before getting back in his truck after breakfast is consumed and the kids are watching television.

As the day gets later and later, I feel the nerves rolling in with a punch. I feel like I'm going to throw up every five seconds. The girls wear jeans and the team jerseys with Benji's number on the back that say Daddy on them. I swallow down the lump in my throat before going into my closet to get dressed. I slip on a pair of tight black jeans. They used to be tighter on me, but they're not horrible. I decide to also grab a black bodysuit that fits perfectly. Buttoning up the jeans, I slide into a pair of white Gucci sneakers.

I move to the bathroom to touch up my hair, which I spent way too much time on. I tried to convince myself I was doing it for me, but in reality, I was doing it for everyone else. To make them see I'm okay, or at least trying to be. My hands shake as I walk down the steps and yell for the girls that it's time to go.

They put on their sneakers at the door while I take the leather jacket and slip it on. I snap a picture of myself and send it to Dr. Mendes with the caption "You can take the widow to the game, but you can't make her wear color." I snort at my own joke before grabbing my keys and heading outside.

I try to control my breathing as I turn down to the parking garage where the families park. The girls are so excited they have been bouncing off the walls all afternoon long. They wouldn't even take a nap. I'm hoping they want to crash in the second period so I can leave. I grab the badge I was sent on Wednesday before we make our way over to the family suite.

The team has three whole sections of suites that they have made into one big one. It always has food and drinks, but then there are about a hundred seats in front of the suite for people to sit and actually watch the game. My neck burns as I get closer and closer, the chatting of everyone around me fades away and all I can hear is my heart thumping in my chest. "This is it," I say when I smile at the security guard at the door, who nods at me when he sees the badge.

As soon as I walk in, I want to turn around and walk right back out the door. Maybe this is too fast. Maybe I should have waited to come back. My eyes quickly fly around the room like a deer in headlights. I think my knees are about to give out when I hear my name being called. Looking over, I'm shocked to see it's Christopher's dad. "Dakota," he says, the smile on his face beams, "hi." When he gets close enough, he bends to kiss my cheek. "Hi." He bends to kiss the girls on the top of their heads. "Look at how big you two got."

"I skate," Luna says.

"Do you?" Justin says. "How fun. Maybe you can come skate with me sometime."

She nods before he stands back up to talk to me. "How have you been?"

"Good," I answer as I look to the side and see Caroline, Christopher's mom, talking to a beautiful woman with blond hair. She is deep in the conversation, but when she sees me, her eyes light up as she touches the girl's hand to stop her from talking and walks to me.

"Oh my goodness," she says softly, coming in to hug me. "I am so, so happy to see you."

"It's great to see you." The nerves that I had in my body before somewhat fade away. I thought it would be awkward to see everyone, and everyone would somehow make me feel like a poor widow. The crowd claps, and the lights turn on and off.

"Who wants to go down to the glass and maybe get some pucks?" Justin asks the girls, who both jump up. Every single time he's been at the game, which is pretty often in the past couple of years since he retired from coaching, he's almost always taken the girls down to the glass for me.

"Me! Me!" they both say at the same time, clapping their hands.

"I want to, I want to!" Luna shrieks out, making Justin smile at her.

"Is it okay if I take them?" he asks, and they are already sliding their hands in his.

"I want Christopher to give me a puck," Rain states as her eyes light up.

"Well, I think we can arrange that," he says, walking out of the room with the girls. My eyes wait until the door closes behind them before I turn back around to talk to Caroline.

"I'm sorry, I've been rude." She laughs. "Koda," she says my name, "this is Christopher's friend, Keely." She points at the girl, and I try to hide the shock on my face.

"Oh, hi," I say, holding out a hand to shake hers. "Nice to meet you, Keely." My throat feels like it's going to close in. The back of my head burns as if I just poured boiling water on it.

"Thank you." She smiles at me. "So is your husband on the team?" she asks, and I swear I think Caroline is going to faint when she asks me that.

"He was," I say. "He passed away this summer." I wait to see if her eyes light up when I say it. But all she does is put her hand to her mouth.

"I'm so, so sorry." Her voice is low, and I feel so bad for her.

"That's okay." I put my hand on her arm. "You didn't know. It's okay." Wow, I didn't think this would happen. It's the first time that I'm okay with discussing my husband being dead. I mean, it's not like I go walking around in the supermarket and say, "Excuse me, my husband died."

The kids come barreling back in after that, both of them holding two black pucks in their hands. "Look what Christopher gave me," Luna crows.

"Justin said to make him sign it." Rain looks up at Justin, who has his hand on her shoulder.

I don't say anything else because the door opens, and I see more of Justin's family enter the room. Everyone is very nice to me, and not one person looks at me with the sadness or pity that people usually have in their eyes. That is the worst. Justin comes over after a couple of minutes and hands me a glass of white wine. "Caroline said to go sit down and enjoy the game."

I look over and see she is sitting down with the girl while they tell her stories, but then the roar of the crowd is almost deafening. "Guess they are taking the ice." I turn and look at the girls, who run to the front of the chairs looking over the glass. I make my way through the crowd of people to sit down on the chair right behind them. Caroline joins me a couple of minutes later and then Keely sits next to her.

The minute his number is announced, you can feel the thunder of the crowd under your feet. Keely stands up and holds up her phone, taking a video of him. The smile fills her face as a video plays on the Jumbotron. I watch his face fill the screen and then hear the kids cheer with their hands over their head as they call his name, "Uncle Chrissy!" Luna looks over at me and points at the screen, like I can't see his blue eyes that look like they are staring right at me and not at the twenty-four thousand people standing for him.

The spotlight goes to the door of the bench, and then he's there, walking like he's on a runway, before he slides onto the ice. He looks left and right with his hand in the air, saying hi to everyone. I clap my hands along with everyone else, and then I stand, looking over at Keely, who has hearts in her eyes. My stomach burns a touch, and I put my hand to it as the game starts. *I cannot be jealous of this woman*, my head screams.

For the whole game, the kids are either playing in the kids' suite right next door or watching the game. I look over and see Justin holding Luna sometimes before she squirms away. By the end of the third period, I'm getting up to leave when Rain comes over. "Can we wait to say hi to Christopher?"

"Honey, it's late," I say softly. "Plus, we don't know if he'll come right out."

"But—" she says, and I hold up a hand.

"We can stay for twenty minutes." I show her my watch. "When it says ten fifty-eight, we have to leave."

"Okay." She nods at me while Luna crawls into my lap and sits here, exhaustion written all over her face. My foot goes up and down as I wait nervously, and when it turns to ten fifty-eight, I look over at Rain, who is fighting sleep.

"Baby," I call softly, "we can call him tomorrow and see if he's busy."

"Okay," she mumbles, getting up, but at this point, Luna is dead asleep on me. I turn her around and hold her under her bum.

"We're going to head out," I tell Justin, who stands with his brother Matthew.

"Let me help you to the car," he offers, and I shake my head.

"No, we're good. The kids wanted to see Christopher, but their glass carriage is quickly turning into a pumpkin."

"We are going to see you tomorrow, right?" Matthew says to me. "Family lunch." Every time Christopher's whole family is in town, they have a Sunday family lunch. I've been to mostly all of them.

"Oh," I say, looking down at Rain, "I have to check."

"You sure you don't need help?" Justin looks worried.

"I've got them," I tell him, and he just nods and kisses my cheek. "I hope I see you tomorrow."

I say goodbye to Caroline, who kisses Luna on her cheek softly and then hugs Rain. "It was nice meeting you." I smile at Keely. The whole night she has been very friendly and super sweet, so hating her has been knocked off the table.

I walk out of the suite, heading down to the garage. The arena is almost empty with just a couple of people walking around. I take the escalator down to the parking lot. The doors leading to the offices and the locker room are closed as I head down the hallway toward my parked car.

I'm opening the back door of the SUV, and I'm about to put Luna in when I hear my name being called. Looking over my shoulder, I see Christopher rushing out wearing a black suit with a white button-down shirt without his tie. "Hey," he says, jogging over to us. "My father just texted me that you were out here all by yourself."

"I'm not by myself," I tell him. "I'm with the girls."

"Yeah, but—" He pulls Luna off me and then turns her in his arms to place her in her seat. He buckles her in and kisses her cheek before closing the door and then squatting to talk to Rain. "Hey there." He pulls her into his arms. "Are you tired?"

"Yeah," she admits. "Will you sign my puck?"

"You bet." He chuckles. "But tomorrow. How about you guys get home to bed." She nods, and he picks her up, walking around to the other side, putting her in. "I'll see you tomorrow."

He closes the door and then walks over to me. "Thanks for staying." He puts his hands in his pockets, and he looks like he's nervous.

"I met Keely." I don't even know why I said that. "She's so nice." I put a smile on my face while my throat gets tight. "I almost apologized to her for taking so much of your time."

"Why would you do that?" he asks. "You should get going." He looks at me, as his hand comes out of his pocket as he takes a step to me. My feet stay glued to the ground as he wraps one hand around my waist. Bending his head to me, my mouth opens as he moves his face to the side and kisses my cheek. "Thank you for bringing the girls," he whispers and then moves his face back a bit, staring at me in my eyes. My hands stay at my sides, while my chest goes up and down quickly as it presses to his. My eyes move from his eyes to his lips and then back up to his eyes. "I'll call you tomorrow," he says before his hand slips away from my waist. He pulls open the driver's side door for me to get in. I get in without looking back at him. My head is going around and around. I pull out of the parking space, looking in my rearview mirror, seeing him watch the SUV before he turns and walks back into the dressing room.

I don't know what the fuck is happening. I have no idea what just happened. Did Christopher almost just kiss me? But the biggest question right now is, did I want him to kiss me?

TWELVE

CHRISTOPHER

I WATCH THE SUV drive up the ramp of the parking garage, then go to the door. Only when the door opens do I turn and walk back to the dressing room. My left hand tingles from it being wrapped around Koda's waist, and my right hand shakes because what the fuck just happened? Looking down at my feet, I shake out my hands before I pull open the door leading to the suites where my family waits for me.

I take a second once the door closes behind me, putting my hands on my hips as I look up at the white ceiling. I take a deep breath. Tonight was an amazing night. The season opener always hits differently. Something was missing in the locker room. Everyone felt it even though no one wanted to say anything about it for fear we would bring the morale down.

When I lined up to skate on the ice during the introductions, it was weird not having him in front of me since he was assistant captain. I had to blink away the tears and talk myself out of vomiting all over the fucking place, I was that nervous. Once I got on the ice, the fans were electric. The whole team played amazing, and it makes it that much better when we win on home ice.

My phone beeps from inside my pocket, and I pull it out, hoping that it's Koda, but then scared if it is. I see it's from my father.

Dad: Hey, we are still in the suite. Did you get to see Koda and the kids?

I answer him right away.

Me: Yeah, I'm on my way.

When I was almost dressed, my father texted me that Koda and the girls just left since the girls wanted to wait for me. I swear to God I almost ran out of the room without my jacket, keys, and phone. I didn't give a shit. The only thing going through my head was Koda and the kids. Seeing her walking with Luna in her arms, sleeping on her shoulder, and Rain holding her hand, I rushed to them, not thinking about anything but being with them. Buckling Rain into her seat and kissing her cheek while she asked me to sign her puck, I knew then and there that all I wanted to do was go home with them and tuck them in even though I've never done this before.

I swallow back the guilt I feel at all of these thoughts. I shouldn't be thinking about this; it should never have crossed my mind. But every time I close my eyes, all I can see is Koda standing before me. My head felt like it was spinning, and I couldn't stop it. Her eyes as she looked at me when she told me she met Keely. I'm not even going to lie, it took me a second to realize who she was talking about. When she said she almost apologized to her for taking up my time, all I wanted to do was tell her how much more time I wanted to spend with the girls and her. How much more I wanted things that I shouldn't want, that I wasn't allowed to want. I rub my hands over my face, trying to rub away the thoughts going through my head.

I walk toward the suite and find my family waiting for me. "There he is." My father gets up from the couch he sits on with my uncles Max, Matthew, and Viktor. I don't know how they do it, but they make sure to be at everyone's season opener. He walks over to me, giving me a big hug and slapping my back. "Did good."

"Thanks," I say, looking around the room and seeing my mother talking to Keely and knowing that by the end of the night, they will never see her again. "Thanks for also taking care of…" I do a chin up toward Keely.

"Yeah, of course," my father replies. "She's a nice girl."

"Yeah." I put my hands in my pockets.

"We should say goodbye, then." My father looks down, trying not to laugh.

"That would be good." I nod, keeping my hands in my pockets. He walks over to my mother and Keely, as Keely looks up at me. Her face fills with a huge smile as she walks over to me.

"Hey," she says, going in for a hug. I take one hand out of my pocket and hug her, waiting to see if my pulse speeds up. But nothing happens. Not one thing happens like it did in that parking garage. I feel nothing. My pulse doesn't speed up. My hands don't itch to touch her face. My arms don't ache to hold her. Nothing is there.

"Hey," I say, "thanks for coming."

"Of course," she says, "it was so much fun."

Before I can say anything else to her, my family comes over, and everyone says goodbye, leaving just the two of us in the suite. "We should get going," I urge, turning and walking out of the suite with her. "Where are you parked?" I ask as we walk down the empty hallway.

"The second floor," she answers, so I walk over to the escalator and go down one floor and follow the signs toward the parking garage. "It's crazy how full this place was not an hour ago, and now it's like a ghost town." She laughs.

"Yeah." I look around, seeing she is not wrong. A couple of security guards are still on duty, but other than that, everyone has slowly left.

"It was so much fun," she gushes again. "Thank you again for asking me to come."

"You're welcome." I inhale as we stop at her car.

"Do you want to maybe get something to eat?" She holds her purse in both her hands in front of her.

I point behind me. "I should get home."

"Yeah, yeah," she says, and I want to kick myself for being such an asshole, "of course."

"I'm sorry, Keely," I tell her softly, knowing at that moment Zoey was right. I was an asshole to even ask her to come. "I should have told you I'm not really looking for anything right now." I swear as soon as I say those words, Koda's face flashes right before me. "It's just that—"

Keely just smirks at me, and one of her hands comes up to hold my arm. "You don't have to say more."

"Ugh," I groan out loud, making her laugh. "I feel like such an asshole."

"Well, I'm sorry to break it to you, but you aren't an asshole." She squeezes my arm before letting me go. "I had the best time, and your family is amazing."

"They have their moments." I chuckle as she turns and walks to her car.

"See you around, Christopher," she says right before she gets into her car. I watch her drive away before turning and making my way to my truck.

Instead of driving straight home, I do a detour and pass by Koda's house. Her SUV is in the driveway, so I know she's home.

I'm usually wired after every game, but this is different on a whole other level. I don't even want to think about why. I fall asleep a little after three o'clock, waking at seven and trying but failing to fall back asleep.

Even when I walk into the Sunday family lunch, I'm very cranky. I look around, seeing it's just the nine of us. When the hockey season starts, the family lunch looks different every weekend, unlike during the summer when it's all of us. "You look tired," my mother observes when I lean down to kiss her cheek.

"Yeah, I feel tired," I admit to her when the doorbell rings. I look over my shoulder at the door opened by my uncle Matthew, who claps his hands.

"Look at these beauties." He leans down, picking up

someone and kissing their cheek. The open door blocks whoever is there. The minute she squeals, I know who it is. It's as if the blood freezes in my veins, but my heart warms at the same time.

He puts her down as she looks around until her eyes find mine, and she bolts toward me. "Uncle Chrissy," she cries as she leaps into my arms, knowing full well I'll catch her each time.

"Hey, pretty girl," I greet, bringing her to me. My eyes are at the door as I watch Matthew bend and kiss Rain and then see Koda walk in. I swear on everything I have that everything leaves my body. She smiles at something he says as she turns to the side to hug my aunt, who is there to greet her. She wears black jeans with a white shirt tucked in and what looks like an army jacket crop top, but the sleeves flare out at the wrists. Her hair is loose and looks like it did last night when I almost fucking kissed her. Luckily for me, Luna squirms out of my arms to go see my father, who has called her over.

"Uncle Christopher." Rain comes over to me right away. I bend and pick her up, just like I did Luna. "I brought my puck," she says, and I shake my head.

"For what?" I shriek, ignoring the pull to look back over at Koda. My heart beats faster and faster as I try not to listen to her voice that seems to be coming closer and closer to me.

"So you can sign it." She turns in my arms. "Mommy, can I have my puck?" She frees herself from my arms, going to her mother, who now stands very close to me but not close enough. I lift the hat off my head to keep my hands busy from touching her. Or leaning into her to kiss her cheek, or to slide my arms around her shoulders while I pull her to me.

"Sorry," she mumbles as she opens her purse and hands her the puck with a silver Sharpie. "I told her you could sign it another time."

"No," my father says, "get it today." He grabs a piece of bread out of the basket.

"This is your idea?" I ask as I take the puck and the pen, signing my name.

"Yeah," he declares proudly as I hand her back the puck. She holds it in her hand and smiles so big I would sign a puck daily if it made her smile like that.

"Thank you, thank you." She turns and walks over to Koda, who has moved away from me and now chats with my aunt about something.

"Mommy, here," she says to Koda as she hands the puck to her. "Can you put this in your purse and make sure you don't lose it?" She opens her purse and sticks it back in, then walks back and places her purse at the door before coming back. She totally avoids looking in my direction, totally avoids that I'm standing right here in the middle of the room, and she has yet to say hello to me. She probably thinks I'm a fucking creep as she walks back over to my aunt and mother, continuing the conversation. My hands ball into fists beside me as I try to talk myself out of going up to her and asking her if I can talk to her.

"You okay?" I hear from beside me, turning to see my father looking at me with a weird expression.

"I'm fine," I snap, not paying attention to anything because I'm trying to calm myself down. I just need a minute to myself. "I'll be back," I tell him, walking toward the stairs and going up them, where I hope to just sit for a minute and get myself together. I find the bathroom, locking the door, and sit on the edge of the bath, hoping like fuck whatever is going on inside me stops. Knowing that whatever it is, I need to get over it because it will never happen. Knowing that whatever I am feeling I have to stop. I don't want to have these feelings. I lean forward, my head hanging down. "I can't do it." I look at myself in the mirror, avoiding looking in my eyes because no matter how much I tell myself I can't do it, my heart tells me that maybe, just maybe, I can.

THIRTEEN

DAKOTA

I WALK OUT of my Pilates class at the same time the phone rings in my hand. Turning it over, I see it's Zara Stone calling me. My heart races in my chest as I wonder why she would be calling me. I mean, over the years we have spoken on the phone, but that was only to talk to her about a dress I wanted to buy from her for an event. "Hello," I say, putting the phone to my ear, my hands starting to shake as I do so.

"Koda." Her soft voice comes through, and I can tell she's on speaker. "How are you?"

"Hey." I unlock my door and climb into the driver's side. "I'm good. How are you?" I try not to sound like I'm frazzled by her calling. My immediate thought is something is wrong with Christopher, and I don't want to think about anything bad happening to him.

"Amazing." I swear I can feel her hype energy through the phone. "I guess you are wondering why I'm calling you?"

"Um," I say, starting the SUV, "you can say that." I laugh nervously, closing my eyes, trying to beat back the anxiety that was pouring through my body less than thirty seconds ago.

"I was just chatting with Zoe, and she mentioned she saw you this weekend."

"Yes." I look down at the phone, putting it on speakerphone before the Bluetooth catches. "It's too bad you couldn't make it."

"I know, it would have been amazing to see you." She stops talking for a second. "I hope you don't mind, but she told me you were looking into getting back into the workforce." Three days ago, we went to Sunday lunch, and even though I secretly dreaded being there, I went for the kids. I was doing whatever I could not to be forced to look around and see if Christopher was there. I don't know what was going on with him, but the whole lunch, he was quiet, except when it came to the girls. He sat with them for lunch while I sat at the table with the women, but as soon as I would go to them or say something, he avoided looking at me. To be honest, it made me sick to my stomach. Instead of just grabbing the girls and heading out, I stayed longer than I should have. I'm not sure why, but I did. I mean, maybe I knew deep down why I stayed, but I wasn't going to admit that, not even to myself. I was also very not ready to face Keely if she was there. I mean, I didn't know if she would be there or not, but once I did a quick sweep of the room, I was really happy she wasn't there. Of course, I couldn't just come out and ask him where she was. I also didn't want to, so there was that.

"I am," I admit. "I figured it was time. Of course, my first priority is my girls." That fact is nonnegotiable in my book.

"Obviously not even a question." She wades in, telling me, "My business has always had a *family first* motto." I can hear her moving around on her end. "With that said, I would like to know if you are interested in meeting with me to discuss a couple of things. I know you have a background in fashion, and you used to be a personal shopper." She mentions the last job I had before I got pregnant with Rain, and Benji and I decided I would be a stay-at-home mom.

"Yes," I reply, nervous now, "whenever you can."

"I'm good to fly down there tomorrow if you can meet. We are in New York now."

"That would work, but I feel bad you have to come all this way. Would a Zoom work also?"

"Whatever you want to do. I'm open to coming down there and meeting, or we can do it via Zoom…" She trails off. "I'm going to be very honest with you." I hold my breath. "I want you to come and work for me. I love your style, I always have. I've told you this throughout the years. But I don't want you to think I'm giving you the job because of whatever." She doesn't mention Benji, and I'm happy she doesn't say his name. "I found out you were going to be throwing your hat in the workforce, and I'd like you to hang your hat at Zara's Closet." She mentions the online company she started so many years ago. She's now sought after by the biggest stars to style them.

"Wow," I say because it's still… wow. All I can do is blink as I think about her speech.

"We have a client roster with a three-year waiting list, and I know that adding you will help bring that down. You can work from home and set your own hours."

"I don't know what to say." The tear I didn't know was forming falls over my lid. "This is—"

"It's too much," she groans. "I promised Zoe I would go in lightly, but you know us. It's balls to the wall each time." I can't help but laugh as I wipe away the tear. "How about you think about it, and we can touch base tomorrow afternoon?"

"I would absolutely love that," I tell her. We hang up shortly after that, and I'm almost in a daze the rest of the afternoon.

I text Dr. Mendes after the call and right before I start dinner.

Me: Do you have an emergency space for me tomorrow?

Her reply is almost right away.

Dr. Mendes: I'm free from eight to ten. Feel free to come by when you drop off the girls.

"This is good," I tell myself as I make my way over to pick up the girls. "This is very good."

As soon as I get the girls, I get home and make dinner while the girls watch a bit of television. They devour the tacos as if they didn't snack when they got home. Only when Luna pushes her plate away do I get up.

"Okay," I say, grabbing the dinner plate off the counter,

"time for homework." I look over at Rain, who nods before getting off her stool and going over to grab her schoolbag. I wipe down the counter before she plops her bag on it. "Luna, go get a workbook." I point at the stack of workbooks I bought a couple of weeks ago. She was so jealous that Rain got to do homework she was fit to be tied. I printed out a couple of sheets for kindergarten kids and she excelled at it. So I ordered a couple of activity books for her to do while Rain does her own homework.

I toss the rag into the sink with the plate before I wash and dry my hands. "Okay, what do we have here?" I ask as I grab her folder with all of her homework in it. A spelling test from two days ago showing she got them all right. "Look at this," I say with a huge smile on my face, "one hundred and two percent." I turn the page around to show Rain and Luna.

"I got the bonus word." She smiles. "You have to sign it." She gives me instructions as I nod and sign my name.

We go through her words for this week, even though she has all week. She does her twenty minutes of reading before it's time for a bath. This is our new normal, and I have to admit the girls are doing better than I thought they would. To be fair, in the last months before Benji died, he stopped joining us for dinner, even when he wasn't on the road. He would tell the girls he had to practice, so they never really asked questions. I was the only one who knew he was lying. He would occasionally show up to tuck them in, but I could have counted on one hand when that happened. I was living in a world of hell, and I made sure no one knew the truth. It was my burden to live with, but I was finally letting it go.

The next day, I arrive at Dr. Mendes's office just after eight, coffee in hand for me and one for her. "Good morning." She looks up from her desk with a bright smile on her face, like always.

"It is a good morning." I hand her her white cup of coffee before I sit down with my own. "I don't think it's been this good of a morning for a long, long time."

"I didn't know what to expect," Dr. Mendes says, sitting in the chair facing me. "Anytime anyone asks for emergency sessions, things usually are not good."

I smile at her as I take a sip of coffee. "This might be one of those rare times, then." She waits for me to tell her more. "I have a job offer." Her eyes go big in surprise. "I know, that's the exact look I had."

"How did all of this come about?" she asks.

"On Sunday, I woke up and started my list for the week. What I wanted to do for the girls and the other what I wanted to do for me." She nods while I talk. "I was going to learn to skate for the girls." I shake my head, knowing I would have tried and I would have fallen on my ass, but I would have tried, and that is all that mattered. "And then I put find a job for me."

"Okay," she murmurs, not sure she is following.

"And well, I was talking to someone about it, and their sister owns Zara's Closet." Even she knows the name because she gasps. "I know," I say excitedly. "She called me, and she offered me a job."

"That's incredible." She takes her own sip of coffee.

"We are going to have a Zoom meeting today at one,"

I confirm. "I have a list of questions I'm nervous to ask, but I figured that she called me, so she might give in a bit." I reach for my phone and open the list of questions. "I mean, it's all little things, but my main thing is being able to be there for the kids. I'm not going to be missing one thing they do. I'm talking every school event. I want to go on field trips, obviously." I smile. "I'll probably curse and hate every minute of them, but that is what I want to do. I want to make sure I sit at the dinner table with them every night." The smile on my face is still there, but the tears in my eyes are forming.

"I want to tuck them in. I want to wake them up. I want to prepare lunches even though by now I'm pulling out my hair because Rain's not eating any of it because she's already fed up with it." The tear rolls down my face. "But I am going to be there for each moment of their lives because when they look back on it, that is the only thing I want them to remember." I sniff.

"What I don't want them to remember is their father choosing not to be there. I don't want them to remember that their mother fell apart when it happened. I don't want them to remember I spent time before he died trying to find proof he was an addict, but each time telling myself that maybe it was in my head. I don't want them to remember I was so tired of being so happy all the time that it hurt to smile. I want them to know that every single time I smiled, it was because I was happy. So if she can be okay with all of this, then I will take her job." Fuck, after saying all that, my chest gets tight, and I have to cough because of the pressure. All of that came out and I didn't do it as a sobbing fucking mess, so to me, that's progress. I did it with a smile on my face, even if tears were rolling down my face. I also did it with a little less hatred than I thought I would be doing it with. I've noticed the hatred has started to fade away a little each day. I mean, don't get me wrong, I hated Benji with every single cell in my body, but I was able to compartmentalize it so my girls never felt my hatred toward him.

"I think anyone who gets to hire you would be really lucky to have you." I inhale deeply at her words.

"I think so also," I agree with her. "I think so also," I repeat. The smile on my face is huge as I take another sip of coffee.

I leave with a clearer mind and almost skip toward my SUV, and when I get off the phone with Zara six hours later, I now have a job.

It is strange, but when I sit down that night after the girls are tucked in, the only person I really want to talk to is the only person I was not talking to since Saturday. Before I can talk myself out of it, I send him a text. I don't know if I should or not, but I also know I'll be seeing him on Saturday with the girls, so this will be less awkward.

Me: Sandra Bullock was also great in Miss Congeniality.

I hit send before I can erase it, and at that text, I hang my head. "Smooth," I scold to myself, "very smooth."

FOURTEEN

CHRISTOPHER

MY PHONE VIBRATED from beside my plate, and I turn it over to see that it's Koda. I look around the table at the guys since we are having a team dinner before our game tomorrow in Detroit. I look over to my right at Cole to see if he's paying attention to me, but he's locked into a conversation with Nick. My eyes go back down to read the text, and I shake my head, trying not to laugh too loud and get eyes looking at me.

Koda: Sandra Bullock was also great in Miss Congeniality.

I haven't texted or called her since I saw her last Sunday. Every morning, I want to text her to see how the girls are doing, but I stop myself each time. If she needs you, she will text you, I repeat the same thing every morning. Then every night, when I want to call her after I know the kids have gone to bed. But now she's texted me, so I have to answer her.

Me: You have no idea what you're talking about.

I put the phone down and try to pay attention to the conversation going on beside me, but all I can think about is Koda. Seeing her on Sunday with my family and having the girls with me felt so natural. It also fucked with my head because I knew it shouldn't feel natural. Nothing about this situation is natural. The phone buzzes next to me, and I pick it up again. This time, my heart picks up speed.

Koda: She went undercover to save the Miss America pageant.

Me: She drove a bus, a big-ass city bus to save people.

I'm about to put the phone down, but I see the bubbles with the three dots come up, and I know she's texting me back. I stare at the screen for a couple of seconds before her reply comes through.

Koda: She had to learn how to walk in heels and juggle.

Me: Did you miss my text about the huge-ass bus she had to learn how to drive? And then she hit the carriage with the cans. Speed will forever be her number-one movie.

Koda: Okay, fine, what about The Lake House?

I roll my eyes before I answer her.

Me: Even she wants to pretend that movie never happened. That was fucking horrible, I think more horrible than any other movie out there. It was not a good comeback for either her or Keanu.

"Who are you texting?" Cole asks from beside me as he leans in to grab the bottle of beer he is having with his burger.

"Is it that chick you brought to the season opener?" Andreas asks from in front of me.

"Kelly." Cole snaps his fingers, coming up with the name.

"It's Keely," I correct him, but I also don't tell him if it's her or not.

"Keely," Cole says, "that's what I meant." He takes a bite of his burger, and I put the phone down to eat my own. "So it's going good?"

"It's okay," I lie through my fucking teeth. "She's a cool girl."

He just nods as he chews, and I take a bite of my burger, hoping the conversation stops right there. Nick is the one who changes the conversation and instead talks about the game tomorrow. I don't pick up my phone again until we leave the restaurant and walk back to the hotel.

Every single minute that goes by, I'm anxious to get to my room to take out my phone. I take out the phone the second the door closes behind me. I see I missed three messages from Koda, and the last one was sent twenty minutes ago.

Koda: Yeah, The Lake House was not their finest moment.

Koda: Two Weeks Notice, now that was a great one. Hugh Grant was good in that one. I mean, not as good as Love Actually or even Notting Hill, but still decent.

Koda: Okay, The Proposal. She raps in that and everything. Plus Ryan Reynolds makes everything better.

I can't help but laugh at the way she's going all in with Sandra Bullock.

Me: Is she your favorite actress?

I don't know if she's still up or not, and when I look over at the side table clock, I see that it's only eight thirty. I kick off my shoes, heading toward the king-sized bed in the middle of the room. Falling on top of the white covers, I sink straight down to the mattress with the flimsy pillows. I grab the two beside me and tuck them under my head.

Koda: No, I don't think so anyway. I don't know if I have a favorite actress. Why? Do you?

Me: I mean Margot Robbie is not bad on the eyes. Gal Gadot is another one. Oh, Scarlett Johansson. Charlize Theron is another one.

I put the phone on my stomach before grabbing the remote to the television from the side table and turning it on, switching channels, trying not to think about the fact I'm texting Koda and it has nothing to do with the girls.

The phone vibrates.

Koda: So you choose the movies according to if there is a hot girl? Interesting.

Me: I mean, not necessarily. But if my sisters are going to turn on a movie, it's good to know I have something to keep me invested.

Koda: Last movie you watched.

Me: Barbie.

Koda: What? You went to the movies to watch Barbie?

Me: I did. I took Penelope and forced Maddox to

come with me. I promised her I would take her last Christmas when she told me about it. I obviously didn't really think how bad it could be. Maddox had no idea what we were doing. He spent the morning on the ice with me, and then I sprang it on him. He hated every single second of it. He didn't talk to me for a whole month. I think he even blocked me.

Koda: Bahaha, he did not.

Me: He did. Every time I texted him, it came up green. Only when I saw him a month later at the family vacation did I grab his phone. Little shit blocked me. The Funcle.

Koda: Do you even know what a funcle is?

Me: You bet your ass I do. I had to google it to make sure, but it's like a dad, just hotter and cooler.

Koda: Does it really? I thought it was a gay uncle.

I gasp.

Me: Are you fucking with me right now? That's a guncle.

Koda: I am not. I honestly thought it meant gay uncle. I think I heard Andy Cohen use it, so I assumed.

Me: I'm not gay.

Koda: Really? This is shocking information.

Me: Koda.

Koda: Christopher, there is nothing wrong with being gay.

Me: I know that. Why would there be? I'm just saying I'm not gay.

Koda: So you really aren't gay?

Me: Koda, you've met my dates.

Koda: Maybe they were your crutch.

Me: How the hell did we go from Sandra Bullock to me being gay?

Koda: Well, you are good-looking, hot, and you dress like you're a GQ model, so it could have gone either way.

Me: I'm happy to announce that I'm one hundred percent heterosexual. I like women. I love women, actually.

Koda: You are trying really hard to convince me that you aren't gay. Is there a reason for that?

I don't bother texting her. Instead, I call her, and she answers right away, and I hear the laughter from her side. "You are just fucking with me."

"Who, me?" She feigns innocence, but I can hear the teasing behind it, and I fucking love it. "I would never do that to you."

"Yeah, right." Those are the only two words I could come up with. Her laughter is shooting straight to me. "Are you done?"

"Just about." Her laughter fades. "That was fun."

"Was it?" I ask, thinking if I can give her this escape, then I would do it over and over again.

"It was." Her voice goes soft. "How was your day?"

"I'm in Detroit," I tell her, "got here this afternoon. What about you? How was your day?"

"Amazing." I can hear the smile in her voice. "I had an amazing therapy session, and I got a job."

"What?" I ask, shocked. "No way. Where?"

"Zara's Closet." The second she mentions my aunt's

business, all I can do is let my mouth hang open. "I was talking to Zoe on Sunday about maybe getting something to pass the time. There is only so much I have left to do around the house. The kids are both at school, and I have nothing left to keep me busy, so…"

"How is this going to work?"

"It's all online based, really. Unless I have to go meet a client, but from what Zara said, most of that is done via Zoom these days." Her voice is so free and excited, I wish I was in front of her.

"That's amazing. We have to celebrate when I get back." I ignore the way my head laughs at me. I'm trying to get in any way I can, apparently even throwing myself at her.

"We don't have to do that." She chuckles. "It can be a dual celebration."

"Of what?"

"My new job," she says, and then I know it's taking everything in her not to burst out laughing when she says the next thing, "and the fact you aren't a gay uncle, but instead a hot one."

I shake my head. "Whatever. I'm back Friday morning, so we can go out Friday night."

"Sounds good," she agrees. "I'm off to bed."

"Same," I tell her, but I don't want to end the call. "Have a good night, Koda."

"You too. Good luck tomorrow."

"Thanks," I say, and she hangs up. All I can do is look at the phone when she sends another text.

Koda: I promise to stop fucking with you. Unless

you don't want me to.

Is she flirting with me? I look at the text over and over again. The biggest question is, do I want her to flirt with me? And do I want to flirt with her back?

I throw my phone on the bed before I answer her back that I want her to fuck with me. I want her to fuck with me whenever she wants to fuck with me. I want her to fuck with me morning, noon, and night.

I get off the bed and pull off my sweatshirt and also my T-shirt, tossing them on the desk under the television. Before walking to the bathroom and turning on the shower, I try to clear my head. I think of the game tomorrow as I unbutton my pants and push down both my pants and my boxers at the same time before my socks join the pile, and I step into the water. I let the rain shower wash over me, putting my head down so it can roll down my neck. The tension in my neck is getting tighter and tighter when all I can do is picture Koda. I place one hand on the shower wall and the other on my cock. The water runs down my shoulders, over my chest, and straight down to my balls as I stroke myself. I can hear her voice calling my name, the way her eyes darkened when I got closer to her. The way her mouth opened when I leaned in to kiss her cheek. The way her mouth might have tasted. The way she might taste. The way she would slide down my cock while I would watch her pussy take me all in. The way her tits would bounce up and down, the way I would lick my thumb to play with her clit. It doesn't take more than that before my balls get tight, and I come on the shower floor. I tug my cock a couple more times before

I'm done. "What the fuck did I just do?" It's a question I don't know if I can answer. It's also a question that is so loaded there is not a right or wrong answer. The guilt that I just jerked off over my friend's wife comes barreling through me so fast I can't stop it, making it even harder to breathe, let alone think.

Grabbing the white towel hanging on the rack, I wrap it around my waist before walking over to my black carry-on bag, unzipping it, and taking out a pair of black boxers. I walk back over to the bed and grab the phone, seeing it's a little after nine when I pull up Stone's number.

Stone answers after two rings. "Hey."

"Hey." I pull the covers back and slide into bed. "I have something to say, but I also need you not to judge me."

"No can do," he answers right away, "this has never been a non-judgment zone."

"What?" I snap. "Since when?"

"Since you just said don't judge me. I'm going to obviously judge you. It doesn't mean I'm going to stop having your back, but—"

I groan.

"Going to judge you."

"Oh, for fuck's sake." I close my eyes. "I'm being fucking serious."

"So am I." He laughs. "What has gotten into you?"

I rub my hand over my face. "I have no idea, to be honest." I try to get the right words, but there are no right words for this. "I think I have feelings for Koda." I close my eyes the minute I say the words. At the same time, my stomach falls to my feet. Thinking this and saying it are two different things.

"I'm sorry." I can hear his confusion. "What did you just say?"

"I know. I know." My head goes back before I put my hand on my head.

"Did you just say what I think you said?" he asks, his voice in a whisper like if he whispers, no one else can hear it.

"You think I want this?" I snap, frustration in my voice.

"Christopher," he says my name, and I'm not sure if it's a warning or a what the fuck. "What are you thinking?"

"I'm thinking that she's a great fucking mom. I'm thinking that Benji is" I start to say but correct myself, "was a stupid fuck for everything he put her through. I think that she's kind and she's sweet and she's so…" I stop before I say she's the sexiest woman I've ever met in my life.

"You think you are falling for her, or you have already fallen for her?" He laughs. "Because the way it sounds, you are already half in love with Koda."

"Jesus Christ, Stone," I hiss, "who is next to you?"

"Um, my wife, but I've paid her five dollars so everything I say near or around her is like an NDA type of thing."

"You are so dumb." I shake my head.

"Don't listen to him," Ryleigh says. Then I hear the

ringing coming and see it's a FaceTime alert.

I press the button, and they come onto the screen. Both of them are in bed, same as me. "I won't say anything because I don't have a big mouth. Him, on the other hand." She points at Stone. "Like *The Gazette*." He gasps while I laugh. "So you like Koda?"

"You can say that," I admit to her, "but it's wrong."

"Why?" she asks, and Stone just looks at her with his mouth hanging low.

"That's his best friend's girl," Stone explains.

"But he's not here." She points at him. "So is it even an issue?"

"You bet your ass it's a fucking issue," Stone snaps. "She's off-limits."

"Why?" Ryleigh asks him. "Benji is dead. It's not like he's on vacation or in jail. He's literally gone, never coming back. She's going to end up getting with someone. So it might as well be someone who is a semi-decent guy."

"Semi?" I say, insulted. "What the fuck? Why semi?"

"I mean, you are still going for your best friend's girl." She shrugs. "Other than that, you are a decent guy."

"Um, thanks," I say, not sure what the fuck is going on.

"Are you saying that if I die, you are going to get with my best friend?" Stone asks her, and Ryleigh looks around, moving her head side to side like she's going through his friend list in her head, making Stone's face look like it's about to explode.

"If I had to, I guess there are a couple I could possibly,

maybe, go for," she decides, then looks at the camera. "You aren't on that list."

"I'm hurt," I reply, putting my hand to my chest. "Before he has a coronary"—I point at Stone—"can we focus on one problem at a time?"

"Yes, let's," Ryleigh agrees.

"We are going to have words later." Stone glares at her. "And you better get your pen and paper out because I want a contract drawn up and notarized." Ryleigh laughs at him.

"What are you going to do if I don't follow it after you're dead?" Ryleigh crosses her arms over her chest. "Come back and haunt me?"

"You bet your ass." Stone doesn't even take a second to think about it.

"Can we get back to Christopher, please?" Ryleigh redirects. "Listen, bottom line, you are both free to do what you want. She has nothing holding her back, and neither do you. The question is, will you be able to get past the fact that she was Benji's first?"

"Yeah, remember that," Stone reminds me, "she was his first." He looks at Ryleigh. "Like, how did this even happen? You've known her for what, ten years, and all of a sudden, you are like, I like her."

"I've known her, but I've never known her like that. I've always known her with Benji," I say softly, "but now it's just her and the girls. I don't know how to explain it. It's just different."

"Fuck, man," Stone says, "I don't know what to say. The reality is that she's by herself now."

"I would never, ever go there if Benji was alive."

"I know you wouldn't. Fuck, everyone knows that, and if they don't, then they don't really know you at all." Stone shakes his head. "I think you need to figure out if you can get through the whole Benji at the back of your mind every time something happens."

"Whatever you do," Ryleigh advises, "remember there are two girls in the middle of this."

"And they're amazing," I point out, and Ryleigh just smirks at me. "What's that look?"

"Nothing, it's just that I think you have your answer," she says, looking at Stone, who side-eyes her. "Jesus, you aren't even dead yet, and we are arguing about me moving on."

I can't help but laugh. "Okay, I'm going to go and not be in the middle of this," I tell them. "Thanks for the talk and not being judgmental, asshole," I direct to Stone, who grabs the phone and hangs up on me.

I turn the lights off and slide down into the bed, turning my head to the side and wondering what it would be like if Koda was mine.

FIFTEEN

Dakota

"HELLO," I ANSWER my phone at the same time I apply glitter at the corner of Rain's eye.

"Hey," Christopher replies. "What time are you guys headed out?" I look over my shoulder at the clock on the stove.

"We should be out by six," I tell him. "It's almost five. I have to feed the kids, and then we are going to go. Why?"

"I told the girls I would go with you guys," he says. "Did you make dinner?"

"I did not," I admit while I move to the other eye and put some glitter on that one. "I was going to probably order."

"Okay, I'll call in a pizza order and pick it up, so it'll be faster. I'll be at your place by five thirty. Is that enough time?"

"Should be," I say, grabbing the crown of fake flowers I sewed together for the past month for Rain's costume.

"See you then." He disconnects. The past two weeks have been, I don't even know what word can describe it. I started working at Zara's Closet last week and love every second of it. I didn't think it would be an easy transition, and I expected to feel overwhelmed, but in the end, I felt like this was what I needed. It was so good to get out of the same routine I was doing, day in and day out. I felt accomplished at the end of the day. I start after ten in the morning, so I still have time to go to therapy and my support group. Some nights, I'll work on a couple of things, but I'm not overextending myself.

The other thing that has been a constant is the phone calls with Christopher. Usually, it starts with a *good morning* text, and he asks about the kids. But then at night, when he knows they are in bed, he calls me to shoot the shit, like he says. We have nothing in common; he likes one thing, and I'm on the other side. The only thing we have in common is we both think we are hilarious. Me more so than him. Even though I'll never admit it to him, he's pretty snarky. It's the nighttime phone calls that I've come to look forward to. Although, when he's on the road, the phone calls happen at three, right before I pick up the girls. But it's an everyday thing, and I'm trying not to overthink it. Except all I do is think about it.

I pin the crown of flowers on her head and then show her what she looks like in the mirror. She gasps, "I look like a fairy." She moves her head from left to right, swinging the little ringlet curls we started on as soon as she got home from school. "I'm going to go and get my dress on."

"No." I shake my head. "Wait until after dinner so you don't dirty it.

"Luna," I call her name, "come and do your hair." Luckily for me, she wanted to be a cat this year, so all I need to do is tie her hair in a ponytail, put whiskers on her face, and paint her nose pink.

I'm putting everything away when the doorbell rings. "That's Uncle Christopher!" I shout from my bathroom as I hear the kids run to the door.

"Pizza!" both girls scream. I look into the mirror, making sure I look okay before heading downstairs, telling myself I'm just fixing myself for when we leave the house. I walk down the stairs toward the kitchen and find Christopher in the middle of it, grabbing some plates. It's funny how it's so natural to see him here doing this, yet confusing at the same time.

"Hey." He looks over, giving me a little smirk, and I quickly smile at him and head toward the fridge, looking away from him before he sees my cheeks get pink from his stupid smirk. It started happening last week at hockey practice. He looked over at me and smirked after he said something about one of the kids, and my stomach got tight. I thought it was because I was hungry, but after sitting down that night and thinking about it, it had nothing to do with me eating and everything to do with his blue eyes.

He does the kids' plates, where he cuts up the pieces of pizza before he sits down at the end of the island. He talks to the kids about their day, and when they are finished, he sends me up with them to get them dressed while he cleans the kitchen.

We walk out of the house after I put on my black vest and the girls grab their Halloween bags. "Okay, so when we get home," Christopher declares, "I get first dibs of the candy."

I laugh when the girls don't agree to it. "You should bring your own bag, then," Luna informs him as she lets go of my hand to walk up to the house next door.

"You okay?" Christopher asks from beside me, his hands in his pockets.

"Yeah, why?" I look over at him.

"It's just the first holiday." The way his voice goes soft makes my chest get tight.

"News flash." I take a deep breath. "Benji wasn't here the last two Halloweens," I tell him, and before he can ask me anything, the girls run back so we can walk to the next house.

"How is that possible?" he asks when the girls leave again.

I shrug. "It just is." I can see his jaw clenching as he bites down. I avoid looking at him the rest of the night, and by the time we walk back to the house, he has Luna on his shoulders because her legs are tired.

He kisses the kids goodbye. "I'm leaving tomorrow for a week, so you won't see me at hockey," he says and both the girls groan a bit. "I'll try to FaceTime Mommy so I can see." He smiles over their head at me. "If she answers."

"When haven't I answered?" I joke with him as he gets up from hugging them. I shake my head as he walks out of the house.

The second day he's gone, he calls me earlier than normal. "Hey." I pick up while I'm sitting at my computer looking at a new client list.

"Are you coming to the fundraiser next weekend?" he asks, and I hear the sound of a door slamming on his end.

"I have no idea," I tell him. "I got the invite, but I'm not sure." It's the annual fundraiser the team does, usually to support the children's hospital. I've gone every year, obviously, because Benji had to go. The last time we went was the first time I knew he was taking drugs. I also knew I would never put myself in that position again.

"Why not?" He sounds out of breath.

"I don't know, because I might not want to." I lean back in my chair. "Why?"

"I was just asking. I didn't know if you would be coming or not." He takes a drink of whatever he is drinking. "It's for the kids."

"I'll think about it," I give in. "I was going to have a Sandra Bullock marathon." I try not to let him know that I'm laughing.

"Good God, start with *The Lake House,* it'll end quickly."

"Goodbye," I say, hanging up with the sound of him laughing.

It takes me a whole week to decide to go. Even on the day of the event, I think about backing out. I haven't even really told Christopher I'm going, in case I get cold feet before I go. He hasn't asked me since that phone call, and I haven't brought it up. The babysitter arrives on time, so I go up and get ready.

I tie my hair at the back of my neck in a long ponytail before applying just a touch of makeup. I quickly get into the dress I ordered literally two days ago and had it rushed over to me. Luckily, I knew the designer, and she could do it. I went with an off-the-shoulder, silk mermaid gown with one little cap sleeve on the right side. It has ruching on the left side of the top area. It goes to the floor but shows the side split when you walk. Turning, I look at myself in the mirror before I grab my nude heels with a peep toe.

After I inhale deeply, the sitter calls my name and tells me the car is here. I put my hand on my stomach before I grab my purse and walk out of the room. When I get to the bottom, I ask to zip me up the rest of the way before I lean down and kiss the girls. "I shouldn't be late," I tell the sitter, who waves with the girls at the door.

My stomach is in knots as I make my way over to the hotel where the event takes place. Looking out the window, I try not to talk myself out of turning back and going home.

I don't have a chance to do anything because my door is opened by the doorman of the hotel. I smile at him before getting out and walking into the building. A big sign on the side of the staircase indicates where to go.

I walk up the staircase with a lump in my throat and my stomach feeling like it's going to come out of my feet. I spot him right away; he's dressed in a black suit that I've seen him wear before, but now it feels like it's different on him. He stands with the guys talking but stops midsentence when he sees me. His eyes are on mine as if he doesn't really believe I'm here. I hold up my hand to him, and he leaves the guys to come my way. "What are you doing here?" he asks when he stops in front of me. "You look amazing." His voice is breathless and tight. "I would have picked you up."

"It was a last-minute decision," I tell him, trying to smile but feeling the tears. "I might leave in an hour or ten minutes. The jury is still out."

He just shakes his head. "You say the word, and we'll get out of here." He motions with his head. "But first, you have to say hello."

"Yeah, I was afraid of that," I mumble as he puts his hand on my lower back. I spot a couple of the players who used to play with Benji. They are all super nice to me and friendly, and I've learned that even though they might have known he was on drugs, Benji was responsible for himself. At the end of the day, he was the one who had to look out for me and the girls, not them.

"Hi," Andreas greets me, bending his head and kissing my cheek. "I'm happy you come here," he says with his thick accent.

"Thank you." I smile, taking his affection.

"You alone?" He looks around me to see if I have maybe a friend or a date.

"I'm alone." I hold my purse in both hands to stop them from shaking.

"Good, good." He chuckles.

"Go away," Christopher says from beside me, and when I look over, I see him glaring at Andreas, who just laughs silently.

"What?" He shrugs before he walks away.

"That guy is a tool," Christopher mumbles. "Do you want something to drink?"

"I think I am going to have something to drink." I turn to him, not realizing how close I am to him. When I do turn, I also forget his arm is at my lower back so now I'm tucked into his side. I look into his soft eyes. "I am definitely getting a drink," I whisper.

"I'll go get you one," Christopher offers but doesn't move from beside me.

"In order to do that, one must move." I giggle like a schoolgirl.

"Yeah." He looks into my eyes and then down at my lips. My heart skips a beat as he moves his hand to my hip, squeezing it a second before he lets me go and walks over to the bar. I try not to watch, but I fail. I also remember that I never told him what I wanted to drink, but whatever it is he gets for me, I'm going to drink it.

I didn't even look around at the event space. It looks like an enchanted forest. The lights are dim, so it shows the fake trees that look like they are all white with blue and pink lights. Black tablecloths are over every table with white picket chairs. "Here," Christopher says to me, handing me a glass of white wine.

"Who said I wanted white wine?" I try to keep a straight face when I see his eyes go big as he looks at me and then the glass in his hand.

"You always drink white wine." He holds up the glass. "But I can go and get you something else."

"I'm just playing with you." I smile at him as I take the glass from him. Our fingers graze at the handoff, making my hand tingle from the tips of my fingernails to my elbow. "Thank you," I say, holding up the glass and taking a sip.

"We should sit," he suggests, looking around when he sees people starting to sit at tables.

"Are you here by yourself?" I ask, and his head tilts to the side as his eyebrows pinch together in confusion. "I don't know if you have a date for this thing."

"In the past seven months, when have I had a date?" he asks, and I roll my eyes.

"Keely was at your game," I point out to him.

"That was date one and none," he mumbles, and I try not to let his words get me excited. "Let's go sit with Cole and Brittany." He motions to the side with his head.

I nod as we walk across the dance floor to the table where Cole and Brittany are sitting and talking to each other. "Is this seat taken?" Christopher asks, and Brittany gasps when she sees me.

"I'm so happy you came." She gets up from her seat to come over to me. "I didn't want to pressure you, but"—she kisses my cheek—"I'm glad you came."

"Thank you," I reply, smiling at Cole, who comes to me and also kisses my cheeks.

"Love that dress," Brittany compliments while Christopher pulls out a chair for me to sit in, and I smile at him.

"Thank you," I say to him, then turn back to Brittany, who sits next to me. "It's from a new up-and-coming designer I'm working with," I state proudly, and her eyes almost bulge out of her head.

"You have a job?" she asks, and I nod before taking another sip of wine. "Tell me everything. I feel like I know nothing."

"Yeah." I look over at Christopher, who takes the seat next to me, holding his tie as he sits down. Brittany and I chat back and forth about what I've been up to. The table fills with a couple more people, all shocked and a little surprised to see me, but all of them cordial.

The head of the hospital fundraising committee comes up to give a speech as food is passed out. I finish the glass of wine and another is quickly poured for me by a passing server. I sit with my hands in my lap while Christopher stretches one arm around my chair, something he's done in the past, but I've never been affected like I am right at this moment. I try to focus on the speech, but the only thing I can think of is the heat of his hand near my back. "And with that, I announce that the dance floor is now open," he says as a song comes on.

Cole gets up from his seat, grabbing Brittany's hand and pulling her to the dance floor that's getting full by the second. Christopher pushes his chair away from the table, and I look up at him as he holds out his hand to me. "Let's go."

"Is that your way of asking me to dance?" I put the napkin that is on my lap back on the table.

"This may be why you don't have a date," I joke with him, but even though saying the words as a joke, it bothers me. I put my hand in his as he leads me to the dance floor. He wraps his free hand around my waist, while he tucks the hand he was holding to his chest. I put my free arm on his elbow.

"I don't have a date," he leans in to whisper in my ear, "because I don't want to have a date."

"Good to know." I try to ignore the way the back of my neck heats as he moves us in a circle. "Why don't you want to have a date?"

I swallow down the bile that feels like it's creeping up my throat, trying to get my heart rate back to normal while I'm so close to him. In his arms, it feels weird but also so good. "I—" he says. "I want to have a date," he admits, and my knees about buckle when he looks into my eyes, "but she's unavailable."

I don't ask him anything else. The only thing I can do is stare into his eyes. I could get lost in his eyes. His arm pulls me closer to him as we dance, neither of us saying anything. It's like all we are saying is in the look we are giving each other. His chest rises and falls under our hands so fast it's like he's working out. "I need some air," he says to me when the song comes to a stop. "Want to come with me?"

I look into his eyes. *I want to go anywhere with you*, I want to say, but I don't trust myself, so I just nod. He doesn't release my hand as he pulls us out of the room. We walk down the steps, and anyone looking at us would think we are a couple.

He walks around the staircase toward the side door, pushing it open. The cool air hits me right away, and I shiver. He shrugs his jacket off before I can tell him not to and wraps it around my shoulders. The cobblestone rock on the path makes my heels sink in, so I reach out to hold his arm to steady myself. "Where are we?" I ask as I look around at a little courtyard. It looks like it's in the middle of the hotel as some of the windows have lights on. Potted plants are scattered around the little space, and when you look up, you see the stars twinkling in the sky.

"No idea," he answers me, "I saw a door."

I laugh, holding the jacket closed with one hand as we walk toward the corner of the building where there aren't many lights on. "This is nice," I observe as we finally make it to a pathway that has concrete, so my heels aren't sinking. "It's a little chilly." I look over at him, seeing him put his hands in his pockets. "Do you want your jacket back?" I ask and shiver at the same time, making me laugh at myself. "We might have to share it." He looks at me, his eyes turning a darker blue, his jaw tight as if he's biting down on it. "What's the matter?" I ask as we stop at the corner of the courtyard, where a darkened entrance leads to a door with the word Maintenance on it.

"Nothing," he says, his words barely a whisper.

"Can I ask you something?" The words are out of my mouth before I can stop them.

"Don't you know that you can ask me anything?" His voice sounds like it's in pain. "And in that dress." He shakes his head and takes one of his hands out of his pocket and grabs the back of his neck with it.

I don't know if it's the wine. I don't know if it's the fact that I'm out of the house, dressed in a nice dress, and just slow danced with a man who has been nothing but supportive to me and my girls. I don't know if it's the fact being in his arms stirred something from the depths of my soul. I don't know if it's just the fact that today I put *get Christopher to kiss me* on my list. I don't know what it is, but we are here, and I'm taking the leap. "Touch me," I whisper, stepping toward him, putting my hands on his chest, feeling his heart racing just as fast as mine.

"Dakota." He uses my full name. "I'm holding on by a string, baby." His voice cracks, and the way he just called me baby made every single part of me tingle, especially parts that have not seen action for over a year.

"You said I could ask you anything." My finger taps his white shirt. "I'm asking you to touch me."

"Fuck," he groans before his hands fly to my face, and he spins me around to the darkened corner, pushing my back against the wall. My hand comes up to grab his tie, pulling him to me. "Fuck it all," he says before his mouth touches mine. My hand grips his tie even tighter, while the other one comes up to hold his cheek. At the same time as his tongue touches mine, fireworks go off inside me. His mouth swallows my moan as one hand drops from my face to my neck. His head twists to the other side to deepen the kiss. I'm lost in all that is him. I'm lost in his smell. I'm lost in his touch. I'm lost in his taste.

He pulls back, looking down at me, his thumb rubbing the side of my throat before his mouth replaces the heat of his finger. My hands go to his sides as my eyes close, his tongue trailing up the vein where my pulse beats.

His hand drops to my hip as he pulls me to him, and I feel how much this is doing to him. I arch my back, the jacket slips off my shoulders and pools around my feet, but we are too lost in each other to care. He nips my jaw before his mouth finds mine again. His hands find mine and move them up beside my head. Our fingers link with each other as we kiss. I've never been kissed like this before. I've never wanted to be kissed so badly in my life before. I've never wanted a kiss to go on forever before. He lets one hand go before he grabs my chin and moves from right to left, leaving my mouth to trail down kisses.

"Christopher." His name on my lips feels like I've been saying it my whole life.

"What, baby?" he says softly as my hands slowly fall from beside my head, his eyes looking up to mine. "Tell me what you want."

"I want you to touch me." My hands grip his hips. "Touch me."

"Your wish..." His tongue trails down my neck, making me move to the side to give him better access to it, right down to where my dress sits, before his tongue sweeps in and licks my nipple. My eyes close at that moment, and I pull his hardness into me more, lifting my leg over his hip. "...is my command."

My hands move from his hips to his ass, then up his back. I want to touch all of him, and my only wish is that he was naked so I could touch his skin. "Dakota," he murmurs my name again, and I open my eyes, "last chance to tell me to stop." Instead of answering him, I fist the back of his shirt before I move lower and pull his shirt out of his pants, my hands sliding under his shirt to his back.

He moves his head back up to kiss me. My mouth devours his as I move my hand to the front of his shirt, pulling it all out of his pants. His hand goes to my leg on his hip as he trails his fingertips up it, slowly, ever so fucking slowly. His fingers walk up the trail toward where I want his touch. My hands move at the same pace as his, almost as if I'm mimicking him. I feel his fingers right beside where my panties meet my hips. I sigh when he moves the lace to the side. Dropping my foot to the ground, I open my legs more. He lets go of my lips, leaving me panting. "I want to watch your eyes," he explains, and I just look at him, wanting to ask him what he's talking about, but I'm in a daze. "Right now," he says at the same time his finger runs down my slit, over my clit, and into me. I swear to God I exhale. "That," he announces, pulling his finger out and then pushing it in again, "is what I wanted to see. How your eyes light up when I touch you."

"Yes," I say. My body feels like it's on fire. He could touch me literally anywhere, and I'll light up like a firework.

My hands go to his belt, and he shakes his head. "If you undo my belt, I'm going to end up fucking you into the wall." He slides another finger into me. "And I'm not going to give a shit that everyone is going to hear you come for me." His thumb grazes over my clit, making my knees weak. "I also know that I'm not only going to fuck you once. I'm going to want to fuck you all night long." He slams his fingers into me. "But when I finally get my cock in you, I'm going to want you spread on my bed, and it's going to be after I've buried my face in your pussy and have made you come a couple of times."

"Yes," I agree, thinking about everything he's said, "let's do that." I move away from the belt buckle to cup his cock over his pants, feeling how hard he is. "I want to do all of that."

"You have no idea"—he slides his tongue into my mouth, moving it at the same pace as his fingers—"how fucking bad I want to taste you."

"Then do it." I look in his eyes as he says that, never expecting him to drop to his knees in front of me.

Looking up at me, he pushes my dress to the side. "If you insist," he says, right before his mouth devours me. He moves one leg over his shoulder as his tongue slides into me with his fingers. I swear to God I see white spots when his tongue licks up from my hole to my clit, right before he bites down on it, first gently, and when I moan, he sucks it into his mouth. His fingers work me over and over, and the sound of my wetness drowns out my panting. "You fucking taste like heaven," he praises right before he bites my clit again, this time harder, as my hand goes into his hair. The hair I've wanted to touch for the past month is now between my fingers. "I could eat you all day, every day." He slides his fingers faster.

"Christopher," I pant out his name, "I'm going to—"

"Yeah, I know, baby." He flicks his tongue before my leg drops to the ground, and he stands. "But I want to watch your face when I make you come." He kisses me, and I've never in my life felt the hunger I feel right now. It's barbaric. I want to rip his clothes off. I want him to rip my clothes off. I want him to pound into me over and over again. "Fuck." He lets go of my lips. "Let go, baby," he tells me, knowing I'm holding back. How he knows, I have no idea. I just want this moment to go on. "Your pussy is squeezing my fingers." His lips hover over mine, his eyes on mine. "You can do it, baby," he encourages me at the same time he curls his fingers inside me, pushing me off that cliff. "Come, baby, come for me," he whispers.

My hand goes to hold his wrist to stop him from moving inside me. "Oh no, baby, I'm not stopping until you come on my fingers." My stomach gets tight, it's right there, I can taste it, I can feel it, and it's going to be out of this world. "That's it," he urges, moving frantically, slamming his fingers into me.

"Oh my God," I chant over and over again, moving my head from side to side. "Christopher."

"Right here, baby," he reassures me, and I let go and fly. I come on his hand so hard that my whole body shakes under him. "Fuck, you're soaking me," he hisses as I squeeze his fingers over and over again. The spasms roar through me. "That's my girl." His mouth covers mine as I yell out.

SIXTEEN

CHRISTOPHER

"RIGHT HERE, BABY." I can feel her ready to fall apart, her hand wrapped so hard around my wrist trying to stop it, but nothing will stop this from happening. "Fuck, you're soaking me," I growl between clenched teeth, trying not to explode myself. "That's my girl." I look into her eyes as my mouth clamps down on hers.

I kiss her like I've never kissed anyone before in my life. Swallowing down her scream as soon as she comes. My fingers ride her all the way down off that cliff, her chest rising and falling, her tongue going around and around with mine. I know as soon as her hand lessens its grip on my wrist that she's at the end of her orgasm. Her body goes limp beneath mine as she sinks more into the concrete wall, and all I want is to make her come again. All I want is to peel that dress off her and get to know all of her. Trail my tongue over every inch of her body. Make her scream my name over and over again.

When I pulled her into the corner, I didn't know what

was going to happen. I knew what I wanted to happen. I knew I wanted to kiss her more than I wanted to take my next breath, more than I wanted anything in my whole damn life. Fuck, I never thought that one touch from her and everything would feel like it made sense, and at the same time, it felt like I was a rocket taking off from the stratosphere. I've never in my life lost control the way I did tonight. It was electrifying. But I should have known because that is the beauty that is Dakota.

"Christopher," she whispers my name when she lets go of my lips for one second, and her hand comes up to the back of my neck before I lean in and kiss her one more time. My lips leave hers before I slide my fingers out of her, her eyes fluttering open. Her mouth opens as I bring my fingers up to my mouth and lick them clean. Her eyes move back and forth from my eyes to my lips, then back to my eyes. As her hands slide from the back of my neck to the front of my shirt, her palms open on top of my pecs. I wonder if she can feel my heart pounding under her fingers. I wonder if she knows how much I want her. I wonder what her hands would feel like on my skin.

"You keep looking at me like that and"—I lean forward to kiss her lips again, softly this time—"all bets are off."

"There are bets?" she says with a smirk, but I can see the pulse on her neck beating faster and faster. She's nervous around me. "Who is taking these bets?" She closes her hands on my chest before letting them fall away from me to her sides.

I look down at my feet, not wanting to step away from her, but knowing we have to get back in there before people wonder what happened to us. The last thing I want is for people to gossip about her or us. I bend down to grab my jacket that has fallen to the ground, putting it around her shoulders before I take a step back and tuck in my shirt. "You ready to go back in there?"

"Yes," she confirms, moving her hands over her dress, making sure she looks okay. "I'm ready."

I slide my hand in hers, our fingers linking together as I walk out of the doorway into the courtyard. The minute the lights hit us, I release her hand. I look over at her one last time before we get to the door, pulling it open.

The heat hits us immediately when we both walk in, and I want to hold her hand in mine. Instead, she turns to me and hands me my jacket. "I'm going to go to the bathroom." She avoids looking at me. "I'll meet you back at the table." She turns and walks up the steps toward the party. The need to call her name and make her look back over at me just to see her smile is more than I care to admit.

I shrug my jacket back on before pulling the cuffs of my shirt out and following the same steps Koda just took up toward the bathroom. I push open the door, and I'm happy that it's empty. I go straight to the sink to wash my hands, and only then does it sink in what just happened.

My chest contracts when the reality of it creeps up on me. I kissed Koda, and not only did I kiss her, I fingerbanged her against a fucking wall. What the fuck did I just do? I stare at myself in the mirror, looking into the eyes that remember what she sounds like when she comes. Looking into the eyes that remember how tight she is. Looking into the eyes that remember how hard I got from just kissing her. *You fucked up*.

I take a deep breath before drying my hands with the paper towel and tossing it in the garbage. "Play it cool," I mumble as I pull open the door and step out.

My eyes roam the room looking for her, seeking her out, but my heart knows she isn't far away because it doesn't hurt when it beats. She's talking to Cole and Brittany, and they say something, and her head goes back, and she laughs. I've never been jealous of anything in my life. Not the fact my cousins are better at hockey than me. Not the fact I'm not always the best on my team. But I am by the fact that someone made her laugh, and it wasn't me. I put my hands in my pockets as I walk over to them.

"Hey," I say, looking at her, and when she looks at me, her eyes look like she's pulled a mask over them. I almost have to take a step back. They are void of the look I got less than fifteen minutes ago. Gone is the woman who looked at me with lust, and in her place is a woman who I haven't seen in a while. It's the same woman who tried to ignore me a month ago. "What's everyone laughing at?" I ask them, standing next to her. I leave my hands in my pockets before I grab her hand in mine and drag her out of here and make sure I never stop kissing her until I get that look back.

"Koda got stuck outside in the courtyard when she went to call the kids," Brittany informs me, and I look over at Koda.

"Really?" I ask, and she looks over at me quickly, and I can see her cheeks getting a touch pink. "It's freezing outside," I advise, "I hope you found a doorway to keep warm."

"Nope." She shakes her head. "Luckily for me, someone heard me knocking and came to my rescue."

"That's good." I look around. "We should go and thank him."

"I did already," she replies quickly, "but thank you."

"We should head back in," Cole says, "it's almost done." He turns and wraps his arm around Brittany, and again, I'm feeling jealous I can't do that. I can't slide my fingers with Koda's nor can I wrap my arm around her waist and pull her to me. I can't do any of that, and it fucking sucks.

"After you." I hold out only one hand because I don't trust myself.

"Thank you," she mumbles but avoids looking at me.

We sit side by side, but she turns her back to me to talk to Brittany the whole time. My leg nervously shakes up and down as the time drags on. I see Brittany nod at her as she pushes away from the table. "We are going to be heading out," Cole states.

"Oh, do you guys mind dropping me off?" Koda asks, and I feel like she just literally kicked me in the balls.

"Of course," Brittany says. "If I had known, we could have driven you here."

"I can take you," I blurt louder than I probably should, getting up with them.

"They are two doors down from me," Koda retorts, looking right through me. "It's fine." She smiles at me, a fake empty smile. "Thanks for tonight."

"Yeah," I say, sitting back down, "you're welcome." I grab the glass of water that is in front of me, gripping it harder than I should. "Have a good night." I avoid looking at her as I take a big sip of water.

I wait maybe fifteen minutes longer before I push away from the table and head out, saying goodbye to a couple of people along the way. I walk down the steps toward the front door, handing the valet guy my ticket. Looking over at the door that not too long ago, I pulled her out of.

A couple of the guys come out at the same time, and we just talk about nothing and everything. "See you tomorrow," I say once I see my car come around the crescent driveway. The valet driver gets out, leaving the door open, and I slide in.

I pull away from the curb, heading home, my head replaying the night. Her in my arms, dancing with me, trying to pull her even closer to me, but not too close that she could feel how hard she was making my cock. I turn into the subdivision, and as of late, I drive by her house before making my way to mine.

Pressing the button to the garage and driving in, I don't bother with the light before walking up the steps to my bedroom. Taking the jacket off, I get a whiff of her perfume, and my head hangs as I take my phone out and call her.

It rings three times before it goes to voicemail. Even

though I'm not going to leave a message, I listen to her voice, only when the beep comes on do I hang up the phone. Then I pull up our text thread.

Me: Can you call me, please?

I sit on my bed, looking down at the phone, willing her to call me. My eyes stare at the phone in front of me, urging the bubble with three dots to come up, even if she tells me she can't talk now, I'll take anything.

Instead, nothing comes through. My body falls back on the bed, my arm outstretched to the side, while the hand that holds my phone comes to the middle of my chest. "What the fuck did you do?" I look at the white ceiling. "Did you just ruin everything?"

SEVENTEEN

Dakota

"MOM," RAIN CALLS me from the living room, looking over my shoulder at her as I rinse off the dinner plates, "is Uncle Christopher playing hockey tonight?"

Just his name makes my stomach flutter and then makes the bile crawl up my throat. "I think so." I turn back around to make sure my daughter doesn't see my face flushed with pink from embarrassment.

"Can we watch a bit of the game?" she asks, and I don't turn around and look at her.

"I want to watch Uncle Chrissy too," Luna whines from her side of the couch.

"Okay," I agree, hoping she just goes back to whatever she was watching before she brought up Christopher.

It's been three days since I last saw him or, better yet, since I threw myself at him. God, just thinking about it, and I wish the floor would eat me up. I couldn't believe what I had just done. I couldn't believe not only had I kissed him for the first time, and it was the kiss to end all fucking kisses. Christopher Stone's kisses could make you forget your first name, which is what happened when he kissed me. I have never, and I mean have never, done anything remotely like that in my life. Never have I been that crazy for someone's touch that I forgot where the hell I was. The way I begged him to touch me, I want to cringe every single time it replays in my head, which is a lot. He must think I'm so desperate.

I can't explain or put into words how I felt afterward. I was ashamed, embarrassed, and most of all I wanted more. But nothing could top the guilt I felt, especially when he let my hand go. All the happy feelings I was feeling when it was just him and me and no one else was gone faster than I could blink my eyes. I wanted to rush out of there, but when I walked out of the bathroom, Brittany was there, so I had to pretend and it was so hard. Sitting next to him and feeling him so close made my heart pound in my chest, feeling like it was going to literally jump out of my chest.

I have avoided everything Christopher since then. He's called every single night, but it goes straight to voicemail and he's only texted once. I just can't face him right now, or maybe ever.

"What channel is the hockey game?" Rain asks when I finally close the dishwasher some forty minutes later. My mind has been so spacey every single time I think back on that night, which is pretty much every single time I let myself do it. It usually happens when I'm driving the kids to school, when I'm cooking or cleaning, when I'm lying in bed at night, and most definitely in my fucking dreams. He's everywhere yet nowhere at the same time.

"Let me check." I dry my hands and walk into the living room, grabbing the remote. Once I find the channel, I click on it, and it's a big mistake because there he is in the middle of my screen. The man who has made my knees weak. The national anthem is playing, and he's on the ice of course. His helmet is off, and his hair looks like he just ran his hands through it. I know exactly what it feels like now, and my own fingers tingle to feel it again. His blue eyes look straight into the camera, making my stomach flutter.

"Uncle Christopher," Rain cheers, clapping her hands.

With Luna following her, "Uncle Chrissy."

Turning back around, I walk to the kitchen and open the fridge door, grabbing the open bottle of wine I started on Sunday, taking a glass out, and filling it halfway. If I have to sit down and watch the man of my dreams, yet a man I can't ever have, I'm going to do it by having a glass of wine.

I curl my feet under me and decide that every time they show him on the screen, I'm going to take a sip of wine.

By the end of the first five minutes, my wineglass is empty. Or maybe it's because my eyes automatically go to him if he's on the ice. I wait until the end of the first period before I chase the kids up to bed. It's a little past their bedtime, so they are asleep before their heads hit the pillows.

I start my nighttime routine, which gives me time not to think about anything, so I automatically think of Christopher. "What the fuck are you doing?" I ask my reflection in the mirror. "It's Christopher. Hot Christopher, but still Christopher. It's not like you didn't find him good-looking before you made out with him and he went down on you." I shake my head, turning away from the mirror and turning off the lights. I don't bother turning on the television in my bedroom because I know I'll turn it on to the game. "You can't have him," I tell myself as I fall asleep, thinking and dreaming only of him.

The next night I've just closed the dishwasher when there is a knock on the door. "Go and grab the game you guys want, while I get the door."

Walking to the door and not bothering to see who it is, I unlock the door and then I see him standing there. He's wearing jeans and a thick, blue knitted sweater, his head down but it lifts up when the door opens. His eyes stare at me. "Hey," I say softly, stepping out of the door, not wanting my girls to hear this exchange in case it gets heated.

"Hey." He moves to the side for me to stand out with him. "I didn't think you would answer."

"Well, you knocked on my door at six o'clock." I cross my arms over my chest to try to keep warm with the wind blowing.

"Yeah." He laughs nervously. "I was hoping that." He uses one of his hands to grip the back of his neck. "Listen, Koda." He uses my nickname, and I suddenly hate it, especially after that I heard him call me Dakota. "I'm so, so sorry," he starts, and something inside me cracks a touch.

"You don't have to say anything." I hold up my hand. "Really, if we can both forget what happened." His eyes change before my eyes, and his jaw gets tight. "I should never have." I don't say the words because they would be a lie, and I've never actually lied to him before. "We shouldn't have. We can totally forget that it even happened. No one but us has to know." I pinch the inside of my arm, saying those words.

"Fuck that," he snaps. "I wanted to kiss you. I'm not ever going to say we shouldn't have."

"But you just said you're sorry," I point out to him. He's about to say something when the door opens, and I hear squeals.

"Uncle Chrissy!" Luna shrieks and launches in the air for him. "You came to visit." She puts her hands on his shoulders. "We watched the hockey, and you said two bad words." She holds up two fingers.

His eyes suddenly light up with her. "I did?" he deadpans, rocking her back and forth. "Did I really?"

"You did. You said motherfucker and piece of shit," Luna recites, and I gasp.

"Luna, don't you ever." She looks over at me, like she didn't say them and she just told him what he said.

"You know what, I shouldn't have said those words," he says to her, "and I don't think you should say those words either."

"Okay," she replies softly, playing with the neckline of his shirt, "I won't."

"Mom." The door opens, and Rain comes out. Her

eyes light up as if the whole cast of Disney showed up at her door. "Uncle Christopher." She goes to him, and he bends to take her in his arms also. "Are you coming to play board games with us?"

"Um—" I start to say because I would really like for him not to be close to me at this moment.

"Yes," he answers, ignoring the way I said um, "I was hoping I would get to spend time with you guys."

He takes the two of them and walks into the house, as if I'm not the one who is in charge of said house. "Christopher," I call to the back of his head, my eyes roaming to his ass and I have to think if I touched it at all. I mean, I know I touched his junk and that man is packing. "You really don't have to stay."

"Oh, I know." He puts the girls down. "But I want to." He tilts his head to the side. "That's okay, right?"

"I want Uncle Chrissy to stay," Luna declares from beside him, grabbing his hand in hers.

"I want Uncle Christopher to stay also." Rain follows her sister's lead and puts her hand in his other hand.

"Looks like I got the votes to stay." He looks down at the girls. "So what are we playing first?"

"Uno!" they both shout at the same time, turning and running to the living room.

"Christopher." I stand in front of him, my chest rising and falling as I just take him in. Wishing he didn't look so good or that I didn't want to jump him right here in the entranceway of my house while my daughters are in the other room. I mean, I wouldn't *jump him* jump him, but I would definitely let him kiss the shit out of me.

"What's the matter, Dakota?" he says my full name, and I swear my knees almost buckle. "It's okay if I stay, you know, since we can forget what happened, right?" He uses my words against me. "We can do that, right?" His voice is soft. "Just pretend nothing happened."

"Yes," I hiss out at him, "and stop calling me that."

"Why?" He smirks at me, and I swear I get wet. "It's your name."

I'm about to tell him that maybe tonight isn't a good idea when Rain runs back to us. "Come on, guys." She grabs Christopher's hand and pulls him with her. His eyes shine bright blue while he takes one look at me before turning back and walking to the family room.

I look up at the ceiling and wonder how to get him out of my house. When Rain and Luna both shout my name, I walk into the family room and see them sitting on the floor. The cards are in the middle of them and there is a spot open next to Christopher and next to Luna. "Saved you a spot," Christopher informs me.

Taking three steps to them before I sit down and crisscross my legs, my knees touching his lightly. I try to move away, but he moves with me. The whole game, I try to ignore that he's touching me, then he even moves his hands down his legs to his knees as his fingers graze mine. It's like his hand sends electric shocks through my body. By the end of the game, I have to step away. "You guys play. I'm going to go and make lunches," I lie through my teeth.

I rush away from him to the kitchen. The three of them play again, and the game is very animated. I can't help but look up from the kitchen a couple of times to see that they are all laughing at something. "It's time for bed and a bath."

"Can Uncle Christopher tuck me in?" Rain asks.

"If it's okay with Mom." He avoids looking at me.

"Can he?" she asks, and I just nod.

They each take his hand, pulling him upstairs. "I got them," he tells me. "Relax, for once."

"Yeah, right," I mumble to his retreating back. I feel like I'm a firework that's been lit on fire but hasn't exploded yet. I put away the lunch things before wiping down the island again for the third time.

I hear him walk down the steps and look up to see him coming into the kitchen. "They are waiting for you to kiss them good night."

I nod and walk over to him, stepping toward the staircase. "I'm going to head out." He stops at the base of the stairs. "Come and lock the door," he urges softly, and I follow him to the door as he pulls it open. "Thank you for tonight." He stops and turns back to face me. "For answering the door and letting me stay." It feels like he's going to advance toward me, and I hold my breath, thinking he's going to kiss me. I don't think I even take a breath. "I'll see you soon, Dakota," he says right before he steps out, and the door closes behind him.

EIGHTEEN

CHRISTOPHER

I PULL UP to the airport and get out of my truck, grabbing my overnight bag. "Did you pack a hat?" Cole asks when he gets out of his own truck beside me.

"I did not. Why?" I shut the door and lock the truck before turning to walk to the plane on the tarmac. The stainless-steel stairs are out, and a couple of players are already here and walking up toward the door.

"I think it's snowing there," he states as we walk side by side to the plane.

"In Buffalo?" I ask, shocked.

"That's what I just saw." Cole holds up his iPhone. "It's also cold AF."

I let him walk up the steps before me, grabbing an empty row and putting my bag in the overhead bin. We are on our way to Buffalo for a game tomorrow. "It's snowing in Buffalo."

"It's not that bad," someone says as I take off my cashmere coat and toss it on the seat next to me. Chatter happens around me as everyone gets situated for the fifty-minute flight. When we land, it is in fact snowing.

The wind blows the snow as we step off and head to the heated bus that is waiting for us. I'm getting my key in the hotel lobby when my phone rings in the inside pocket of my jacket. Pulling it out, I see Dakota is FaceTiming me. I'm about to answer it when it stops, and only when I scan my hotel key on the door and step in do I call her back.

When I showed up at her house, I expected her to tell me she was busy and didn't have the time. What I wasn't ready for was her telling me that we should forget whatever happened. There was no way in fuck I was going to forget what we did. Not a chance in hell. I also never expected the girls to invite me in. Was it a cheap shot to just go in? You bet your ass. But there is no place I want to be these days other than with her and the girls. I know there is something else there I have to talk about. I know I'm treading on ice so thin that it's cracking and my foot is already in the water. I know that everything in my head tells me it's wrong, yet my heart tells me a different story. A story I'm not sure I'm ready for.

The sound of the ringing fills my room as I shrug off my jacket. I see that she connected and I'm expecting to see her face, but instead it's Rain who comes on the screen. "Hey there." I smile at her.

"Uncle Christopher," she says, her smile so big that her eyes light up, "guess what?"

"Ummm, you got a hundred on your spelling test?" I guess the first thing that comes to my mind.

"No." She shakes her head. "I scored three goals today."

I gasp, "You what?"

"We had a hockey practice today," she starts, "and at the end, we had a little game, and I scored three goals."

"That's a hat trick." I sit on the bed, looking at her, and my chest fills with pride. I honestly have never felt this feeling in my life. I know I feel pride for my nieces and my nephews, but this one, this one just feels like my chest is going to explode. "Did Mom throw a hat on the ice?"

She giggles and looks up at Koda. "She didn't."

"I didn't have a hat." I hear her voice, and another thing happens, but that is more south. Just her voice and a little laugh, and my body suddenly awakens.

"I'll be there for Saturday practice. We can go out after and celebrate," I say, and she looks up at her mom.

"We are going to celebrate," she tells her even though I know she can hear. "Bye, Uncle Christopher," she says and then hands the phone to her mom. "Here."

"I want to talk to Uncle Chrissy," Luna whines.

"Here you go." Koda hands her the phone.

"Hey, princess," I greet her when she comes onto the screen, "how was hockey?"

"I didn't fall," she states proudly, "not even once."

"Look at you, you're a superstar." She nods, agreeing with me. "You get extra chocolate chips on Saturday."

She gasps, turning to Koda. "I'm getting all the chocolate on Saturday." I can't help but laugh at how different the story can change from me to her.

"Is that so?" Koda says as Luna hands her the phone.

"Hi," she says, looking at the screen, "sorry about calling, but Rain had to talk to you."

"You never have to be sorry about calling me. How are you?" Besides looking gorgeous, I don't add.

"Good," she replies, "I'm about to start dinner."

"Okay, I'll let you get on that. Can you call me later?" I stare at her to see her reaction, knowing she won't want to. "I have something to tell you." The back of my neck gets hot. "It's important." I'm really throwing everything out there for her.

"I have some work to do after the kids go down." She tries to come up with an excuse.

"It won't take long, I promise."

"Fine." She finally gives in, and I know she's just doing it to get it over with. "I'll call you when the girls go down."

"Talk to you then," I reply, wanting to say a lot more, but I have to tread lightly because she already has one foot out the door and the second is very close to following it.

"Bye." She hangs up without a second thought.

I get a text from Cole right after I hang up.

Cole: Dinner downstairs in the restaurant, no one wants to go out in the snow.

Me: Sounds good. What time?

Cole: Thirty.

I look at the clock and see that it's going to be five thirty, so it gives me enough time to go downstairs, have dinner, and get back to my room in time for her to call me, knowing the girls go to bed at seven thirty.

Me: Meet you down there.

I toss the phone aside and take off my suit jacket and hang it up, since I'm wearing it for the game tomorrow. The same with the pants as I slide into my tracksuit and running shoes, making it downstairs in twenty minutes.

A couple of the guys are shooting the shit when I pull out a chair and sit down. Dinner is a bit of chaos since they weren't expecting the team to be eating in the dining room. I make it back upstairs by seven and decide to take a quick shower while I wait for her.

Sliding into a pair of white boxers, I slip into bed and turn on the television while I wait for her to call me. I'm giving her until eight thirty before I cave and call her.

I flick through the channels, my head trying not to go crazy with what I'm going to say to her. At seven fifty-seven the phone rings, and I swear my hand flies out so fast I'm surprise that I don't drop the phone.

I press the green button, putting it on speaker. "Why didn't you FaceTime me?"

"I don't know, you said to call you." I press the camera button. "Are you FaceTiming me?"

"Yes," I answer as I see the little white words telling me it's connecting.

I see that she's sitting in her bed with her hair tied on top of her head. "Are you in bed?" I ask right away.

"Yes, I—" she stumbles with her words.

"You lied to me." I can't help but laugh at her nervousness.

"I did not lie to you," she snaps, "I have work to do. I'm going to do it after this phone call."

"I call bullshit." Which earns me a glare. "You tried to get out of talking to me, so you lied and said you had to work."

"Again, didn't lie," she hisses. "Is this what you had to talk to me about that was so urgent?"

"No." I snicker. "But it's fun when you get mad."

She pffts out. "Now that we've got you annoying me out of the way, we can get on with whatever it is you have to say so I can get to doing what I need to do."

"We need to discuss what you said yesterday," I tell her. I can see her walls come up but I'm ready to knock them down. "I think you misinterpreted what I was saying."

"I don't think anything at all," she quickly adds in, "and I don't think we really need to talk about this."

"Then you are shit out of luck." I sit up and see that her eyes go from my face to my chest, her cheeks getting a light pink, and I love that I have this effect on her. "Because there are a couple of things that have to be said, and I'm going to say them."

"I don't want you to say them." She takes a deep breath in. "I don't think we should go there."

"Too bad." I shake my head. "You want to forget that it happened?"

"Yes," she replies without even thinking about it.

"So you didn't want me to kiss you?" I ask, swallowing down, hoping like fuck she is honest with me. "Because I'm going to be very honest. If you didn't want me to kiss you and then I kissed you, I'm…" I feel sick to my stomach. "Jesus, I'm not that guy to take advantage of you or anyone."

"Christopher," she says softly, "that's not at all what I meant. You didn't take advantage of me; you would never do that."

"Listen, I don't know what the right and wrong thing is to do right now," I admit what is on my mind. "I have never been here, but I know a couple of things." I watch her face as I talk. "And I'm going to say them and then you can do what you want with them."

"Okay," she agrees softly.

"There is nothing I wanted more in my life than to kiss you the other night. I've wanted nothing more than to kiss you for the last two fucking months, or maybe it's been longer, I don't know. But I knew if I didn't kiss you when I did, I would have regretted it for the rest of my life." Her mouth opens in shock. "The only reason I told you I was sorry was because I thought you regretted it."

"I didn't regret it," she finally says, her voice in a whisper.

"You didn't even look at me the rest of the night." I can't help that my voice cracks. "You avoided looking at me and refused to let me drive you home. It killed me that I had one of the best kisses of my life and then thought you didn't want it."

"Christopher, I was so embarrassed."

"What?" I snap. "For what?"

"Good God, I let you go down on me in a dark doorway," she croaks out. "What the fuck was I thinking?"

"Are you asking me?" I smile at her. "Because not

going to lie, baby, if you would have dropped to your knees, I would not have said no, so there is that."

"What?" It's her turn to ask me.

"Baby, I want to touch you all the fucking time," I admit. "I want to kiss the shit out of you. I want to hold your hand and then kiss your fingertips. I want to worship your whole fucking body, like literally inch by fucking inch." I can see it in her eyes that she wants the same thing I want. "I lost total control the other night, and for that, I'm sorry also. I should have protected you. I can't even think about what would have happened if someone saw you in that state." I shake my head, my blood boiling. "No one gets to see you like that but me. That's mine, and it's yours. I was so fucking far gone for you, I didn't even think twice."

"You wanted me that bad?"

"Fuck, I want you that bad," I admit. "Like right now, my cock is so hard it hurts." She gasps. "A little TMI but"—I put my head back—"it's like a constant state when I'm next to you or I see you."

"I've never done that before." She takes a big exhale. "I've never, ever wanted to be touched so bad in my life. The minute you kissed me, it was like I forgot everything. My name, where I was, what I was doing. The only thing I wanted was to be closer to you."

"You can't say things like that to me when I'm here and you're there."

"Why not?" She laughs for the first time tonight, and my cock gets even harder.

"Because I can't touch you," I admit. "The things I

would do to you."

"Really?" She smirks. "Care to tell me?" She giggles and then hides her face.

"Don't do that. Don't hide from me."

"This is all very new to me," she admits.

"We are both in uncharted territory." I smirk. "And there is no one else I want to be uncharted with than you."

She tilts her head to the side. "Same." Finally admitting it makes me want to go and shout it from the rooftops.

"I'm really fucking happy you called me back tonight," I say softly.

"I'm really fucking happy that I did," she counters, and all I can think of is the next time I see her and the kiss I'm going to lay on her.

NINETEEN

Dakota

MY PHONE RINGS from beside me as I'm scrolling through pictures from a new designer. Looking down, I see it's Brittany calling me. "Hey, Brittany," I answer after two rings.

"Hey, Koda," Brittany says cheerfully. "How are you?"

"Good, just working." I lean back in my office chair and look around the room. When I got the job with Zara's Closet, I worked on the island for most of the day, but after two weeks, I thought I needed a proper office. So here I am in the little office I created right off the main entrance. It's a room Benji used to use for his own office. Where he would store the jerseys he needed to sign or do video interviews. I swapped out all the dark furniture he had in here and replaced it with everything bright. A white desk replaced the oak one that is now in Eddie's home, along with the big brown leather chair he sat in. Mine is black with a white fur throw on the back. A vase of pink roses sits at the corner of my desk. Fresh flowers have been a staple in the home lately, especially in my office. The girls have even gone as far as asking me to buy them little vases, and they cut two or three flowers to put in their own rooms.

"I won't keep you long. I'm just calling because all the wives are going to the game tomorrow night, and then we are going out to the bar."

I tap the back of the pen on the pad I was writing on as I listen to her. "Before you say no, it's not a couples thing." We both laugh. "The whole team is joining us after."

"Um." I look out the window at the sun that is shining. "I need to see if I can get a sitter."

"If you can get a sitter, does that mean you will come?" she asks with hope.

"Sure," I say. I'm not sure why I'm saying yes, but it'll be my thing to do for myself this week.

"Yay," she cheers gleefully. "Perfect, I'll pick you up tomorrow."

"Sounds good. I'll let you know if things work out," I say, disconnecting and then texting the babysitter right away.

Me: Hey, I know it's last minute, but would you be free tomorrow?

She answers me right away.

Morgan: I am free. What time would you need me there?

Me: Five should be good.

Morgan: See you there.

Me: I'll order pizza.
Morgan: Sounds good.

After I send her a text, I think for a couple of minutes before I pull up his name.

Me: Are you going to the bar after the game tomorrow?

I know he's away in Buffalo for a game tonight for two reasons. One, the kids made me make a calendar of the games and put it on the fridge, and two, when he called me yesterday to talk, he was in the hotel room. I didn't want to call him back, and I definitely wasn't ready to see him shirtless, but I figured I would bite the bullet. It's a good thing I did because I found out he didn't think I was a hussy for what happened. In fact, he lost as much control as I did, and to know I made him do that makes me want to do it over and over again.

My phone beeps with a message.

Christopher: I said I would make an appearance. Why?

I smile when I read his answer.

Me: Brittany just invited me, and I said yes.
Christopher: Cool, I'll drive you home.

I put my head back and laugh. I'm about to answer him when another one comes in.

Christopher: And if you pull the same stunt you did last week, I'm still showing up at your door.
Me: Message received.
Christopher: Glad we are in the same territory together. I don't care if that makes no sense, you get it.
Me: I do. Talk later.

Christopher: You bet your ass.
Me: Stop thinking of my ass.
Christopher: I just put on my jock strap and now I'm at half-mast. Do you know how painful this is?
Me: Hahahaha. I'll stop talking now.
Christopher: Good choice and also thinking of your ass and now other parts of you, which is not good for me.
Me: Then stop talking to me.
Christopher: Never.

I put the phone down, and for the rest of the day, a smile is on my face. I also feel lighter, which is strange but something I'm okay with. The girls and I gather around the television that night to watch the game. We've decided to do a picnic and have popcorn and snacks on the floor. The minute that Christopher's face fills the screen, I smirk. By the end of the second period, both girls are fast asleep on the floor, and it takes everything out of me to get them to bed. I watch the rest of the game in bed, and they end up losing four to two. Turning off the television and lying down, I think about texting him, but I'm not sure if I should.

I mean, we have made it clear that we both want each other, at least naked. But I don't know if I should text him and say good night or not. I literally spend over an hour thinking about it back and forth when my phone beeps from the bedside table. Reaching out, I grab it and see it's from Christopher.

Christopher: Just got on the bus. I'll see you tomorrow morning.

I smile, knowing he's probably going to get back after three o'clock in the morning, and he'll still wake up at six to come with the girls to hockey.

Me: I'll make you coffee. See you tomorrow.

The following morning, I get dressed, and my whole body is a stack of nerves. I don't know what is going to happen. Does the phone conversation change the way we are with each other? Are we going to be shy toward each other? When we walk out the front door, he's outside waiting for us, a smile on his face when he sees us, and then he pulls two hats from behind his back and throws them in the air, and they land at Rain's feet. "That's for your hat trick," he says while she bends to pick them up.

"I'm going to hang these in my room," she informs me.

"Oh, here we go," I mumble as he opens the back door to let the kids get in.

"Hey," I say when I get close to him, handing him one of the two cups I'm holding in my hands.

"Hey," he replies, coming close to me and kissing my cheek, something he's never done before. "Thank you." He takes a sip while the girls buckle themselves in.

When he closes the door, he looks at me. "I hope it was okay I kissed your cheek." He takes another sip. "I figure before they see me stick my tongue down your throat, they should see me kiss your cheek."

"Good call." I can't help but giggle as I get into the driver's seat.

He doesn't reach over to hold my hand, and even when we sit next to each other, he doesn't drape an arm over me or kiss me. But he does look over at me a lot, leaning in, and talking to me about the kids, but then slyly kissing my cheek. He even reaches over a couple of times and squeezes my knee.

When we go out to breakfast, and he sits next to me in the booth, it's the first time he holds my hand. I mean, not my whole hand. When I put my hand on the bench, he follows suit and his pinky slides with mine. It's silly that his touch can light me up like it does.

He drops me off with another kiss on the cheek and one for each girl before he heads out to take a nap. I tell the kids I'm going out that night, but I don't mention the hockey game.

I dress in blue jeans, which I've worn before, and I also know that they look fantastic on my ass with a long-sleeved black bodysuit. My hair is loose, and I curl it just a bit, adding a touch of mascara. Instead of sneakers, I opt for black high-heeled booties, putting on my cropped leather jacket to finish the look.

I kiss the kids goodbye when Brittany texts me that she's on her way. I smile when I get in the car and she says, "Damn, you look hot."

I laugh while I put on my seat belt. "I feel good today," I tell her and see her smile get soft. Many people ask me throughout the day how I'm feeling. And I often want to get angry with them and snap, but I've learned from the group that not everyone knows how hard it was for me. They only know what I told them or what Benji told them, and it wasn't much. I put on a farce for everyone, just to make sure I protected him. Something I didn't even know I was doing. Something I wish I could go back and change, but alas, we are here.

I walk into the suite and say hello to a couple of people while I grab a glass of wine and go and sit down. During the whole game, my stomach was in knots, especially after the game when we walked into the bar that was closed just for the team.

We walk to the bar where I order another glass of wine. A couple of the wives tells stories, and I laugh. My eyes look over to the door every single time it opens, as I try not to draw too much attention to myself. I take a sip of my wine when the door opens, and Cole comes walking in wearing his suit with no tie. Right next to him is Christopher, dressed the same way Cole is, but obviously hotter.

His eyes scan the room as he looks for me, and only when he sees me does he smirk. He walks around Cole, who has stopped right next to the door, when he spots Brittany talking to someone.

It takes him five steps to get to me. "Hey," he says, putting his arm around my waist and bending to kiss my cheek. The smell of cedarwood makes my mouth water. "You look sexy as hell," he compliments softly in my ear before letting me go.

"You're not looking bad yourself." I look around to see that no one is paying any attention to me. "You hungry?"

"I could eat." He looks around, spotting a couple of tables open. "You hungry?"

I bring the glass of wine to my mouth. "Not for food."

I can't help but laugh when I see his eyes go dark.

"Oh, I see how it is." He nods at me, and if anyone was looking at us, it would be like two friends just chatting away.

"Let's grab a table." He puts his hand on my hip and squeezes. I grab my jacket and bag that I put on the top of the bar and follow him to the table. We sit, and it's just the two of us. "Who's with the girls?"

"Morgan," I say, trying not to fall for him even more but probably failing. This man has so many layers to him, I don't think he's not going to surprise me. "Good game."

"Always a good game when you win." He leans back in his chair but then gets up to shrug off his suit jacket. He sits back down and moves his chair even closer to me. "Did you have fun?"

I put my elbows on the table and interlock my hands. "I did." I can't help but smile. "I had a lot of fun." I tilt my head to the side. "Having more fun now."

"Are you?" He puts his own elbows on the table.

"Most definitely," I assure him, and then stop talking when the server comes over, and he orders himself a burger.

He's about to say something when the chair in front of him is pulled away, and then so is the one next to me. Brittany and Cole join us. Our food arrives, and we laugh and chat the whole time, and finally, when it's almost midnight, I look over at him. "I should get home."

"We should also," Brittany says.

"I'm headed out also. I got her." He looks at me and

pushes back from the table, grabbing his jacket while I grab mine. As we walk to his car, we say goodbye to Brittany and Cole, along with most of the team.

He takes his keys out of his pocket, and the lights on the car blink as it unlocks. He looks around for a couple of seconds before reaching out, and instead of opening the car door for me, he pushes me against it, taking me by surprise. "I've waited all fucking night to do this." His voice comes out thick as his hand flies to my face, and I have no time to prepare for his mouth hitting mine. His tongue slides into my mouth, and the kiss is hot and wet. My hands go to his chest, the kiss making the top of my head tingle to the top of my toes. It's over faster than I want it to be. "You should get in the car."

"I would, but you are pressing me against it." I lean forward and kiss his neck. The action shocks me just as much as him.

"I like your lips on me," he shares softly, "like you are claiming pieces of me." He pushes back a bit, leaving me room to step away from the door so he can open it.

I get into the car and watch him walk around to his side of it. He starts the car and puts on his seat belt before making his way to my house. Neither of us really says anything, and when we pull up to the house, I'm nervous yet excited. He gets out of the car and walks me to the door. I have my hand on the door when I turn to him. "You going to stay?"

I can see his eyes change. "Dakota," he says my name, and it's almost as if he's in pain, "I can't touch you in his house."

It's as if he poured ice-cold water on me. Everything I was feeling earlier is gone, and in its place is anger. "Excuse me?" I say, giving him the benefit of the doubt. Maybe I didn't hear it right.

"I want to, God, you know I want to, but I just can't touch you in his house."

I swallow down the lump that is now crawling toward my throat. "Fuck you, Christopher," I snap, shocking him, "this isn't his house. It's my house." I point at myself. "He lost this house the minute he started using drugs instead of coming home to this house."

I quickly turn and walk into the house, closing the door behind me. The lone tear rolls down my cheek as I walk into the house toward the family room and find Morgan watching a movie, waiting for me. I wipe the tear and put a smile on my face. "Hey," I say, "was everything okay?"

"Yeah, they went to bed before the second period." She gets up, and I walk her to the door, holding my breath when she opens it and steps outside. I wait for her to get in her car before I close the door and walk over to the step. I sit down on the step and stupidly wait for him to come back, but after fifteen minutes, I give up. Taking off my shoes and walking upstairs, I go through the motions and try not to think about my heart that hasn't even healed yet but is broken once again.

TWENTY

CHRISTOPHER

I SKATE INTO the neutral zone next to Cole, who passes me the puck, but I miss it, and the defenseman steals it from me. I'm so frustrated I slash his stick with mine, and I see the referee's hand go up in the air. "Motherfucker," I mumble while I lift his stick and touch the puck with mine, stopping the play.

"Number eight Pittsburgh, minor penalty, slashing," he says, chopping his right arm.

"Fucking bullshit call, Pete," I bark when I skate by him.

"Dude, are you okay?" Cole asks when he skates over to me, pushing me to the box and making sure I don't go after the referee.

"I'm fine," I huff, going into the box and slamming the door. I remove my helmet and gloves, grabbing the green Gatorade bottle and squeezing it, squirting water into my mouth.

I watch the Jumbotron while they replay the slashing

play, and all I can do is shake my head. It's a horrible, fucking rookie mistake, and I shouldn't be fucking taking stupid-ass penalties. It takes the team one minute and four seconds to score the goal. I put my helmet back on and my gloves, skating with my head down from the penalty box over to the bench.

"Stone," my coach says from behind me, "cut that shit out." He glares at me, and all I can do is nod. I look at the game, trying to hide my disgust that I let my team down. We end up losing five to two, and I barely listen to what the coach says in the locker room. This road trip has been disastrous, to say the very least. Our last game against Nashville was even worse. I got three penalties that game and even dropped the gloves to fight. Now this game, I got two. Anyone who knows me knows that isn't the way I play. I think I got a total of eight the whole last season. Now I have six in two games. It's been a long fucking week, to say the least.

I head out to the bus waiting to take us to the plane and head straight home. It's a three-hour plane ride, so we will get home after one o'clock. The plane ride home is pretty much silent. No one is really talking, as a couple sleep while others watch shit on their phones. I sit with my head against the plane, looking out the window, thinking about this whole week.

How I went from being on top of the fucking world to walking with the biggest chip on my shoulder. I don't even know what to say. All I know is that I'm fucking miserable. Actually, I'm worse than miserable, but I can't come up with a word that would make it feel worse.

It's been five fucking days since I last saw or spoke to Koda, and it feels like an eternity. I fucked up in a way that I don't think I can come back from. There was nothing I wanted more than to take her in the house and kiss the living shit out of her, but I couldn't cross that line. Benji bought her that house. They made a life for themselves in that house. He kissed her good morning in that house. He kissed her good night in that house. I know it's probably stupid, but I can't fucking help it. It's enough that I have this guilt I'm with her, making it feel like I'm being disrespectful to him. I just couldn't do it. I just can't do it. Closing my eyes, all I can see is the hurt on her face, making my chest tight. She was straight-up pissed the fuck off, and she let me know it. She told me to go fuck myself and slammed the door in my face. I got back in my car and pulled away, driving to my house, but I couldn't even go inside. Instead, I drove back over to her house and sat in my car for about an hour, trying to convince myself to call her or go and knock on the door. Each time I would get the courage, the guilt would creep up and grab me.

In the end, I went home and lay in bed all night long, watching the hours creep by. The next day, I busied myself with working out in my home gym for hours, trying to tire myself out so I could just crash that night. Even though I crashed early, the dreams were all of Koda. Her smiling at me and then her with tears running down her face. The days following weren't much better, and now I was returning home to an empty house.

We touch down a little after one thirty in the morning,

the wind gushing through me hair as I walk from the plane to my parked truck. Tossing the bag onto the seat beside me, I make my way home. Taking the new route I do now, which includes driving past her house, the pressure on my chest makes it really difficult to breathe. My house is dead quiet when I arrive as I make my way from the mudroom off the garage toward my bedroom, not turning on a single light.

I toss my bag in the closet as I strip down, leaving everything in the middle of the floor. I lie on my side, hoping sleep comes to take me, but only when the sun rises do my eyes give in and shut. When I wake up, I turn to the side, seeing it's past one o'clock in the afternoon.

I grab my phone, and I have over forty missed texts. I blink my eyes a couple of times, opening up the text app and checking to see if any are from her. My stomach sinks yet again when I don't see her name.

The top of the text thread starts with my uncle Viktor.

Viktor: You want to give me a call?

I sigh when I go to the next one from my father.

Dad: Call me when you get up. And I mean today and not in a week.

"Ugh." I roll over from my side to my back, feeling like I'm ten again, and my father is going to ream my ass.

The next one is a text chain with my uncles Matthew and Max.

Matthew: What the fuck was that play?
Max: That was a peewee move if I ever saw one.

"Thanks for that," I say and make the mistake of clicking the cousins group chat.

Michael: The fuck is in your head?

Stone: That was so bad.

Dylan: Like you guys haven't made dumb plays before. STFU.

Chase: Why am I in this group? I don't even play hockey.

Stefano: I don't even watch hockey.

Romeo: There was a game????

Xavier: Can we just not jump down his throat?

Tristan: I can't leave this chat nor can I comment on anything because I'm married into the family.

Stone: But seriously, what is wrong with you?

Michael: He threw down his gloves. The fuck was that all about? Who does that?

Dylan: He was protecting his player.

Michael: Can someone please kick him out of this group chat?

I laugh at the end of that but don't reply to any of it. I get up, going to the bathroom, washing my face, and brushing my teeth before heading downstairs to make myself a coffee. I'm taking my first sip of coffee when my phone rings. Looking down, I see it's my dad.

"Hello," I answer, putting it on speakerphone as I walk toward the couch.

"Hello, my ass," he snaps. "I told you to call me when you got up."

"You didn't even give me a chance." I lean back on the couch. "I just woke up."

"It's the afternoon."

"Yeah, I had trouble falling asleep," I admit.

"I bet you did after those last two games." He stops talking, and I don't have anything to add, so he continues. "What the fuck is wrong with you? Dropping your gloves, what are you… five?"

"Wilson drops his gloves every fifth game," I point out about my cousin Franny's husband, Wilson.

"He's not my kid," he hisses. "What the hell is going on with you? You have never been that type of player."

A heavy sigh comes out of my mouth. "I don't know, Dad," I say softly. "I mean, I know, but I—"

"What is going on?" His tone changes. "Do you need me to come out there?"

"Yes," I reply but then quickly change my mind. "No. Fuck, I don't know, Dad." My throat feels like it's closing in on me, and I can't breathe. I sit back up, putting my coffee down on the table in front of me. "Dad, I don't know what to do."

"Whatever it is, we can get through it." The worry in his voice makes me feel even worse. "Just talk to me."

I put my phone down on the table so I can rub my face with both my hands. "I don't know how to say this."

"Christopher." His tone is tight. "Whatever the fuck it is, we are here for you."

"I don't know about that." The thought that he is going to be disgusted with me is almost too much to bear, but I also know if I don't tell him something, his ass will be on a plane within the hour, and then he'll be in my face, making me tell him.

"Wow," he says. "After all this, you think I don't have your back?" His voice is almost broken. "You don't think we have your back?"

"It's not about having my back, Dad. It's about the fact you might be disappointed in me."

"Never," he quickly adds, "I could never."

"Never say never." I try to laugh, but it comes out pitiful.

"Why don't you let me be the judge of that?"

"Okay." I take a deep breath in and then slowly let it out when I say the words, "I think I'm falling for Koda." My eyes close when I say those words, waiting for his reaction.

"You think you are falling for her, or you already fell for her?" Fuck, I should have known he would see right through that.

"I'm pretty sure I've one thousand percent fallen for her," I confess to him. "It's so fucked up, I know. She's Benji's wife."

"She's not anyone's wife," he points out. "He's not here."

"You know what I mean."

"I know what you mean, but I also need you to see what I mean." He doesn't give me a chance. "If Benji was still here and he was married to her, would you be falling for her?"

"Probably not," I say, shaking my head. "I would never cross that line. She's a beautiful woman with a heart of gold, and I've always thought that, but I also knew she was off-limits."

"Exactly."

"But…" I sigh.

"But nothing." His voice is soft again. "You don't get to choose who you love"—I close my eyes—"or who you fall for. Look at your mom. I knew without a doubt I should have stayed away from her, but I also knew that it would have killed me to do that. I also knew without a shadow of a doubt that there was no way I would ever love someone the way I love her." He trails off. "But, son, it's not just her you have to think about."

"I love those girls like they were my own. That is for damn sure."

"Okay, so I don't know what the hang-up is."

"Dad, he died seven months ago."

"Is there a rule book that says when it's a right time to fall for someone?" He laughs at his own joke while I roll my eyes. "If this happened two years from now, would that be better?"

"Yes," I reply, but then I think about her maybe falling for someone else in those two years, and I feel like I'm going to be physically sick. "No. I don't know."

"What does she have to say about all of this? Surely, this isn't coming out of the blue."

"I might have fucked up."

"You might have?" He laughs. "Well, now I know why you sucked so bad on the ice. What happened?" he asks. I leave out the whole going down on her in public because he's still my dad, and it's awkward, but I definitely tell him about not going into the house.

"Shit," he says. "I mean, I get it. I don't think I would have been able to do that, but did you talk to her before that?"

"Dad, I just admitted to you for the first time that I'm falling for her. You think I've admitted it to her? What if she thinks I'm a creep?"

"If she thought you were a creep, she wouldn't stick her tongue down your throat." I groan. "You need to put your big-boy pants on and have a conversation with her. She needs to know what you are comfortable with, just like you need to know what she's comfortable with. Nothing will be solved if you run away from her."

"I'm not running away. I was away for work."

"Did you call or text her?"

"I was giving her space."

"You were being a scared punk-ass bitch." He doesn't skip one single beat. "And then you took it onto the ice and let your team down."

"This pep talk is amazing, Dad. We should really do this more."

"Just keeping it real, son." He laughs. "Now I'm going to let you go so you can call her and talk to her. I'm also coming down there this weekend."

"You don't have to do that."

"I'll give you until next weekend, and then I'm coming down."

"Fine." I sigh. "I'm going to let you go."

"Talk to her and not in a punk-ass-bitch way. In a way that is actually communicating."

"Again, Dad, you really should do motivational speaking." I chuckle. "Love you," I say, hanging up. Then I take a big breath before pulling up her number and calling her.

I don't even know if she's going to answer me or not. I look down at the phone, willing her to pick up and then making a plan for going over to her house. I'm almost going to hang up when the phone connects. "Hello," she breathes heavily, as if she ran to the phone.

"Hey," I say softly, my heart feels like it's beating normal for the first time this week, "it's me."

"Hey." Her voice stays neutral.

"I was wondering if I could come over and we could talk." I look down at the phone, wishing I would have FaceTimed her so I could have seen her face.

I wait for what feels like an eternity, waiting for her to tell me to go fuck myself, but instead, her words shock me. "We're gone."

TWENTY-ONE

Dakoda

TALKING TO CHRISTOPHER was not on my agenda today, but if I didn't answer the phone, I would have to tell my mother why I wasn't answering it. So now I am here in my teenage bedroom on my bed, talking to the man I've been thinking about obsessively. "We're gone."

"Where are you?" he asks so quickly.

"The girls were off this week, so I decided to come up to my parents' house for the week." I close my eyes, hoping he doesn't think I ran away from him, which I did, but he doesn't need to know that.

"Oh," he says softly, and I close my eyes. "Okay, when are you going to be back?"

"Sunday night," I tell him.

"Can you call me when you get back?" The question doesn't surprise me. I knew we would have to talk, but I didn't know when it would be. I also didn't think it would have been this long before we talked. But I know he's been on the road traveling because we've been watching his games with the girls.

"Yeah," I give in.

"Give the girls a kiss for me," he urges, sounding so defeated, and even though I hate it, it serves him right.

"I will," I reply and then just hang up. I fall back on my bed and close my eyes, wishing I was home so we could have this talk and get it over with. I don't know what the talk is going to do exactly, but I know I want it out of the way. For both our sakes.

The phone rings again on my chest, and I pick it up, seeing he's calling me back. "Hello," I answer right away.

"Hey." He sounds nervous. "I was wondering if you would go on a date with me?"

I swallow the golf ball that was stuck in my throat before that now feels like a baseball. "No." I close my eyes when I say the word. "I don't have the time when I get back." I give him some bullshit excuse. "I'll be swamped with work emails since I'm not really working this week."

"Okay," he stumbles, "yeah, of course. Call me when you get back." He disconnects first this time, not giving me a chance to say anything else.

"What the fuck was that all about?" I look at the phone that has the lock screen of me and the girls on their first day of school. "Why the hell did you say no? This is literally what you've wanted."

I swipe up and go to my call list, seeing his name and calling him back. I sit up on my bed, waiting for him to answer. Even though he answers after one ring and a half, I have to think he didn't want to answer. "Hey," I say before he can even say hello, "I'm coming back this afternoon." I shock myself at this decision because I was supposed to be here for the next four days. "So if you want to go out and get that talk out of the way tonight, we can do that."

"Yeah," he agrees right away. "Yeah, let's do that. I'll pick you up at seven. Is that good?"

"Works for me," I confirm, looking at my watch. If I leave now, I'll get home by four thirty, which would still give me enough time to get ready.

"I'll see you then," I say, hanging up the phone before either of us changes our minds. I run down the stairs toward the kitchen to find my mother, who is cleaning the lunch dishes. "Hey," I start, walking in, "I'm going to head back home."

I look around, wondering where the girls are. "What?" my mother asks, shocked. "Why?"

"I just—" I start to say and then stop. I haven't really told anyone but Dr. Mendes about Christopher. "Thought I would get back home and—"

"If you have to go home for work, then you should go," she says, drying her hands. "Would it be okay if we kept the girls here?"

"I don't want to do that to you."

"Oh, please, it's been so fun having them here." She smiles at me. "Why don't you go home and, I don't know, go out."

"Mom," I gasp, avoiding looking at her.

"What?" Her voice goes high. "You are a young

widow with two kids. There is nothing wrong with you going out and having fun. You aren't the one who…" She doesn't say the rest of the words. "Now, go pack your stuff and get on the road." She smiles and blinks away tears. "We will bring the kids home on Sunday."

"Okay," I agree, hugging her. It takes me about five minutes to pack my stuff, and the girls aren't even sad to see me go. They both hug me and wave at the window when I pull out. I make it home in less time than I thought it would take me. I walk in and go straight to my bedroom, emptying my bag in the closet before looking for what I should wear. I don't even know where I'm going, but I figure I should dress nice.

I pull up Dr. Mendes's contact and send her a quick text.

Me: What does one wear on a date with her dead husband's best friend? Asking for a friend.

I move my hangers, checking my options when she answers me back.

Dr. Mendes: Three red bows, one on each of your nipples, the other one on your vagina. If that is not an option, go for red. It screams have sex with me.

Me: Forget I asked you.

I put my phone in my back pocket before I grab a red pantsuit I've never worn. Holding it up, I then walk over to my bodysuits, grabbing a lace one that dips very low in the front and lower in the back. I put the outfit on my bed before rushing to the bathroom to take a shower and do my hair. I straighten my hair and part it in the middle, tucking it behind my ears before putting on some smoky eye shadow and mascara. I go back to get dressed before applying the lip gloss. I slide on the bodysuit first before I grab the pants that fit me perfectly, tight all the way down to my ankles. The bodysuit is sexy and shows off my cleavage just enough to make him want it but not enough that I'm giving away the farm. I put the jacket on to finish the look, pushing the sleeves up a bit before stepping into my black sky-high shoes that are not made for walking. They are made to put on, walk to the car, and then to the table. I apply my lip gloss and then take a picture of myself to send to Dr. Mendes.

Me: Went with the red option.
Dr. Mendes: I see no bows.

I laugh and put the phone in my handheld purse, walking downstairs and already regretting the shoes decision. I don't have a chance to second-guess anything because the doorbell rings. I ignore all the butterflies in my stomach and walk to the door, hoping I don't vomit all over his shoes. I pull open the door and I can't help but smile when I see him, even though I want to stab his toe with the heel of my shoe for being a dick the other night. "Hey," I greet him, ignoring how satisfied I am when his mouth hangs open.

"Um," he stammers, and I stand here as he holds out a huge bouquet of roses for me, wrapped in white paper. "I got you these," he says of the flowers, "and I got these for the girls." He holds up his other hand that holds two smaller bouquets. "They told me they like flowers in their room."

Now it's my turn to stare at him with my mouth open.

"Um, thank you. The girls are staying at my parents' place until Sunday." I reach for them with both my hands. "I'll get them in water, and then we can go."

"They have the little water things at the bottom," he mentions, "so they are good until tomorrow."

"Great." I walk away from him to the kitchen and place them on the counter. He doesn't follow me in, and when I walk back, I see that he's staring at me with his hands in his pockets. He's wearing dark navy-blue pants that I know have to be custom made because they fit him perfectly, showing off his huge thighs. A baby-blue button-down shirt that has three buttons at the top open, showing you his neck, and a navy cashmere coat.

"You look," he says when I get close enough, "really fucking good." I stand in front of him.

"Thank you." I look down when he steps into my space.

He puts his hand around my waist, pulling me to him. "Thank you for giving me a chance," he states softly, bending his head and kissing my cheek. He lets his hand fall from around my waist, opening the door for me to step out, and then closing it after him. He slides his hand in mine before walking down the steps toward his car. He opens the door for me, and I have to push down the disappointment that he didn't try to kiss me. I watch him walk around to the driver's side and get into the car. I look over at him, and I admit I've fallen for him. I just don't know what to do about it.

"Where are we going?" I ask when he pulls out of the driveway.

"Just a little place I like. It's good food and private enough that we won't be bothered."

I nod, looking out the window, trying not to look as nervous as I feel. We get to the restaurant, and he stops in front of the valet sign. The door is opened by a man as I step out and see Christopher walking around the back of the car. "The keys are in the car," he tells the valet, grabbing my hand and pulling me away from the guy who nods at him. "Asshole."

"What?" I ask, laughing.

"He was literally drooling over you," he snaps, pulling open the door for me to walk through it, the heat hitting me right away. "I wish I could have walked in front and behind you because I'm pretty sure he was checking out your ass."

"Christopher," I say his name, laughing, "he was not."

"Yeah, right," he counters, walking in, "you didn't see his eyes go right down your shirt."

I gasp, putting my hand on said shirt. "We have a reservation for two," he says to the hostess, who is wearing a black dress. I look around the dimly lit restaurant that has maybe ten to fifteen tables. All tables are round with four chairs with hanging chandeliers over each one, which have three crystal vases with water and floating candles, making the mood even more romantic.

The hostess pauses at a table in the corner, and Christopher stops to pull out my chair for me. "Thank you," I say, sitting in the chair and then watching him shrug off his jacket and put it in the chair beside me, before pulling the chair from my other side out.

"Don't you dare take off that jacket," he mumbles when I watch him sit down. I've never felt more confident or sexier than I do at this very minute.

"Excuse me," I say, pushing my chair away from the table, "I'm going to the restroom." I turn, walking away from him, ignoring the stinging in my eyes. I spot the bathroom in the corner of the room, and when I push the door open, I'm glad no one is in there. I exhale and then inhale. I use the back of my thumb to wipe away the tear. Dr. Mendes's words play over in my head. "He's not here anymore, so you aren't doing anything to him."

I look at myself in the mirror before walking back out, finding Christopher's eyes on the bathroom door. I walk to him and pull out my chair. "Are you okay?"

"Yeah." I nod. "It's just I've not been on a date in a long, long time." I pull my chair in.

"We can get out of here and go get pizza if you want." He puts his hands down on the table, ready to get up and just walk out.

"Not a chance in hell." I smile at him. "I'm here, and you're here, and we are going to talk about a couple of things."

"Okay, but if at any time you want to go, we can go." He puts his hand on mine. "Even if we are mid meal."

I laugh as the server comes over and asks us if we want still or sparkling water. I listen to the special but my head is more focused on the way his fingertips are playing with mine. "Are you going to drink wine?" Christopher asks while he picks up the menu.

"I can have a glass or two," I reply, picking up my

own menu. "Are you going to have one?"

"I would, but from the minute I got my driver's license, my parents said if I had even one drop of alcohol, I wasn't allowed to drive. It's silly, I know, but"—he shrugs—"I won't put you in danger. I won't put myself in danger, and I won't put anyone else in danger."

"Have you always been this perfect?" I ask, shocked at his confession.

"I mean, you did tell me to fuck off last week, so I'm going to go out on a limb and say no." He leans back, making his shirt go tight on his chest.

"I did." I close the menu. "I think we should get that out of the way."

"You mean you want to hear my excuses before we continue, in case you want to kick me in the balls?"

I can't help but laugh. "Something like that."

"Listen, I know I could have worded it differently, but the fact is still that no matter who lives in the house now, it was Benji's."

I swallow when I see the guilt all over his face. "Let me share a couple of things with you. Last October, Benji got home from out of town. I think you guys were in Vegas, maybe LA, not sure, but at least in one of those places, he had a threesome." I watch his face to make sure he didn't know about it and just didn't tell me, but the way his eyes darken, I know he would never have been okay with Benji doing that to me. "The reason I know is that he butt dialed me." I blink. "I heard the three of them. Not for long. I got the gist of it, so I hung up."

"Dakota," he says my name, and it feels like it's being ripped from his chest.

I hold up my hand. "Then he got home, and I pretended nothing happened. I smiled at him and let him kiss my lips. Until the kids went to bed, and then I walked into our bedroom where he was lying on the bed, somehow thinking I would have sex with him, I'm not even sure. He looked up, and all I did was toss him my phone. He didn't understand what I was saying, so I told him to check my call log. When he did, he knew. I also told him I would never forgive him for doing that to me. He then informed me that not only was it not his first time, he'd been doing it to me since we started dating." Christopher hangs his head. "He pulled up his phone like it was a trophy and showed me every single girl he had stored in his phone by state. And if that wasn't bad enough, he showed me pictures. Because what good is show-and-tell without the showing. It was then I knew my marriage was over, but then I knew something else was going on with him. So the cheating was the least of my worries."

"Can you stop, please?" he says, his eyes filled with tears.

"That's the man you are comparing yourself to." I don't stop. "I've known you as a friend for a long fucking time, Christopher. I don't know you as well as I knew Benji, but I can bet on my life that you would never, ever do that to someone you say you love. So when you stood there and told me you couldn't do that to him, it made me angry for two reasons. One, because it's not his house. It hasn't been his house for a while, and two, I was pissed he was taking something else from me." I take a deep breath, and I'm proud I did all that without sobbing. "Now, that's to say you aren't the only one who is feeling guilty about this. So before this goes forward, you have to make a decision. Will you ever be okay knowing I was Benji's once?" He opens his mouth. "You don't have to decide now. For tonight, I want to sit down at a table with a hot man who thinks I'm just as hot as him. I want to drink wine and see if I can still flirt." He smirks at me. "If you give me anything, at least give me tonight."

TWENTY-TWO

CHRISTOPHER

ALL I CAN do is look at this woman in front of me. This strong, independent, classy woman. The nerves that were all in my stomach bringing her here have turned into bile, listening to her tell me her story. My hands clench into fists with each word that comes out. "So before this goes forward, you have to make a decision. Will you ever be okay knowing I was Benji's once?" I start to open my mouth, not sure what I'm going to say, but wanting to say at least something. "You don't have to decide now. For tonight, I want to sit down at a table with a hot man who thinks I'm just as hot as him. I want to drink wine and see if I can still flirt." All I can do is smirk at her. "If you give me anything, at least give me tonight."

"Are you done?" I finally ask when she reaches over to grab her glass of wine and bring it to her lips.

"Yes." She nods, smirking back at me. "For now, I think."

"Good." I tap the table with my finger. "Before I say

anything else, it needs to be said that you are way hotter than me tonight and every other day." She rolls her eyes at that. "With that said, I also have to tell you I had no idea what Benji was up to with the women." I shake my head. "Never, and I mean never, would I have been okay with that."

"I kind of figured that," she says softly. "Again, it wasn't your place to do anything about it. He did that. I mean, in the last couple of months, he didn't really try to hide it from me. Some nights, he didn't even come home until six o'clock in the morning."

I hold my hand up. "You are going to need to stop talking because, at this very minute, I'm wishing I could drag him back up and beat the ever-loving shit out of him." I swallow back the anger. "You said that I have to make a decision, and you're right." Her eyes just watch me, and all I want is to lean over and kiss her, except I'm not sure if I should. I'm not sure she wants me to. "But with that said, you also have to decide what you want in all this. You kept saying I had to make a decision, and you are wholeheartedly right, I do. You have a say in this also, so what do you want?" I move my hand on the table to put it on hers. "You don't have to decide now. For tonight, I want to sit down at a table with the woman who drives me crazy. With the woman who, with just one look, gets me so hot and bothered I don't even know what is going on around us." I wink at her. "For tonight, it's just you and me. Good food, with great fucking company." She smiles bigger. "Also, you're not taking off that jacket because I swear to God I've already been at half-mast since you opened the door, and it's about to go from fifty to a hundred." She puts her head back and giggles, making my cock immediately go to one hundred and fifty. "Well, it's at a hundred." I lean over and kiss her neck. "I like you wearing your hair like that."

"Yeah?" she asks as she moves her hand from under mine, to put it on top. "Why is that?"

"Easy access to this part." I move my hand from the table to touch the back of her ear, and she shivers under my touch. "Then it leads to this." I move my finger down her neck to underneath her jaw. "Then right about here, where I can feel how your heart beats for me."

"I know you said you were at half-mast before." She looks around, speaking softly, "I'd like to let you know, even if I wanted to, I can't take off my jacket because my nipples have been hard since the minute you touched my hand." She leans into me, and my body moves to her. "And I can tell you right now," she whispers in my ear, "I'm wet for you." She kisses behind my ear, and now it's my turn to shiver. "I guess you can say I'm at a hundred."

"I was a hundred the minute you laughed," I admit, and her eyes get hazy with lust.

She's about to say something when the phone rings from her purse. She reaches out to grab the handbag and unzip it. "It's my mother." She looks at me. "She has the kids."

"Answer it," I tell her, wondering if the girls are okay.

"Hey, is everything okay?" she says, and I can see the worry on her face, "Saturday morning, why?" she questions her mother, and then she laughs. "I was hoping she wouldn't remember. It's all good. Text me once you guys head out." She says goodbye and hangs up.

"Everything okay?"

She nods, putting her phone back in her purse. "Rain asked about hockey on Saturday. And then threw a fit that she was missing it." I smirk at her. "So they are coming home Friday."

"She loves being on skates," I state proudly.

"She always did, but didn't have anyone to—" She shakes her head. "Not tonight."

"Not tonight," I agree with her. "There is a lot we need to get into, so how much did you miss me this week?"

She picks up her glass of wine. "Not even a bit." She tries to hide her smile. "Maybe just like." She holds up her hand and uses her thumb and forefinger to pinch just a bit. "And then maybe the next day a little more." She opens her fingers. "But then I remembered why I was mad at you, so it went to zero." She closes her fingers, and I can't help but laugh at her. "But by the end of the night, it was always this much." She uses both hands to show me.

"Good." I chuckle. "Just so you know, I missed you too."

"Obviously." She takes a sip of her wine, trying to be serious but then just laughing silently. "I'm pretty fucking spectacular."

"That you fucking are." I don't know how it happened. I don't know when it happened, but Koda is under my skin, and I want her even more under my skin.

MEANT FOR HER

I SLIDE MY hand in hers after putting my jacket on. Her fingers slide into mine like she's always done this, like she was born with my hand in hers. My thumb rubs her hand while I walk side by side with her. The valet guy sees me walking outside, so he grabs my keys and rushes to get my car. I turn to her, standing right in front of her. I wrap my free arm around her waist and pull her to me. "I want to take you home with me," I declare as she slides her hand out of mine and puts both of them on my chest. "Literally nothing more I want in this world than to take you home with me. I'd take you to bed and wake up with you." She looks down. "But I'm not going to do that because I respect you too much. You deserve to be worshipped, but more importantly, you deserve to be shown how much you mean to me."

"Christopher," she says my name, and once again, it shoots straight through my heart and down to my dick.

"No, I'm not going to bend on this. When we go there, and we will get there, Dakota." She smirks at me. "It's going to be the last time it'll be a first for both of us."

"What do you mean?" Her fingers tap my chest.

"I can't see the future," I admit, "but if it's going to be anything like right now, right here at this moment, I know there will be no one else after you, which means there will be no one else for you."

Her eyes go big. "So that is something else you have to think about. It's not a game I want to play, but it's a game I'm going to fucking win because the result is something I can't imagine losing."

"Tonight is the best date I've ever been on," she confesses, looking down and then looking back up. "You know why?" I wrap both hands around her waist, pulling her flush to me. "I'll tell you why. Because I knew without a shadow of a doubt there was no one else you wanted to be sitting in front of you. Never, not once, did your eyes stray from mine to look around the room to see who was there or who was looking at you. You had eyes just for me, and I've never, ever had that." She smiles so big her eyes crinkle as she moves her hands from my chest to my neck. "I never knew how much I liked that until now. So thank you for that."

"Anytime, baby," I assure her, bending my head and kissing her lips softly. "I'm at one hundred and seven."

"I know." She laughs. "I can feel it."

"Great." I know I should be embarrassed, but I'm not. She fucking drives me wild, and she needs to know that.

"Also, you should know I want to have a make-out session in your car." She pulls away from me when my car stops right beside us. "Like a hot-and-heavy one."

"Are you trying to kill my dick?" I ask as the valet gets out of the car and rushes over to open her door, but I step in front of him, grabbing the handle. "I got her." I look over my shoulder, making sure I block all access to Dakota that I can. When she is in the car, I close the door, turning to look at the guy. "Thank you." I slide him a twenty-dollar bill before walking around the car and getting in.

I pull away from the restaurant, heading in the

direction of our houses. Pulling into the subdivision, and then, instead of driving toward her house, I drive toward mine. "Where are we going?"

"You said you wanted a hot-and-heavy make-out session in the car." I turn to her, worried she changed her mind. "I'm not going to have your neighbors talk about you making out in a car, so I'm going to go to my house. We will drive into the garage and make out with each other, and then I'll drive you home."

"What is wrong with you?" She shakes her head, and I twist my head to look at her. "You can't be that perfect."

"I mean, I'm not going to say I am because if you talk to my sisters, they can tell you exactly why I'm not perfect." I press the button to open the garage door. "I'm far from perfect." I put the car in park and shut it off before pressing the button to shut the door.

"I don't know about that. You are pretty fucking perfect to me," she states, taking off her seat belt and turning in her seat, her back toward the door. "All of you is pretty perfect."

I undo my seat belt and then reach over to grab her face in my hands. Her hands fly to my face at the same time our lips meet. Her tongue slides into my mouth, and I swear to God I see fucking stars kissing her. She kisses me back with everything she has. I let one hand leave her face while pressing the button to make my seat extend all the way back. The whole time our tongues are fighting a match, but in the end, we're both winners. When it's all the way back, I grab her and pull her over the middle console and into my lap. I expect her to sit on my lap, but instead, she turns to straddle me. Her back leans against the horn, making us both jump and then laugh hysterically. "I should have taken the truck. There is much more room in the truck."

"Nothing like getting a heart attack while making out." She leans forward, and her smile fades when she kisses me again. This time, it starts out slow, us both taking our time, but it's not long before it's hot and heavy all over again. Her hands roam up and down my chest while my hands roam up and down her back toward her ass.

"I should get you home," I tell her when she grinds down on me, making us both moan, "before I forget everything I said earlier and end up fucking you on the hood of the car." Her eyes literally close halfway when I say that. "Okay, so the second time I fuck you will be on the hood of the car." I kiss her one more time before she gets off me.

"Going to have to make a list," she mumbles once she buckles herself up and I turn on the car.

"What list is that?" I ask, pulling out and she shocks the fuck out of me when she answers.

"Places I want to have sex." My foot hits the brake, jerking us both forward.

"Excuse me?" I shake my head, not sure I heard her.

"I never thought about it before you said you were going to fuck me on your car." She points at the hood. "But now that I think about it, I kind of want to get fucked on your car and maybe other places."

"Dakota," I say her name through clenched teeth. I'm sure my jaw is twitching.

"What?" she says, looking over at me. "It's something that came to my mind."

I shake my head and pull out of the driveway and head over to her house. I get out of the car to walk to the door. She takes out the key and opens it but doesn't step inside. "Thank you for tonight, Christopher." She gets on her tippy-toes to kiss me on the lips before turning and stepping into the house.

I watch her smile at me as she closes the door, and when she almost has it shut is when I speak. "I want to see that list," I tell her, and her eyes fill with lust, "because I have my own as well." I wink at her before walking down the steps and then looking over my shoulder. "Night, baby."

TWENTY-THREE

Dakota

DR. MENDES: GOOD luck today.
Me: Thank you.

I put my phone down and take a deep breath before I pick it back up and search her name. My heart beats so fast I think it's going to come out of my chest. Then my throat feels like something is stuck in it, so I cough a couple of times.

The sound of the ringing fills my office as my legs move up and down nervously. When the ringing stops, her voice comes on. "Hey, Koda," she answers softly, "so nice to hear from you."

"Hey, Zoe," I say, smiling, "am I catching you at a bad time?"

"Never," she replies. "What's up?"

I take a deep breath in and exhale slowly. "I need your help."

"Anything." She doesn't even stop to think. "What can I do to help?"

I close my eyes when I say the words. "I'm thinking of selling my house."

"Oh my," she says softly.

"Actually, I've decided I want to sell my house." I laugh nervously. "And I want to buy a new one."

"That's a big step." I don't know why I was nervous to call her. Maybe it's because I finally made the decision last week. It was a strange one really. I sat down on the couch in Dr. Mendes's office, and I just blurted it out, "I think I want to sell my house." I didn't even know that it was on my mind until the words came out of my mouth.

"It is," I agree with her, "but with the three of us. This is a lot more room than we need. I don't use the basement really, so all that space is wasted. Plus, it's a lot of work to maintain such a big house on my own."

"What do you think you are looking for?" she asks, and I hear her shuffling papers around.

"I want to stay in the same neighborhood if I can, but chances are I won't be able to," I state sadly. "I want four bedrooms for sure. A kitchen with a great room right off it is really a must."

"It's almost what you have now, but way smaller." She chuckles.

"I don't need a seven-bedroom house." I laugh. "The playroom is nice, but it's not something they always use. As of right now anyway, when they get older and become teenagers, I'm sure their needs will change."

"Okay, why don't I work on this and see what I come up with, and then we can go from there. I don't think it'll be a problem to sell your house. It's in the top neighborhood with a great school district."

"That's good news."

"Let me see what I can pull up, and we can go from there." Her voice is cheerful. "We are going to get you that house."

"Thank you." I breathe a sigh of relief. "Oh, and, Zoe, if it isn't too much to ask if you could maybe not say anything to—"

"My lips are sealed, as always." She doesn't even make me skip a beat. I mean it's not like I'm not going to tell Christopher; it's just I don't want him to think it's because of him.

"Amazing. I'll look for your email."

"You should get one by tonight," she assures me before we disconnect.

I look down at the phone. "One down, one to go," I say before I pull up Christopher's name.

Me: Hey, can you call me when you get a chance?

I press send, not sure if he's in practice or not. So I fire up my computer, taking a sip of my coffee when the phone rings and I see it's him. But of course he doesn't call me, nope, he's a FaceTime guy.

"Hello there." I smile as soon as I answer it, his face filling the screen, and I can see he's in his gym.

"Hello to you," he replies and his smile does all types of things to me. "What's up, baby?"

It's been two weeks since our first official date. I want to say we've been on another one, but he's been on the road for a week and then add in the kids and, well, it hasn't been easy. That isn't to say we haven't had any make-out sessions. Yesterday morning after I dropped the kids off at school, I swung by his house to say hello, and I literally jumped his bones in his entranceway. Then there were a couple of hot-and-heavy parking lot make-out sessions when he met me at the grocery store, and another when I was in the Target parking lot. I even forgot why I was there.

"Are you busy for dinner?" I smile as I ask.

"Not for you. Why?"

"No reason. The girls want you to come over and Rain has something that she wants to talk to you about."

"I'm off today, so how about I swing by before you get them at school and we can go together?"

I tap my finger on the desk. "Stop thinking that."

"What do you mean?" I ask and he laughs.

"It's the look like you would do dirty things to me, and I'm thinking of doing the same dirty things to you. So now I'm riding my bike with a hard-on."

I can't help but giggle. "How did you know that was what I was thinking?"

"Your eyes get this glaze over them. It's going to be amazing to see what happens when I sink my cock into you."

"Oh my God," I moan, "pick me up at three."

"Are you going to make out with me before we get the kids?" he asks, and then I just stare at his smirk.

"Pick me up at two forty-five," I correct and he bursts out laughing. "Goodbye."

I hang up and start tackling my emails, and by the time I look back at the clock, it's almost two forty. I rush up, going to brush my teeth before sliding my boots on and seeing that he's just pulling into the driveway. I grab my jacket and rush out the door toward him. He's wearing a tracksuit with his hat backward. "Hey, baby," he greets when he sees me.

"Hi," I say breathlessly when I get near him, wrapping an arm around him and looking up to kiss him. His lips brush mine before he opens the truck door for me. I wait for him to get into the truck before I lean over and take his hat off, just to run my fingers through his hair, before placing it back on his head.

"My girl likes to play with my hair?"

"She does," I confirm, smiling at him. "Oh, wait. Am I your girl?"

"Smart-ass," He laughs out.

"Does that mean you're my boy?" I ask but then shake my head. "Sorry, my man."

"I'm whatever you want to call me." He pulls into his driveway and rips the seat belt off me.

"I'm going to miss this," I say once I get in his lap. "The whole make-out sessions in the car when we finally do the deed."

"Speaking of the deed," he says, "I'm getting tested."

"Um, okay," I reply softly.

"Are you on birth control?" I nod. "Good. So when we do the deed, I'm not wearing a condom."

"Um."

"Unless you aren't okay with that, then I will, but I don't want anything between us," he says, so I cover his fingers with mine.

"I haven't had sex in over a year, and I was already tested. I have an IUD, so we are safe on that part."

"Good. Now kiss me." He smiles as my lips find his and we make out for over twenty minutes and get to the girls with seconds to spare.

"Uncle Chrissy!" Luna yells, running out toward him. He swings her up and turns her, making her laugh even more.

"Hey, princess," he says, kissing her cheek, "how was school?"

"Okay," she replies when he puts her down. "Tommy called me a girly girl."

"And what did you do?" he asks her as we wait for Rain.

"I didn't say anything to him, I went like this." She outstretches her arms by her sides and bobs forward. "That scared him, so then I called him a girly girl."

"Good," Christopher says, and I just shake my head.

"Not good," I quickly interject, "that wasn't very nice."

"Well, he wasn't nice first, so it doesn't matter," Luna tells me.

"You can't argue with that," Christopher adds as Rain comes out and skips to us.

"Hi," he says to her, kissing the top of her head, "how was school?"

"Good," she says with a huge smile. "I have something for you." She looks up at him and he looks at me. "It's at home."

"Okay," he says, the four of us walking over to the

truck.

"What are we having for dinner?" Luna asks as soon as she sits down in the truck.

"I was thinking some tomato soup and grilled cheese." I look in the back at the girls, who give me their approval. "You good with that?"

"Yeah," he responds to me as he makes his way back to the house.

The kids step in before us and take off their things. We have a routine, so Christopher just pulls out the stool and sits there with us.

"I'm going to go and get your thing," Rain states, looking at him and going up to her bedroom.

"What's going on?" He looks at me, and I just shrug, but my eyes start to get dry and burn.

"Why don't you go in the family room and wait for her?" I motion with my chin, and he does as I say but looks over at me four times before he sits down.

Rain comes back downstairs with her hands behind her back as she goes to him. "I made you this," she says. Her voice is low, and everything in me just stops moving. You could hear a pin drop in the whole house. She sounds so nervous and scared as she sits next to him and hands him what is in her hands.

"What's this?" he asks, looking down at the card she made him last week at school.

"There is going to be a father-daughter dance at school," she starts softly, "and some people are bringing their uncles or grandfathers." Her voice trembles. "I want to bring you. It's on Friday at the school," she tells him what is written in the card.

He looks at her and then looks up at me, the tears already running down his face. "Of course," he says, putting his arm around her, "it would be my honor to take you." He kisses her head, and she gets up and runs to me.

"Mommy, Mommy, he said yes," she almost screams, and I wrap my arms around her, my own tears falling on top of her head.

"I heard." I look over and see Christopher still sitting on the couch, looking at the handmade invitation. He opens it and reads it again, before he closes it. "Get your homework started," I tell her and then make my way over to Christopher, who is still in the same spot. "Hey." I sit beside him and he looks at me, and I see his face is ravished. "Are you okay?"

He shakes his head. "No. This—" He holds up the paper. "There are no words for this." His voice breaks at the end of it. The emotions ripping through him are raw and real and beautiful. Seeing the way he loves my children makes me fall even more for this man.

I put my hand on his knee. "She thinks the world of you," I tell him softly. "She was scared to ask you." He just balks at it and then leans forward to put his elbows on his knees.

I search his eyes, wondering if this is too much for him, but knowing better. This man is the best man I've ever met. Hands down the most thoughtful, most caring, most perfect. The most fucking everything and, apparently, he's now mine. Or better yet, ours. "I would walk through fire for her."

Right here in the room where I found my husband dead from an overdose, where I thought my life would never be the same, I realize I've done the impossible. I've healed myself, and I've also fallen in love.

TWENTY-FOUR

CHRISTOPHER

AS SOON AS I park the truck in the driveway, I pull up Uncle Viktor's number. He of course answers within seconds. It's like the phone is stuck to his side. "What's up?" His voice is soft, and I hear the television in the background. I can just picture him sitting on the couch watching some game or another.

"Um," I start to say, but then all I do is close my eyes. "Something amazing happened tonight." My heart contracts in my chest. "I was asked to go to a father-daughter dance." My voice breaks at the end, and I feel exactly how I did when Rain came up to me in the family room a couple of hours ago.

"That's a big deal," he states softly. "Are you okay with that?"

"I'm more than okay with that." I put my head back on the seat. "I'm just—"

"Feeling guilty that you are taking his place," he says the words I don't want to say.

"In the past couple of weeks, I've found out a bit more about Benji that I did not like. I also came to the realization that if I knew the person he really was, there is no way I would be friends with a guy like that." Truth be told, if I had found out what he was actually like before he passed, there was no way in fuck I would have even spoken to the guy, let alone have him be one of my best friends.

"That's a lot to unpack."

"It is, but it's the truth. He wasn't the man I thought he was. But with that said." I swallow down. "I have serious feelings for Dakota, and I can wholeheartedly say I'm in love with Rain and Luna." I know I'm in love with Dakota, but I don't want him to know before she knows.

"Serious feelings sound like a big deal." His voice is judgment-free and exactly how I knew it would be, yet I was still scared to bring it up.

"We've been on one date with each other," I admit to him, "and I know that I want a million more."

"So you don't have serious feelings for her. You are in love with her." His question or statement goes unanswered. "Christopher, you have stepped in and given them support. There is nothing, and I mean nothing, wrong with that."

"I know." I exhale. "I know, it's just that. I'm angry that if he was still here, he wouldn't see the beauty in front of him."

"The only thing you can control is what is in front of you now. You can't lose your energy on things from the past. You have to focus on the here and now."

"She's so fucking special, Uncle Viktor. Like hands down the best person I've ever met. She's had all this shit happen to her, and instead of wallowing, she's a fucking warrior."

"She has no choice," he reminds me. "She's got two girls who have already lost a parent. She's not going to just fall and leave them alone."

"She would never." I jump to her defense quickly, making him laugh.

"You obviously did something good if she asked you to the father-daughter dance." He changes the subject from Dakota. "It's a great honor."

"It really is." I smile. "I'm going to take her to dinner before the dance, just her and me."

"You are a special man, Christopher. Proud of you."

"Thanks, Uncle Viktor, for everything."

"When are you going to stop thanking me?" He laughs. "It's getting on my last nerve."

Now I'm the one laughing. "I'll talk to you later," I say and hang up, getting out of the truck and walking into the house.

I'm about to call Dakota when my phone rings, and I see it's Stone.

"What's up?" I answer after one ring.

"What's up, my ass," Stone snaps. "You haven't called me in what... two weeks?"

"I was on the road last week." I quickly add, "And then I was busy."

"Busy?" He snorts. "I see your game has picked up and not gone down the tubes. We are all proud."

"Shut the fuck up; it was a couple of games." I walk up the stairs to my room, and for the first time ever, my house feels so empty.

"I think they almost scheduled an intervention. The Bat Signal was unleashed, and I think even the phone chain." I can't help but laugh at that one. One thing I can expect from my family is for them to be in your face when they think you need it. "So what's going on?"

I sit on my bed and think about telling him about Koda. "Not much."

"How is Koda," he asks, "and the girls?"

"Good." I don't say much more. "Rain asked me to a father-daughter dance tonight."

"Stop it."

"Yeah." I nod and put the invitation that she handmade down on my bedside table.

"That's amazing." His voice goes high. "Shit," he hisses, "you have to practice your mean face."

I can't help but laugh. "What the fuck are you talking about?"

"For all the boys who look at her," he snaps. "You have to make sure they know that if they fuck with her, they are going to get you."

"Oh my," I whisper.

"Make sure they know she's off-limits, and you aren't afraid to fight them." He stops talking for a minute before he continues, "And then you can trip him when he walks by you by accident."

"You know she's six, right?"

"Better to start now so they know," he advises softly.

"I have to go. Ryleigh is giving me the look that says if I don't stop talking, she's going to kick me, and not in places I like."

"Hopefully, when she kicks you, it makes your brain go back to normal." I hang up on him and then FaceTime Koda.

I lie in bed that night, wondering what it would be like if we all lived under the same roof. The night of the dance, I put on a black suit and light pink tie to match Rain's dress that Koda told me she was wearing.

I grab the corsage I had made of tiny roses with a light pink bow out of the fridge before taking off to pick her up. I arrive and walk up the steps, my hands shaking with nerves as I ring the doorbell.

I hear running from the other side of the door, and as I look down, I take a deep breath and wait for it to open. "Hi, Uncle Chrissy," Luna greets me, moving out of the way so I can come in. "Rain is coming," she says as I close the door behind me. "Momma and me are doing mani and pedis."

"Oh, fun," I reply and look at the stairs, seeing Koda coming down wearing jeans and a white T-shirt. She's wearing stuff that is casual, yet my cock wakes up.

"Hi." She smiles at me. "You look nice."

"Thank you." I walk to her and wrap an arm around her waist, bending to kiss her cheek. This time closer to her lips than before. "You smell nice."

"So do you." Her eyes brighten as she stays in my arms a bit longer than she should, but neither of us pays attention until we hear footsteps on the stairs. I look up to see Rain walking down wearing a white, long-sleeve shirt with a light pink skirt that ruffles and goes down to her ankles. Her hair is pinned back as she smiles at me.

"Don't you look beautiful," I praise, crouching down in front of her. "I got you this." I hold up the clear container.

Her eyes go big as her mouth hangs open. "For me?" she asks, and I nod, taking it out and putting it on her wrist. "Mommy, look." She holds her wrist backward to show her.

"Very pretty," Koda says with tears in her eyes, but they are happy tears because her eyes shine bright. "We have to take a picture." She pulls her cell phone out of her back pocket as we pose for pictures in the foyer. I pull Luna and Koda in for a selfie at the end, the four of us with huge smiles on our faces. "See you two later." She puts her hand on my chest and leans in to kiss my cheek and then down to kiss Rain's.

"Shall we?" I hold out my hand for Rain after she puts on her jacket and makes a fuss not to squish her flowers. I walk out holding her small hand in mine, opening the car door for her, helping her in, before I get behind the wheel.

I hold her hand even when we get to the restaurant, helping her take off her jacket. I sit in front of her and smile. Not sure how to start a conversation, but once the nerves wear off, it's just me and her.

"Do you think I'm going to be able to play hockey on a team next year?" she asks as we wait for our food.

"I don't see why not. Is that what you want?"

She nods. "I'm excited for the winter camp." She mentions the winter camp that takes place over Christmas break. She'll be on the ice every single day doing on-ice and off-ice training. "I'm going to skate every day."

"You might get sick of it," I tease, and she shakes her head adamantly, making me laugh.

We finish eating and head over to the school. The first thing we hear once I open the school's front doors is the music. Balloon arches are set up from the school's entrance to the gym. We stop at her locker for her to put away her jacket, and she makes sure she looks down and her flowers are all right.

She slips her hand in mine as we walk toward the gym, stepping in and seeing that half the lights are on, while the other half are off. Round tables are all around the outside of the floor, leaving a big open space for dancing or better yet for kids to chase each other, which is what a couple of them are doing. White and pink lanterns hang from the ceiling, which is why half the lights were off.

"Do you see your friends?" I lean down to ask. She nods her head and points at a group of girls in the corner twirling in their dresses. "You can go and say hello to them," I urge her. She nods at me and slowly slips her hand out of mine going toward them.

I put my hands in my jacket as I watch the girls all giggle together. I see Rain hold out her hand for all the other girls to see her corsage. "Did you upstage all the dads?" someone asks from behind me, and I turn to see Cole walking into the dance.

I laugh. "Not sure about upstaging."

"I knew I was forgetting something," he says, standing beside me. "I'm surprised to see you here. Thought for sure she would ask Eddie."

"He's in Florida," I reply, my eyes never leaving Rain, making sure she's in my sight the whole time.

She comes over to me when the DJ asks everyone to get on the dance floor. She puts her hand in mine as we walk over to the dance floor. I look down at her, the immense feeling of pride hitting me right in the chest.

She wraps her arm around my waist when a song comes on, and we dance side by side. She smiles up at me, and then the dance switches to a fast dance. I stand to the side with the other dads while the girls bop up and down.

Three hours later, we are walking out of the gym, and she's going on and on about her friends loving her flowers. When I open the car door for her, she looks up at me. "Thank you for being my date." She giggles when she says that. "It was the best."

"Thank you," I say, bending to hug her, my arms wrapping around her, pulling her to me. "It was the best night ever." I kiss the top of her head while she gets into the car.

By the time I pull in the driveway, she's passed out cold. I open the door and carefully unbuckle her seat belt. Picking her up in my arms, I rest her head on my shoulder, and the door opens before I have a chance to ring the bell.

"Hi," Koda says, standing there in her loungewear set, "is she out?"

"She is," I confirm softly as I walk up the steps toward her bedroom. It's been a couple of times when I've been over, and they've fallen asleep, so I carried them upstairs. Her night-light is on in her room, and when I put her down on her bed, she wakes up just a little.

"Watch my flowers," she mumbles as I slip her shoes off.

"Should we leave her in the dress?" I look over at Koda, who nods. I move Rain enough to get her cover over her, then slip her corsage off her wrist and put it on her bedside table.

I follow Koda out of the room, wishing I wasn't going home to my house. "How was tonight?" she asks as we walk down the stairs toward the front door.

"It was the third-best night of my life," I tell her honestly, standing in front of the door. She looks down blushing, hopefully thinking of the other two nights I was talking about. "She's the best."

"She is," she agrees with me. I take a step to her, wanting to kiss her with everything I have, but instead, I lean down and kiss her cheek. "Thank you for taking her."

"Lock up after me, yeah?" I say, walking out of the house with what feels like a boulder sitting on my chest.

I pull out my phone and text my father first.

Me: Tonight was hands down the proudest I've ever felt.

I send the text and attach it with a picture of the two of us that I took when we were at dinner.

I'm walking into the house when the phone rings. I

look down and see it's my dad, and he's FaceTiming me.

"Hey," I say once we connect, and I look and see it's my mother and my father. My mother looks like she's blinking away tears.

"Hey," she replies softly, looking at me, "that picture is going in a frame in the house."

"I think so also." I kick off my shoes in the mudroom, and the smile on my face is plastered there. "Tonight was so much fun."

"Tell me all about it," my mother urges softly. "I want to know all about it." I tell her the little things that made it so good. The having dinner with just her, her holding her hand in mine, and being proud I was by her side. Her just being fucking her and being the best kid I've ever met.

"Well, now you know," my father says when I finally stop talking.

"Now I know what?"

"What it means to love someone so unconditionally that you would brave the storm just to keep them okay. You would do things you wouldn't do for anyone else but them." His smile mimics mine. "Now you know how I felt when I met Caroline." He looks at my mom. "Best thing I ever did in my life." She blinks her eyes and leans forward to kiss his lips.

"Dad," I say, "I'll never try to take Benji's place."

"Totally different scenarios," he counters. "They are old enough to keep the memories of Benji with them, but at the same time create ones with you that are totally different."

"I'll do whatever they want me to do, whenever they want me to do it."

My parents share a look and then turn to smile at me. "We can't wait to see them again. Maybe we could come down soon and visit."

"That would be great. Let me talk to Koda."

"Okay, honey," my mother says, "love you."

"I love you too," I say, smiling at her. "You too, big guy."

My father laughs. "Proud of you," he praises, and for the first time, I understand him. I give him a chin up and hang up the phone, and then quickly text Koda.

Me: I miss you.

She replies right away.

Koda: You just left.

Me: I know, but I thought you should know.

Koda: Consider me in the know. Also.

I look down at the screen, wondering if she hit send too early.

Koda: I miss you also. Thanks for taking her to the dance.

Me: It's me who should be thanking her.

Koda: You can stop being perfect now.

Me: Trust me, the things I'd like to do to you now are not making me perfect.

Koda: Stop turning me on right before I go to bed.

I'm about to answer her when my phone rings, and when I put it to my ear, I can only laugh when I answer it.

I'M WALKING INTO the house three days later after practice when I get a text from Dakota.

Koda: Do you think you could meet me quickly?
Me: Where?
Koda: 375 Peterbourgh.
Me: When?
Koda: Now, if you're free.
Me: Be right there.

I get into the car and put the address in the GPS, seeing it's about fifteen minutes away.

Me: Be there in fifteen.
Koda: I'll be waiting.

I start the drive there, wondering what is going on. I pull up to the house thirteen minutes later and see Koda's car parked in the driveway of a two-story house.

I park on the street at the curb, looking up at the house that has four massive windows in the front, two on each side. On the right side, you see the living room, and on the left, you see the staircase going up to the second floor. I stride up the paved walkway to the brown front door, stepping up the two steps.

The door opens right away, and Koda stands there wearing a pair of black pants with a thick white knitted turtleneck sweater. "Hi." She smiles big at me, and I step in beside her, bending to kiss her lips.

"Hi," I return softly, looking over her head, seeing a living room with two white chairs and a gray armoire stacked with books.

"Thanks for coming," she says, slipping her hand in mine.

"Of course," I reply as she walks with me trailing her, holding her hand down the small hallway toward the kitchen and family room.

"Look at the kitchen." She runs her hand over the white granite island with three stools. "Isn't it perfect?" She smiles so big, and I look around at the staged living room.

"You have to see upstairs." She pulls me back toward the front door, walking up the stairs to the second floor. "There are four bedrooms." I look at the doors once we get upstairs.

"What is all this?" I ask as she walks into the master bedroom. I see the king-sized bed in the middle of the room against the wall, a bench in front of the bed with pillows on it. She slips her hand out of mine, taking a step deeper into the room, going to the window that faces the side of the house. "Where are we?"

She puts her hands to her mouth and then squeals, "This is my new house." Whatever I thought she was going to say, it's definitely not what she actually said.

"What?" I gasp, my mouth open as I look around.

"I put an offer in on the house two days ago." She jumps up, just like Rain did in the gym. "And they accepted it right away. It's mine after they come and take all their staged shit away."

"You bought a house?" I look around the room.

"I did," she confirms and guilt washes over me.

"But what about—"

"It's too big," she explains, "but this." She turns in the room. "This is so us. I can picture making breakfast with the girls in the kitchen. I can picture putting Christmas greens around the stairs and seeing the lights twinkling outside."

"But what about the other house?" I ask, and she rolls her lips.

"We put it on the market last week, and I've gotten two offers, and now it's a bidding war. Which is shocking since I had to disclose that someone died in the house." She snort-laughs at the last part, shocking me even more.

"Koda," I say her name. "What about the girls?"

"The girls are okay with it. We sat down yesterday, and I told them that the house was a bit too big for just the three of us. Christopher, we barely use half the house."

I take steps to her. "You really are serious about moving?"

"I really am serious about moving. It'll suck to pack all the things up, but I think that—" I put my arms around her waist. "I know it's the right move for us." She puts her hands on my chest. "I didn't think I would find it so fast, but the minute your aunt sent me the link and I clicked on the photos, I knew it was mine." She beams with happiness. "It's mine."

"It's the perfect house," I say, bending my head and kissing her lips, thinking it's going to be just a soft kiss. But she slides her hands up my chest, around my neck, and into the back of my hair as her tongue enters my mouth. The kiss goes from zero to a hundred in a matter of seconds. Her hands move from my head to my back, roaming down to my ass. "Dakota."

I release her hips just to say her name, but her hands

are at my waist. My hands have a mind of their own, and they are cupping her ass and bringing her toward me, my cock hard on her stomach. I swallow her moan, but her hands are pulling up my T-shirt as she moves her fingers into the waistband of my sweatpants. "Christopher," she says my name, and it shoots straight down to my balls. Her fingertips make my whole body shiver. "That night." She gets on her tippy-toes, kissing the underside of my jaw. "When you touched me." I swallow, but it's getting harder and harder to breathe or focus for that matter. "I regretted one thing," she admits, nipping the bottom of my jaw. "Do you want to know what?"

"Baby," I hiss, "I can't even breathe right now with your hands on me."

"Do you know what that does to me?" Her fingertips go deeper into the elastic of my pants. "How sexy it makes me feel?" I close my eyes when she kisses my neck and then licks it. "For the past month, all I've thought about was what I would have done to you." I feel her fingers at the elastic of my boxers. My stomach contracts from her touch. "How I would have taken you in my mouth." She nips under my chin, and I swear to God I'm shaking, and when her fingers finally touch my cock, I think I'm going to come from one touch. "Hmm," she says, rubbing the precum around the head of my cock. "I want to taste you."

"It's yours." The minute I say those two words, she drops to her knees in front of me. "Fuck," I growl when she pulls the pants down under my hips, my cock bouncing free.

"Is this mine?" She looks up at me with those innocent green eyes, but you can see the sparkle at the same time. She grips the base of my cock in her hand. "This is mine, right?"

"All of me is yours," I tell her, and she leans in, licking the top of my cock like she's licking an ice cream cone.

My knees about buckle under me with just one touch. "You like that?" she asks, but I'm too focused on what she is doing with her mouth to answer her. "What about this?" She twirls her tongue around my cock and then moans. "Or this?" She bends her head to lick my cock from my balls all the way to the tip before sucking the head into her mouth softly. "Oh, yeah, you like that," she says as my cock jerks in her hands.

"You continue like that, and you'll see how much I like it when I come all over your face." I'm joking, but her eyes darken. "Fuck, you want me to come on your face?"

"I want you to come when you want to come, where you want to come," she declares, taking a bit more of my cock into her mouth. "On my face." She moves down a touch more. "On my tits." She grips the base of my cock and works her hand at the same time as her mouth. "On my stomach." I swear I close my eyes. "In my pussy." My head goes back as I think about fucking her, my hips thrusting forward in her hand. "On my back."

"Baby," I moan, putting my hand on top of her head, "you have no idea what you're asking me."

"I know exactly what I'm asking you." She licks the side of my cock before taking more of it into her mouth.

My hand grips her hair, pulling her head back to see my cock sliding out of her mouth before I feed it to her.

"You are asking me to come on your body?" I thrust my cock into her mouth, not giving her any chance to answer me. "It makes me wild when I think of my cum on you, but especially when I think of it inside you." She grips my cock even harder as she jerks me and swallows me at the same time. "With my cock in your mouth, it's the sexiest thing I've ever seen."

She lets go of my cock long enough to say, "For now," before she swallows me back in her mouth.

"I wanted to do this in a better way." Her hot mouth on me makes me forget all of this. "Be romantic, but fuck me, I have no control when it comes to you."

"Christopher." She looks at me, sucking in my head lightly. "I need you to do something for me."

"You can ask me to do anything."

"Lose control with me." The minute she says that, everything in me snaps. I pick her up from under her armpits, and she groans.

"I wasn't done with that," she whines, but my hands are ripping her shirt over her head. Leaving her in her bra as I lean down and take a nipple in my mouth through her lace. "Okay, I guess we can go back to that, after." I chuckle as I move over to her other nipple and suck it, then bite down on it.

"One of these days," I vow when she moans, "I'm going to make you come just by sucking your tits." I move my head down her stomach to the waist of her jeans. "But for today, I want you coming on my tongue and then my cock," I say, unsnapping her bra and tossing it to the side with her shirt. My hand comes up to cup her tits, rolling her nipples between my fingers.

"Christopher." Her knees close together as I move my hand to undo her button and pull down her zipper.

"You have one decision." I stop moving my head up, her eyes have glazed over. "Are we fucking on the bed or the floor?" My hands fall from her tits.

"Not on the bed." She shakes her head. "It's a staged bed." She tries to cover herself, but my hand comes out to knock hers out of the way so I can see her perfect tits, peaked and pebbled for me.

"And?" My hands come back up to play with her nipples. I roll them at the same time, and she has trouble speaking.

"And there might have been other people fucking on the cover." She tries to look at me, but her eyes close just a touch.

"The floor it is," I decide, moving and pulling her pants down her legs. "Lift your leg," I tell her, and she lifts one leg and then the other, leaving her naked in front of me.

"Fuck." My hand comes out to slide through her folds. "Wet for me." All she does is nod her head as I slide a finger into her, her hand gripping my wrist.

"It's not fair I'm naked, and you're not." Her head falls back and rolls to the side as I slide my finger out and slip another one in.

"You want me naked?" I ask, and she nods.

"I want you naked and on top of me," she confirms

MEANT FOR HER

breathlessly. "I want to wrap my whole body around you while you fuck me."

I slide my fingers out of her, bringing them to my mouth and licking them clean. I'm about to reach for my shirt when she slaps my hand away. "You can't have all the fun." She reaches for my shirt and roughly tugs it off me.

She grips my cock, forgetting about my pants. "That's not my pants."

"I know, but it's so pretty." She steps into me.

"Baby," I say, and she looks up at me, "no guy wants his dick to be called pretty."

She laughs. "Okay, fine, it's so big."

I nod. "That's a good one."

"A monster." I roll my eyes.

"Can we get to the fucking, please?"

She smirks at me. "Please." She moves my pants down my legs, where I kick off my shoes and then slip my socks and pants off at the same time.

"Did you make a list?" I ask, wrapping my arm around her waist and feeling her hot body against mine.

"Yeah." Her arms go around my neck.

"And what's number one? Was bedroom floor one of them?"

"No," she answers, "but it's shot straight up to the top of the list as of now."

"Baby, I don't know how this is going to go," I admit, "having you naked in front of me. I haven't had my cock this hard in my whole life. I don't know how long it's going to even last." She smiles big. "That's the spell you've cast on me."

I bend to my knees, taking her with me. "I promise the next time will be a million times better." Her hands go from my neck to my face. "And longer."

"Christopher," she says my name, and it runs straight to my cock.

"My name on your lips is like heaven to me." I bend my head to kiss her. The kiss is wet and hard. "I want to take my time with you."

She puts her finger on my lips. "Christopher, show me," she urges softly. "Show me what I do to you."

My mouth attacks hers as my arm wraps around her waist, and I pick her up and bend her to her back. Her legs open for me as I place her on her back, and she grips my cock, pulling me into her. "Now," she says when I let go of her lips, "please." I kneel in the middle of her legs.

"Okay, baby." I watch her rub my cock up and down her slit. "Watch us," I tell her, and she looks into my eyes before looking down between us. "Watch me fuck you." I move her hand out of the way, gripping my cock and sliding the head into her and stopping because her tightness and wetness are better than I ever imagined.

"More?" she asks, reaching forward to my hips and trying to pull me into her.

"Baby," I grind between clenched teeth, "I need to go slow."

"Christopher, you said you would give me whatever I want," she reminds me, "and I want it all. I want it now, and I want it hard. I want you to bury yourself inside me, and I want it now." She hitches her hips higher, trying to get me more into her.

"Fuck," I swear, losing control.

"I want you, Christopher." The way she says my name, everything I had holding me back snaps. "Please." Instead of inching into her, I slam into her, shocking her as she hisses out, "Yes."

"Look at how you look with my cock stuffed in your pussy," I tell her, pulling out to the tip and then slamming in again, the sound filling the room. She arches her back, holding on to my arms that are beside her. "Fuck, you're tight."

"Well, that's because your cock is a monster," She stops talking when I slam into her. "Yes, right there." I watch her mouth open as her pussy gets tighter and tighter.

"You are squeezing me so tight," I tell her, my balls slapping her ass. "If I was taking my time," I say between thrusts, "I'd pull out and eat your pussy." Her fingernails score into the skin on my arms. "Fuck you with my tongue." Her pussy squeezes me tighter. "Right before you come, slide my cock back into you." It's all I need to say. Her back arches, her head goes back as her hips rise up to meet mine. "That's it, baby," I encourage her. "Come all over my cock." She spasms five times before I finally let go myself and plant myself to the root and explode into her.

TWENTY-FIVE

Dakota

HE PLANTS HIMSELF to the root as my limbs wrap around him, needing him even closer to me even though he's literally inside me. His arms let go as he lies on top of me, burying his face in my neck. "Baby," he murmurs, kissing me softly, "I don't think I've ever come that hard in my life." He turns to the side, bringing him up to me. "Jesus," he pants out, "I'm not even out of you, and I want to be back in you."

"If it makes you feel any better." I kiss the top of his head. "I want you back in there." I wait a couple of minutes before moving away from him. "I'm going to go clean up."

"No." He shakes his head. "I'm going to fuck you again in a couple of minutes." I try not to smile but fail at it. "I just need a second."

I lie beside him, putting my hands on his chest, and then putting my chin on it. "Will you come and get the girls with me?" His hand is rubbing my naked shoulder.

"We can bring them around to see the house."

"Whatever you want." We are in the middle of the bedroom on the floor, our clothes scattered around us, and I don't have a care in the world. Our legs are intertwined as my front is pressed to his side. I've never been fucking happier in my life, lying in the brand-new house I bought for me with the man who I'm in love with. Who I drove crazy enough that he fucked me on my new bedroom floor. It doesn't get better than this, but what he says next might be.

"I have a break in January," he says softly. "Do you think you can get away for a couple of days?"

I put my hand on his chest and rest my chin on it. "I will call my parents as soon as we get in the car," I tell him, and he pulls me up to lie on his chest. "Where are we going to go?"

"Wherever we go, you'll be naked the whole time," he teases, making me laugh, "and we are going to fuck on every single piece of surface in the place."

I roll my lips. "That sounds like a busy couple of days."

"Oh, it's going to be." He kisses me, and his kisses make me weak. I open my legs to straddle him, finding his cock ready for me. "How much time we got?" he asks.

"Enough time for me to come one more time," I tell him, lifting myself up and reaching between us to grab his cock before I slide down on him. His hands grip my hips until his balls hit my ass. "Maybe twice if we hurry," I add, lifting up again and sliding down. His cock is thicker than my vibrator. "Hmm," I moan when his hands cup my tits, and he rolls my nipples.

"God, your pussy is like a grip on my cock," he declares before sucking my nipple into his mouth and holding my hips down on him. "I want to sit up," he says, wrapping an arm around my waist and sitting up with his back against the bed. "Fuck, I went deeper in you, and now I don't want you to move."

"Too bad." I place my feet beside his hips and move up slowly, feeling every single vein in his cock. "It's so good." I move up and down on him, wanting to get him deeper and deeper in me. His hands grip my hips so tight I hope they leave his mark on me.

"What were you thinking right then?" he asks as he moves me up and down on his cock. "Whatever you were thinking, your pussy clenched."

"I was thinking how I hoped you left a mark on me." I put my hand on his shoulder.

"You want my mark on you?" He can barely talk, his jaw is clenched, and I nod. He leans down and sucks my nipple deep into his mouth before letting it go and then sucking right next to it, leaving a red mark on my skin. "And this one also." He goes over to my other tit, doing the same thing. "God, you're so wet it's dripping down." I move as fast as I can, and he sucks his thumb into his mouth before reaching between us. "Time to make you come again," he announces right before his thumb rubs my clit, making me hiss. "She likes this."

"I've never—" I start, getting distracted while he plays with my clit. "I've never—" His cock rubs my G-spot, and his fingers play with my clit. I have no control over what is happening with my body. I am a fiddle, and his cock is the bow. I lean back, arching. "Fuck," I pant out, "fuck." When his cock hits the right area, I moan, "I'm—"

"Give it to me," he demands, rubbing my clit back and forth. I've never in my life had an orgasm build like this.

As he plays with my clit and my G-spot, I close my eyes. "I don't know," I try to say, but it fades out as I come all over him. His hands guiding me up and down his cock, I lean forward, putting my mouth on his. "Christopher," I say as he slides his tongue into my mouth, his hand moving me even faster. I breathe in once, and I let go of his lips. "It's happening again."

"I want you with me," he states, and I can't even say the words, but I would follow him anywhere. He groans out my name, his hands moving me like I'm a rag doll as I come again right after. He slowly stops moving me when my ass is on his thighs, his cock still in me, and my head is lying on his shoulder. Our chests stick to each other as his hand slip from my tits to wrap around me.

"I don't know what you did to me," I say, trying to get my breathing under control, "but I'd like to do that again."

"Anytime." He squeezes his arms harder around me before kissing the top of my head. "We have to get the girls." I nod but I don't move for a couple of seconds before finally getting off him.

"Thank you." I look at him as he gets to standing. I

finally take in his whole body, which is like a walking Calvin Klein underwear ad. His abs are on fucking point, his thighs thick with muscle, his cock like a work of fucking art. Nice, long, and thick, so thick I almost gagged when he thrust into me when I was sucking his dick.

"You keep looking at me like that, and I'm going to have to bend you over and fuck you again."

"You can't say things like that." I practically stomp my foot. "Now I want to be late."

He slaps my ass, laughing. "Put that on the top of your list."

"No," I retort, walking toward the master bathroom, "because I want to be on my hands and knees next time with you pulling my hair."

He stops moving next to me. "I'm going to go in the other bathroom." He points over his shoulder. "Because if you touch me right now, I'm going to forget we have to get the girls, and they'll be sitting there waiting for us, and everyone is going to know we are late because I was fucking you."

"How would they know?" I ask, confused. "We could be in traffic."

"They would know because I'm going to fuck you so hard that you'll have trouble walking." How can just words make me wet? "I can see from your eyes you want that just as bad as me."

"Yes," I whisper.

"Go get cleaned up, Dakota." He motions with his chin, and all I can do is nod at him and head to the bathroom. Only when I'm in the bathroom do I see the two marks he left on my breasts and another of his teeth on my shoulder, and I can't remember when he did that one.

He comes in a minute later. "When did you do this?" I ask, pointing at his teeth marks.

"When you came twice in a row." I nod as I wet a facecloth to clean myself off. "Did I hurt you?"

I look over at him. "You could never hurt me," I reassure him softly, and he bends down to kiss me.

"Do I smell of sex?" I ask, leaning into him when we get to the school parking lot.

"No," he says, "but you smell like me."

"So like sex." I laugh, pulling open the door and getting out.

The girls run out to us, and it's so simple having him here with me these days. We drive to the house, and the kids are just as shocked as Christopher was, but then they choose their rooms.

It takes one week to get the whole house packed up, thanks to Zoe and her magic of knowing people. A group of four people have come in every single day, and we've gone from room to room. The good news is that once the boxes were packed up, they took them over to the new house and unpacked them. It was a godsend. The only room I didn't do anything with was the basement. I made them do all of the packing and rented a storage unit. Even though I didn't want anything to do with the things there, I know my girls will want it when they get old enough. If they don't, then I can give it to Eddie.

He was more than surprised when I told him we were moving, and a little bit angry and pissed that I did it without talking to him. The conversation ended at a stalemate. I had to respect he was mourning his son, and he had to respect I was moving on.

Today is the big day. The day has finally arrived, and I open the door, expecting it to be the movers. It was the movers, but it was also most of the team, led by Christopher. "We are here to pack up things, and you can go to the house and wait for us to get there."

"What?" I look from him to Cole. "But—"

"The only thing that needs to be done is the big furniture, so you can't help anyway," Cole says. "So go over to the house and wait for us there."

"Are you sure?" The team nods their heads at me.

I'm waiting at the house for about two hours when I see the truck pull in. Opening the door for them, I see they filled the truck to the brim. Christopher gets out of his truck and comes to meet me. "Did you guys do everything in one shot?"

"We did," he confirms, stepping in on the plastic floor covering. "It was like playing *Tetris* all over again." His forehead is all sweaty.

He puts his arm around my waist and pulls me in for a kiss. "Hi, baby," he says softly, bending to kiss me, pulling away from me when he hears voices coming closer to the door.

"The couch is first," Cole states. "We tried to put the bedroom first, but it just didn't work out."

"That's fine," I say, walking ahead of them. In the two hours I've been here, I have already placed the pictures up on the walls. The new carpets I bought are out, waiting for the couch. It takes over five hours for everything to be where I want it to be. Christopher is the only one left, the rest of the guys headed out once all the heavy furniture was brought in. Brittany is going to be bringing the girls over in a bit.

"So how does it look?" I ask when he puts out the table lamp at the front door.

"It looks like your home," he says, making me smile.

"It does, doesn't it?" I cross my arms over my chest, basking in the feeling of peace.

He walks over to me and puts his hands on my hips. "Welcome home, Dakota," he declares right before he kisses me, in my brand-new home.

TWENTY-SIX

CHRISTOPHER

"ARE WE GOING to take my car or yours?" I ask Dakota when I step into my garage and look at my pickup truck and my car.

"We can take mine," she says. "Are you sure about this?" The nervousness in her voice is apparent.

"I'm more than sure about this." I walk over to the pickup truck and start it. "It's family skate day, and I want you and the girls there with me." Today is the family skate day, and we've decided she's going to come with me as my plus-one. Not as Koda and the kids, but as Christopher's. She's been nervous for the past couple of days since we decided to actually do it. Sort of let people know we are together but not flaunt it in their faces.

"I know," she starts softly, "it's just that—"

"Baby," I reply softly, "it's going to be fine."

"Yeah, you keep saying that." She laughs.

"You going to be by my side?" I ask.

"Absolutely."

"You going to let me stay after the kids go to bed so we can make out on your couch?"

"Ummm, duh." Her answer makes me laugh.

"Then we will be fine." I hear her inhale. "Baby, it's going to be fine. It's you and me."

"Yeah," she says, not sounding convincing.

"I'll be there soon." I disconnect before I tell her I love her on the fucking phone. It's been over a week since she's moved into her place. Over a week since I've fucked her on her bedroom floor. On her couch. In the bathroom downstairs, in her mudroom before I left for the night. Basically, we've had sex everywhere but an actual bed. I've also been at her house for dinner every night if I'm not at work.

I pull up to her house, parking beside her SUV and making my way over to the front door. She opens it right away, and I can't help but plaster a smile on my face. It's infectious when I'm around her. "Hey, baby." I look at her from top to bottom and see she's wearing a pair of tights that look like they are leather with a white shirt with a team hoodie on.

I wrap my arm around her waist and pull her to me. "I missed you." I kiss her lips softly and then hear the sound of the girls coming toward us. I loosen my arm around her waist but still keep her to me when the girls come in. We've started to show a little bit more affection in front of them. I always kiss her on the cheek when I arrive and they are there, and I hug her more so it's not going to be a shocker when we announce that we are together. When that will be, I have no idea. I'm not pushing it onto them. If they figure it out before we tell them, that would be great.

"I have something to tell you," Koda says quickly but doesn't get a chance to finish talking before the girls come into the room.

"Hey, you two," I say to them, seeing them wearing almost the same tights as Koda, but they are wearing their jerseys.

"Uncle Chrissy," Luna chirps, jumping at me, making me drop away from her mom and catch her. "I'm wearing your jersey," she announces to me, trying to pull the back to the front.

"What?" I ask, then look over at Rain, then to Koda.

"The girls wanted to wear your jersey for the family skate," Koda explains quickly as I stand here tongue-tied, not really sure what to say.

"Look at mine," Rain says, turning around, "it says Stone."

"I see that." My throat closes from the lump that is growing bigger and bigger. "Um." I kiss Luna on the cheek, putting her down and then squatting in front of them. "That's a really big honor," I say, clearing my throat, "it's very special." I look up at Koda, who just smiles at me. "Are we ready to go?"

"I'm ready," they both say, turning to grab their jackets.

"Are you sure you're okay?" Koda asks from beside me, slipping her hand into mine.

"No." I shake my head and look down before my voice cracks. "That was—" I try to clear the frog in my throat. "It's—"

"Yeah, it is." She puts one of her hands on my chest. "It's all of that."

"I'm going to go load the kids," I tell her, leaning forward and kissing her cheek, but also the corner of her lips.

"I'll be right out," she says, turning to grab her leather jacket.

"You look good," I tell her, winking at her and then smirking. "I see the tights will be a challenge."

Her cheeks turn a bright pink. "I've never known you to back down from a challenge."

I put my head back and bark out laughing. "Challenge accepted." I wink at her again before I walk out with the girls toward her SUV. Opening the back door for them, I wait for Koda to come. I walk around the truck with her opening the passenger door for her to get in.

I get behind the wheel, something I've been doing for the past couple of weeks when we've gone out or to hockey practice or to pick up the girls. I drive them.

I make my way over to the arena with the girls chatting about their day and what they did. I pull into my spot, turning the car off and getting out. I open the back door on my side and Koda opens the back door at her side. The girls walk over to the trunk, waiting for me to hand them their backpacks with the skates we packed and their helmets and gloves.

I close the trunk and see the girls waiting for me and look over at Koda. "You ready?" I ask, and she takes a deep breath as she slips her hand in mine.

Our fingers link together. "Now, I'm ready," she says, rubbing her thumb over my thumb. "Shall we?"

"I want to hold Christopher's hand," Rain states, walking to my side while Luna looks at her mom and runs over to hold her hand.

"Here we go." I look at her as we walk toward the silver door. I release Rain's hand for a second so I can open the door, but then she grabs it again as we walk in.

We walk down the hall, the four of us attached in one way or another. When we get to the locker room, the girls release our hands to run in and chat with a couple of the kids. "Hey, guys," I say to the room, Koda's hand squeezing mine tightly for a second. The room goes almost silent and you can literally hear a pin drop. I'm ready to throat punch anyone who says anything mean toward Koda.

I see a couple of the guys look over at us with a smile and then look down at our hands connected, their mouths opening and their eyes looking like they are about to bulge out of their sockets. "Hey," a couple of the rookies respond, trying not to be too awkward.

"Uncle Chrissy!" Luna yells my name as she sits on the bench where I sit, taking her skates out of the bag.

I give Koda a squeeze of the hand before I let her go and walk over to the girls. Rain has her skates already on, waiting for me to tie them. I feel Koda behind me as she waits for the girls to get laced up. The chatter in the room is now back to normal as Rain stands up first and then Luna. "We are going to head out to the ice," Koda says, "see you out there."

I nod at her as she walks out with the girls, her head high, and I couldn't be more proud of her. It took a lot to come back to this arena, and she did it time and time again. But then it took even more courage to come back while holding my hand. She did it, and she fucking killed it.

"Holy shit," Cole says from beside me, "you and Koda."

"Yeah, me and Koda." I sit down, kicking off my sneakers and grabbing one skate, waiting for whatever will come. Knowing it'll for sure be a shock for all of them, but knowing that I'm not going to sit here and take shit and criticism from them. I'll go down fighting for her today and every single day after.

"It's cool." I look up to see Andreas sitting at his spot, not even bothering to get ready. "It's beautiful." I laugh at the way he says it, and I'm not the only one.

"When did this happen?" Cole asks from beside me.

"Not too long ago." I don't give him any details because even if we said we would come out, we really didn't discuss what we would say.

He shakes his head as I lean forward to tie my skate. "You and Koda?" He laughs as he says it.

"Me and Koda," I repeat, looking over at him, the smile now filling his face.

"Happy for you." I sit up, my eyebrows pinching together.

"Well, you weren't going to go there unless you were a hundred percent sure of it." He gets up on his skates. "So I'm happy you found her." He looks around. "And

I'm sure as fuck happy she found you."

"Thanks," I mumble, trying not to freak out at his words. I put my other skate on, standing up and heading out of the room. My head spins from his words.

I see Koda by the benches talking with Brittany as she looks over at me. "Hey." She smiles at me.

"Your girl is out there skating around all of the boys," Brittany observes, and I smirk, looking over and finding Rain right away. She's skating around a couple of the older guys, and she smirks at them.

"Those extra lessons are paying off," Koda declares, folding her arms over her chest. "Totally worth the extra five hours a week we are in the arena."

"I told you," I say, knowing she's sarcastic, winking at her. Brittany's eyeballs almost pop out of her sockets. "Next year, you'll be on skates." I point at her, and she just shakes her head.

"You wish." I skate backward away from her.

"I love a challenge." I smirk at her as she rolls her eyes at me, making me laugh. I skate over to Rain, who is skating like a boss, going to Luna who is getting better and better as the weeks progress. Not as good as Rain, but better.

I see one of the boys telling Rain that she's not that good of a skater, and she looks at him and says, "I'll race you."

I want to butt in and tell the kid he's being a dick, but I just stand here now watching it play out. The kid is a good head taller than she is. One of the rookies, Reed, skates over to them, and he asks them what's going on.

Cole skates beside me. "What's going on?"

"Kid says he can skate faster than Rain," I explain as Reed tells them the rules. I watch him point from one blue line to the other.

They line up behind the blue line, and I stand here with my arms over my chest watching, waiting to see if maybe perhaps I have to go in and trip this kid by "accident."

I see Rain smirk over at him as he says something, and she just shrugs. "Okay, one, two, three. Go," Reed announces, and the two of them take off. The kid makes the mistake of looking over at Rain, who ignores him and just focuses on getting to the line before him. She takes him with a couple of seconds to spare, her hands going up in the air.

"Yes," I hiss, holding my hand in a fist and skating over to her. I hold up my hand for her to give me a high five.

"That's my girl," I praise her and then sneer at the kid. "Punk," I mumble under my breath. "Go get something to drink." I motion with my head toward the bench.

The photographer is on the ice taking pictures, so I skate over to the bench and hold out my hand for Koda, who just stares at it. "I want to get a picture," I tell her, and she comes over, putting her hand in mine as she walks onto the ice. Her hand is in mine as we gather the girls, who stand in front of us. I pull her to my side, wrapping my arm around her waist, her front is stuck to my side so I can put one hand on Luna's shoulder, who stands in front of Koda, and put an arm on Rain's shoulder. I literally have them all in my arms, and I couldn't be happier.

"You okay?" Koda whispers.

"Yeah, baby," I confirm. *This is it,* I think to myself. This is what I've been looking for. This is what all of my cousins have, and it's here right now in my hands. The only thing I can think of is how do I make them know that for the rest of my life, I'm going to do whatever I can do in my power to make them happy. "I'm more than okay."

TWENTY-SEVEN

Dakota

"ARE YOU GOING to tell me where we're going?" I ask Christopher when I grab my bag from the back of his truck and start walking toward the private plane sitting on the tarmac.

"I gave you hints," he reminds me from behind, and I make the mistake of looking over my shoulder to see him smirking at me, which literally now just makes me wet every single time he does it.

I'm lucky I don't trip on my feet as we walk toward the plane. His hand is in mine. "What hints did you give me? I asked what I should pack."

"And I said nothing because you'll be naked all weekend," he repeats what he's been telling me for the last week, "yet you packed a whole bag."

"I wasn't going to come with no clothes at all," I gasp as I walk up the steps to the plane.

"Good morning," the flight attendant says when I board the plane. "Welcome aboard, Mr. and Mrs. Stone."

"Um." I want to correct him, but then Christopher's hands land on my hips. "Thank you," I mumble, walking toward one of the seats.

"We'll be taking off shortly," he informs us before turning and saying something to the captain.

Christopher takes my bag and shakes his head. "This is very heavy for not a lot of things."

"I didn't know where we were going, so I had to have some options." I shrug off my jacket before I sit in one of the chairs. "If you don't stop, I won't put on the special outfit I bought for you." Looking up at him, I see him clench his teeth, and all I can do is look out the window so he doesn't see me laughing at him.

"You know what I'm most excited about?" Christopher asks, sitting next to me. "Having sex in a bed."

I gasp and look over at the flight attendant to see if he's listening to our conversation, but he's too busy closing the door. "Christopher," I hiss.

"Baby," he croons, making all of my body parts melt. He leans over, whispering, "I love sinking into you no matter where it is." His breath on my ear makes me shiver. "But the thought of you spread-eagle, naked on the bed"—I swear I have to cross my legs—"I've been hard all week long."

"Are you done?" I ask, turning my head and coming face-to-face with him. He brings his hand up to cup my cheek, and I swear one day his touch is not going to make my heart race. One day, his kiss isn't going to feel like the first time. One day, I'll get used to him touching me. I don't know when it'll be, but I'm sure it'll be soon.

"No." His lips brush mine. "I'm not nearly done with you." His thumb rubs my cheek. "I don't think I'll ever be done with you." He doesn't wait for me to say anything to him. He just slowly kisses me, his tongue sliding in with mine. My hand comes up to hold his on my face as we make out. It's wet, it's soft, and it's everything. My stomach does all sorts of things. It's been over a month that we've been with each other. A week since we officially came out as a couple, or whatever it is we're calling it. We haven't really spoken about it, or better yet, I've been too chickenshit to ask him what it is. I figure it's past the stage when I call him my boyfriend. As a widowed single mother of two children, I think girlfriend is a bit young for me. "All we need is a bed," he mumbles when he lets go of my lips, "and maybe some whipped cream."

"Oh, I could totally go for some whipped cream," I tell him, leaning and kissing his neck. "Going to add that to my ever-growing list."

"I have a list also," he informs me, and I sit back in my chair and turn sideways to look at him. "There is one thing on there for this weekend. It's just one word. Bed."

I snort out a laugh, shaking my head. "You, naked, and in a bed."

"That's three things." I hold up three fingers.

"It all leads to the same thing," he says, and I don't answer him because the flight attendant comes over and places a tray of fruit in front of us.

We spend five hours sitting side by side, his hand on my knee doing little circles. His hand then coming up and twirling my hair around his finger. Then dropping the hair to rub my neck with his finger. Whatever it is, he's always touching me. When the plane finally touches down, I don't even care where I am. All I want is to rip off my jeans and his jeans and have sex wherever our bodies land.

I walk off the plane, holding the railing with one hand while carrying our jackets in the other. Christopher ducks his head, carrying both of our carry-on bags off. The heat hits me right away, and it smells like ocean air.

"Do you want to know where we are?" he asks as we walk toward the blacked-out SUV waiting for us.

"Nope." I shake my head. "I don't care where I am as long as I'm with you."

"Good answer." He puts the bags in the SUV's trunk before turning and grabbing my face.

"I'm not going to lie," I say breathless. "I want to see the bed, and then we can do everything else after."

"Really?" He smirks, and I nod. "Then let's go."

He opens the back door for me to get in, slapping my ass on the way. "I have another thing on my list," he states, sliding in next to me, putting his arm around my shoulder, "my palm print on your ass."

I look around and then back at him. "How mad would you be if, I don't know, we have sex in the bathroom of the lobby?"

His mouth opens and then closes. "Spread-ass-eagle in the bed, and I'm going to eat you until your juices run down my face."

"You can't say things like that to me right now." I

try to move away from him. "For five hours, you were driving me crazy."

"Five hours," he repeats, grabbing my hand and putting it on his hard cock through his jeans. "I've been in this state for the past week."

"We've had sex four times." I look at him. "Yeah, and I have the bruises on my ass to prove it." I roll my lips. "That fucking doorknob gets me every time." I rub his length. "You shouldn't do that." He looks over as the driver gets in. "I was this close"—he puts his thumb and finger together—"from fucking you on the plane."

"Promises, promises," I huff, and the driver starts driving. "This drive better be like a ten-minute thing, or else the bed will be the second place we do it." I intertwine my fingers with his hand hanging off my shoulder. "Also, thank you," I tell him.

"For all the orgasms?"

"Well, yes." I laugh. "But for this weekend. Four days alone with you."

"I wish it was more," he admits softly, his eyes staring into mine. The vehicle comes to a stop, and I swear I've never jumped out faster. Someone waits for us, and he starts shaking Christopher's hand and then mine. "This way."

"We don't need a tour," Christopher says, sliding his hand in mine and walking as fast as he can, "just the room key."

"Of course." He smiles, handing Christopher the cardboard with two keys inside. "We have you in the villa." I don't even know what else he says because I swear my ears are buzzing. "Enjoy Turks and Caicos."

"Oh, I've never been here," I say, and he smirks.

"I know." He winks at me as we climb into a golf cart that takes us to our villa. Christopher walks up the four steps to the door, scanning the card, and I hear the click.

"Thank you," he says to the bellhop, who places the bags at the door. I step into the villa, seeing the whole back wall is a view of the ocean. I don't have a chance to do anything else because the door slams closed, and I look over. "Naked."

I turn around to face him, pulling my shirt over my head and then unsnapping my bra, before kicking off my shoes and tossing them to the side. I see Christopher doing the same thing as me, the sound of our zippers going down at the same time. "How many rooms is this villa?"

"I have no fucking clue." He pushes his jeans and boxers down his legs, his thick cock ready for me. "We just need a fucking bed."

I slip the jeans over my hips, and by the time I'm done, he stands in front of me. His mouth crashes onto mine and he wraps an arm around my waist and hoists me up. My legs wrap around his waist. "You know you can just place me on your cock in this position."

"Oh, I know. We did this two days ago."

He walks through the house, and I whisper, "I need you so bad right now."

He walks into the bedroom, and all I can see is that three walls are all glass, and a bathtub is outside. "We're going to fuck in that tub," he tells me right before he tosses me on the bed. "Now spread your legs"—he fists his cock—"and show me how wet you are."

I scoot back, putting my head on the pillows before spreading my legs for him. I used to be shy when it came to sex, but with Christopher, knowing that I drive him crazy is just so much better. I spread my legs and cock up my knees. "I'm soaking," I tell him, rubbing a finger down through my slit.

"Put two fingers in yourself." He stands at the edge of the bed, his eyes on my fingers, his hand on his cock. I do what he says. "Now take them out and move up to play with your clit." My eyes are hooded when I follow his instructions, and my clit is hard and slippery when I move my fingers from side to side. "You have no idea how fucking sexy you look right now," he tells me. "Your pussy is glistening."

"Yes," I say, about to put my fingers back inside me.

"It's my turn," he says, kneeling on the bed. He plants himself between my legs, his middle finger coming out as he moves to my clit and does little circles. "I love this part of you." He moves my clit up and down. "Your pussy clenches down so hard when I play with this and my cock is in you." He moves it side to side, and my legs open even more. "Want to feel?" he asks. I reach out to touch his cock, but he doesn't let me. "First, I make you come on my finger and my tongue, then you get my cock."

"Christopher," I moan his name, "please, baby." I raise my hips.

"I love when you call my name." His eyes gloss over

with lust. "But hearing you call me baby."

"Trust me, I know," I say, trying to focus, but he's rubbing my clit in little circles before he runs his finger down my slit to my pussy and slides it in me.

"Yes," I coo, and he just chuckles.

"If my baby wants to come, I will make her come." He bends down, and while looking into my eyes, he licks me from ass to fucking clit. "I'm going to spend the whole weekend making you come." My body shivers as he slides another finger into me. "I'm going to fuck every single part of your body." I arch my back, my hands coming to grab my tits. He slides his tongue into me with his finger. "Fuck, you taste like heaven." His tongue moves in and out with his fingers, and I wish I could spread more. "Baby, you're all tense."

"I need you to make me come and then fuck me hard." I hold my legs under my knees. "Please, Christopher." I'm about to cry with need.

He slides his finger out of me but only to move closer to me, holding his cock in his hand. I lift my hips to reach his cock as he slides the head in. "Fuck," he hisses, "I'm going to give you a little at a time."

"No," I moan in frustration, "I want it all."

He grabs my ankles and places them by his head before leaning forward and slamming into me. I see stars, I'm sure. "Yes," I hiss, but I can't say anything else because he's slamming into me over and over again.

"This what you want?" he asks through clenched teeth.

"No," I say, grabbing his arm, "I want it harder."

"Fuck, baby, I'm going to hurt you," he worries, but his speed picks up. "You are already so fucking tight."

I move my hand to my clit, moving it from side to side. "Harder." I can barely say the word, he slams into me so hard I come all over his cock, moaning out his name. I don't say anything else because he fucks me without pause, going deeper and deeper each time until I'm coming again. In the middle, he whispers my name before his cock gets even bigger in me, and he comes.

He collapses on top of me. His body and mine are covered in sweat, and I feel like I ran a sprint. My legs fall off his shoulders as he buries his face in my neck, pulling out his cock a bit and then slamming it back in. "Fuck, I'm still hard."

"I can tell," I say as he slowly pulls out and then slams back in again.

"It's the bed."

I shake my head. "It's my pussy," I tease and lift to match him, "that's got you this hard, not the bed." I turn my head to find his lips.

"You're wrong," he corrects as he pumps his cock into me. "It's my pussy."

TWENTY-EIGHT

CHRISTOPHER

"THE WATER IS getting cold." We're sitting in the outdoor bathtub and have been for the past couple of hours. I'm leaning back against the tub with Dakota in my arms in front of me, her back to my chest, her legs tangled with mine. The waves crashing in the distance fill the air as the sun slowly moves toward sunset.

"Do you want to add more hot water?" I ask softly as I trail kisses up her shoulder to her neck. Her hair is tied up on top of her head.

"Do you want to get out?" I kiss her naked shoulder, not moving my arms from around her. "We are all shriveled up." She holds up her hand.

"There is one thing that isn't shriveled." I kiss behind her ear.

"Oh, trust me, I know." She turns her head toward mine. "I've felt it digging in my back for the past five minutes."

"Well, if you sat on it, then it would not be in your

back." I smirk.

"I've sat on it twice already since we've been in this tub." I lean forward to kiss her smiling face. "Once facing you, the other not facing you."

"Hmm," I moan as I slide my tongue into her mouth. "I might need you to refresh my memory."

She laughs now, her laughter filling the balcony. "You are funny." She kisses my lips, then buries her face in my neck.

For the past two days, we've been here and have never left the room. We've either been having sex, sleeping, or eating. All done either naked or with the robes that came with the room.

"Are you hungry?" I ask as I slide my finger with hers in the water, picking it up and kissing her fingertips that are really shriveled. "What do you want for dinner?"

"Are you asking me to suck your dick?" she asks, and now both our chests shake while we laugh.

"No," I finally say. "When I want you to suck my dick, I'll just say suck my dick."

"Glad we got that talk out of the way." She turns in the tub to face me, moving farther away.

I take her foot in my hand, and I can see she has something on her mind. "What's going on?" I ask.

"I know that we are, you know—" she says and then looks down. I stop moving my fingers until she looks back up at me. I just stare at her, at her beauty, at everything she is. "You know we are having—"

"Sex," I fill in the blanks.

"Yeah, we are doing that. But I was wondering if, you

know, we are just"—she points a finger at her chest, then me—"are we just having sex with each other?"

I sit up. "Are you saying you want to have sex with other people?" My heart pounds.

"No." She shakes her head. "I'm asking if we are exclusive."

"What kind of question is that?" I almost snap.

"Well, I don't know, we never defined this."

"Didn't we?" I tilt my head to the side. "I think I remember saying I'm yours, and you're mine."

"Was I there for this conversation?" She smiles, and I can see she's happy with the direction of this discussion because her eyes light up. I also know I'm going to marry her. I knew before I was in for the long haul. Now with her sitting in front of me, her face pink from us fucking, her body with my marks on it, the way I feel when I wake up with her in my arms. I know no one else in the world is supposed to be by my side for the rest of my life.

"I think you were there. Baby, whatever you want is what we do." Her eyes lighten even more. "I don't care what you call me. I just know that I'm yours and you're mine. Also, FYI, there is no fucking open relationship," I snap, and she giggles. "I don't know how much clearer I need to be."

"I think you are pretty clear." She's about to come to me when we hear a phone ring from inside the house.

I can see the worry hit her face right away. "That's my mom." Jumping out of the tub, she grabs the towel near us and runs into the house. I get out and grab the other towel, following her inside.

"How high is her fever?" she asks as she sits on the bed, her eyes coming to me. "That's really high," she states, grabbing the robe and then slipping it on before she presses the FaceTime video. She sits with the phone in her hand. "Hi, baby." She smiles. "How are you feeling?"

"I'm sick," Luna says, and then she coughs, "and my throat hurts."

"Oh, baby, I'm going to try to call the doctor to see if he can see you today, but if anything, Grams is going to take you to the doctor tomorrow."

"Okay, Mommy." I sit next to her and see Luna lying on the couch, her cheeks pink and her eyes drooping closed.

"I'll call you tomorrow," she says to the phone and then hangs up.

"What's the matter?" I ask.

"She has a fever of one hundred and two. Her throat hurts, and she has a little cough. I think it's probably strep." She puts her phone to her ear. "I'm going to see if I can get her taken into the emergency pediatrician." She listens to whatever is being said on her side. "Shit, they are full for today." The worry fills her face as she presses something on her phone. "I have to make an appointment online." Her fingers go crazy over the phone. "Got it. Tomorrow morning at ten thirty. It's the earliest appointment I could get." I nod at her before I grab my phone and call my sister Abigail. "What are you doing?"

"Calling my sister. She's a nurse," I reply, and before

she has a chance to say anything, Abigail picks up.

"Eww," she hisses, "why are you calling me naked?"

"I'm not naked," I say in my defense. "Listen, Luna has a fever of a hundred and two, her throat is sore, and she has a cough."

"Okay," Abigail says, confusion on her face.

"What can we do?"

"Well, for one," she states, "give her acetaminophen for the fever. Then you take her to the doctor."

I roll my eyes. "Could it be strep?"

"It could be, but you won't know unless she gets a throat culture." I nod.

"Okay, bye." I hang up the phone on her as she's about to ask me a question. I know what she's going to ask me, and I'll get back to the gossip later. It takes her a second to send the text, and I think about not answering it, but I know it'll just get worse if I don't.

Abigail: Are you on vacation with Koda, or did she call you?

Me: Later.

Abigail: I'm calling Mom and Dad.

Me: Snitches get stitches.

Abigail: I'll tell my husband that, and you can deal with him.

Me: I'm more scared of Gabriella than I am of Tristan. I'll call you tomorrow.

"What are you doing?" Koda asks from beside me as I start to implement my plan.

"I'm getting us a plane, then I'm getting us a doctor who is going to go see her now," I say, pulling up the phone number to the private plane we took down here.

"What?" she asks, her eyes wide.

"You aren't going to be able to relax here when she's sick," I tell her, "and frankly, neither will I, so we'll cut the trip short."

"You would do that?"

"I don't see any other option, do you?" I ask, and she shakes her head. "It's a good thing we didn't unpack."

She laughs while I get on the phone with the private plane company. It takes an hour to get everything situated. We are strapping ourselves in when I look over at her. She's wearing exactly what she wore two days ago and so am I. "We should land at around nine," I tell her, and she nods.

"It's my mother," she announces when her phone rings right as the flight attendant closes the plane door. "Hey." She puts the phone to her ear. "Wait, what?" Her eyes fly to mine. "Okay, we will be home in five hours," she tells her mother. "Kiss them for me."

She hangs up the phone as the plane starts heading down the runway. "Did you send a doctor to the house?"

"Yeah."

"Just yeah," she says breathlessly, "just like that?"

"Well, I don't know what else I'm supposed to say." I look into her eyes. "I may have overstepped, but the thought of her being sick and not getting help until tomorrow is unacceptable. So I called the team doctor, who knew a friend who did me a favor."

Her hands come up to cup my face. "I'm going to need you to stop being so perfect." She sniffles back tears.

"I'll try, baby," I say as she kisses my lips.

For five hours, she sits beside me with her head on my shoulder. "I owe you two days," she whispers.

"You owe me nothing," I tell her, kissing her head. "If anything, I owe you."

When the plane touches down, we rush to the truck and head straight to her house. Her mother comes out of the living room. "Hey," she greets us, "they are upstairs sleeping." She points upstairs, so Dakota rushes up the stairs toward the bedrooms.

"I can't believe you flew back so fast." Her father comes out of the living room.

"It was easy to get a plane," I lie to them. I had to beg a pilot to take us back home and pay them double. But I would have done whatever it took to get her home.

Her parents go to the door, grabbing their jackets. "We are going to head home." Her father helps her mother put on her jacket.

"Are you sure?" I ask, looking up to see Koda coming back down the stairs.

"Yes," her mother affirms, and Koda comes over to hug them both and thank them for coming.

I shake her father's hand, and her mother hugs me and squeezes my arms. I walk out with them, grab her bag from the trunk, and then return inside. I see she's not there, so I place the bag on the carpet. "What are you doing?" she asks when she finally comes down the steps.

"I'm going to head out," I tell her, and she shakes her head, coming to stand in front of me.

"No, you're going to come upstairs and get into bed

with me." She puts her hands on my chest.

"The kids—" I start to say.

"The kids are sleeping, and they will be just as happy to see you as they will to see me." She gets on her tippy-toes. "And I don't want you to go home."

"But—" I start, but she wraps her arms around me.

"But nothing. Stay with me. I'm not ready to let you go yet."

"Are you sure?" I ask, knowing I would do anything for her.

"More than sure." She smiles at me. "We just can't sleep naked."

"Then I can't stay," I joke, and she laughs. "I'll go get my bag."

"You packed pj's in your bag?" she asks, and I shake my head.

"But I have shorts." I rush back out to grab my bag, coming back in and seeing her waiting for me by the door. I grab her bag and my own as I walk upstairs to her bedroom.

I put my bag on the chair in the corner of her room and take her bag to her walk-in closet. "I'm going to go check on the girls one more time," she whispers, and I nod.

When she returns, she walks over to her closet, and changes into her pj set. I have my basketball shorts on with a T-shirt. "What side do you sleep on?" I ask nervously.

"Any side you are on." She winks at me, making me laugh. I slide into bed, and she rolls into me. "It's not the same." She looks up from my chest at me. "I like the skin to skin."

"You aren't the only one who likes skin to skin." I roll toward her as she cocks her leg over my hip. "Go to sleep, baby." I kiss her lips, then she buries her face in my neck as I turn over on my back.

I barely drift off to sleep when I hear Luna crying. Koda stirs from my chest, getting up. I blink my eyes open and get out of bed to follow her. "You are hot," Koda says, touching her cheek to Luna's forehead. "I'm going to go get your medicine." Luna just nods at her.

"I'll stay with her," I tell Koda as she walks downstairs to the kitchen.

"Hey there." I walk over to the side of her bed and sit on the twin-sized mattress. "I heard you weren't feeling well."

"I'm hot," she whines, and when I lean forward to touch her forehead, she slides into my lap.

I turn to put my back against the headboard as I cuddle her, rocking her back and forth. "Mommy is going to make you feel all better," I say. When Koda comes back into the room, I'm about to get up when Luna shakes her head.

"Here, take this," Koda urges, holding a syringe filled with red liquid in her hand. "You'll feel better after this." Luna opens her mouth and takes it all, then asks for water.

She hands her the water bottle, and I feel like I shouldn't be here, but I also know I don't want to leave. I'm about to do the handoff to Koda when I look up at her, and she looks at me as if I'm the only person in the world. Her eyes are soft, and she smiles at me as Luna lays her head on my chest. "You're incredible," she says softly. "I hope you know that."

TWENTY-NINE

DAKOTA

THE FRONT DOOR opens as I'm taking the roasting pan out of the oven. "It smells so good," Christopher says. "Wash your hands."

"Okay," the girls reply, running to the bathroom while I look over and see him walking into the kitchen.

"Hey." I put the baking dish on the top of the stove, taking off the baking gloves when his hands rest on my hips. "Did you wash your hands?" I turn in his arms, seeing him smirk. It's been almost two weeks since our trip was cut short because Luna was sick. Two weeks of him staying over when he's in town. So far, it hasn't been much, and if I'm honest, I miss him a ridiculous amount when he's gone.

"I did not," he admits, leaning in to kiss me softly on the lips. Then hearing the girls run our way, he lets me go to wash his hands in the sink. Even though he's been here in my bed when the girls wake up, and he holds my hand when we sit or go anywhere, he still hasn't kissed me in front of the girls. I don't know if he's giving them a chance to get used to him or if he's just not ready yet, but whatever it is, I won't push him.

"What's for dinner?" Rain asks when she walks into the kitchen, wiping her wet hands on her black tights. It was an impromptu night of hockey. When they got home from school, Christopher asked if he could take them to the rink to skate. I didn't even have a chance to answer before the girls had their bags ready to go.

"Roasted chicken and veggies." I grab the plates. "Are you hungry?"

"Yes." She nods, going to her stool that is next to Christopher's. Something she started doing when he started sleeping over. The four of us sit down at the counter talking about the day, when out of the blue Rain turns to Christopher.

"Were you and my dad best friends?" The question shocks us both. My fork falls from my hand with a clank on the plate. Christopher's face pales just a little, but then he quickly turns to her.

"Yes," he answers softly as my heart races faster and faster. "Yes, he was."

"Was he nice to everyone?" She looks over at Christopher, waiting for him to answer.

"He was," he says, smiling at her. "One year, when the rookies came in, he made sure that he took them out for dinner and gave them his number."

"Did you do that too?" she asks, and I pick up my fork, not to eat anything but to keep my hands busy.

"I did," he says.

"What was the nicest thing he did?" The question is so pure, and I hold my breath. The only two things Benji ever did that were nice were give me my girls.

"He did a lot of things that were nice," Christopher says. "But I think the nicest thing would have been when we went to visit some sick kids in the hospital, and he paid for the family to come to one of the games," he shares, sniffling. "He was also a jokester." He pushes the plate away from him as he turns with fondness in his eyes, and I see the tears are there. "One year, when we were back from summer vacation, I walked into the locker room, and he had taped all my equipment together with three rolls of tape." He laughs. "And then he shoved little pieces of tape in the fingers of my gloves. It took forever for me to get them out." He is animated with his hands, making the girls laugh.

"What did you do?" Rain asks, the smile filling her face.

"The next year—" He starts, laughing at himself. "I filled his skates and his gloves with gum." Even I laugh. "It took me over three hours to chew all those pieces. It was stuck to his socks, and he tried to peel them off, but they were wet." He throws his head back and laughs. "He tried to shake it off his hands, and one flew in another skate. We didn't know whose skate until Cole stepped out of his skate and stuck to the floor." We all laugh at the memories. "It was a good time." He leans back in his chair.

"That's funny," Rain says before she changes the subject, and I see that Christopher has gotten quiet. After all of this, I have to remember that he lost one of his best friends. No matter how much I feel toward him, he needs to be able to talk about it. He's been so incredible to give me what I need, I somehow forgot I have to be that for him also. I also know it's time to have the talk I've been scared to have with him. It's sort of the last little piece I've been keeping to myself. But if this is going to happen, and I really want it to happen, he has to have all of it.

"Okay, finish up," I say to the girls. "It's late, and neither of you have taken a bath yet."

I push away from the island, avoiding looking at Christopher as I walk over to the sink.

"I've got this," he states from behind me. "Go get the girls settled."

"Okay." I put my plate in the sink and walk around him, gathering the girls and pushing them toward the stairs.

My hands start to shake when they finish their showers and get into pj's. They shake even more when I hear him coming up the stairs to say good night to them.

"Good night." I kiss Luna on the cheek before walking out and coming face-to-face with Christopher. "I have to use the bathroom," I say, my voice shaking as I bend my head and make my way to my bathroom.

I walk to the sink, turning on the cold water as my neck gets hot. "It's going to be fine," I tell myself, not sure my heart will be able to handle it if it's over.

I close my eyes, not ready to think about it for much longer before I chicken out again and don't tell him. I was initially going to tell him on vacation, but then I just wanted it to be about us. About him and about me. Call me selfish, but that is all I wanted.

I unlock the door and step out, coming to a halt when I see him sitting on my bed with his hands on his knees and his head hanging down. "Hey," I say softly, looking at him for the first time, seeing his face ravaged.

I take a step toward him but stop when his words come out almost broken. "I'm sorry," he says, halting me again in my steps. "I didn't know what to say when she asked me about him."

Oh. My. God. "It's her dad, and she needs to be proud of him until she's old enough to know better. Until then, I can't be the one to tell her the truth." If I didn't think I loved this man before this moment, then I would have fallen in love with him right now. Right here, in the middle of my brand-new bedroom that is practically ours since he has some of his clothes in the chair in the corner. Along with his razor on the side of his sink and a couple of suits in my closet.

"But if you want, when we talk about him, I'll try to do it when you don't have to hear it."

"I would never do that," I say, standing in front of him now, his hands coming to my hips and pulling me closer. "There is something I need to tell you." I take a step back and out of his reach, knowing if he touches me, I'll forget what I have to say. "And I know that it can be shocking, but I figured that this thing between us is getting a little serious."

"You can say that, baby." His voice is soft. "I don't

know what you call a little serious, but we'll discuss that after you say what you have to say."

I try not to get too wrapped up in what he's saying and how he's saying it. I also try to focus on the words I want to say. "When Benji died, I found out a lot of things," I say nervously. "Things that were not easy to come to terms with." I look at him but then look down at my fingers, wringing them. "Some things I knew before." I can't stop the tears from pouring out of my eyes, but it's not because I'm angry about what I discovered. It's because I'm not sure if he'll look at me the same way after this. "Three weeks after he died," I say and look at him, "there was a knock on the door. I opened it, and there was a man I had never seen before. I had no idea who he even was." I take a deep breath. "He informed me that he was Benji's friend."

"His friend?" Christopher asks, his eyebrows pinched together.

"His friend," I repeat. "But in reality, it was his drug dealer." My hands shake when I see his eyes go big. "He was there to collect on his debt."

Christopher shoots to his feet. "Excuse me?" His voice is thick with rage.

"It seemed that he fronted him with some stuff." I hold up my hands and shake my head at the same time. "And now he wanted to be paid for said stuff."

"What is his name?" His voice fills with venom, but I ignore it, continuing with the story.

"Benji owed him close to two hundred thousand dollars," I whisper, "and now that debt was mine. Ours.

Mine and the girls."

"Dakota," he growls through clenched teeth.

"So I called Eddie up when he left. I was a fucking mess and had no idea what to do. Obviously, I had money in the account, but I wasn't going to go to the bank and ask them to give me two hundred thousand dollars in a bag." He takes a step toward me, but I hold up my hand, shaking my head. "Eddie came over and tried to calm me down. Told me not to worry about it and he would take care of it. I didn't know what he meant until I found out that Benji has always struggled with substance abuse." I see more shock fill his face. "Started when he was sixteen. They got a 'handle on it'"—I use air quotes with my fingers—"as Eddie said, when he was nineteen. I have no idea if he was ever not fucking high. It was also the day I let Eddie know I never wanted to see him again. He could see the girls, but for me, I would never sit down at a table with him again. I would never share the same space as him. Instead of helping me when he saw a problem, he pushed it under the rug. I could forgive a lot of things, and maybe in time, I'll change my mind, but for now, I don't want to talk to him. He calls every Sunday to talk to the kids, but that's where it ends." I tremble. "I paid off the debt. I wrote a check and told him that was all he was getting from me." I put my hand in front of my mouth to stop the sob. "That is who I think of when I think of Benji."

"Baby." Christopher cups my face in his hands. "How could you do that?" I wait for the anger to come in his voice. "How could you put yourself in danger like that?"

His head shakes side to side. "Why didn't you call me?"

"And tell you what?" I ask. "There was nothing to say. You would have probably gone apeshit over it, paid the debt off, and lied to me about it."

I can see in his eyes that what I just said is what he would have done. "I was coming back," he says, "and I was staging an intervention." Now his words are the ones that shock me. "I didn't give a shit what he said or what he did. I was taking him to get help." I see the tears escape his eyes. "I never got that chance."

My hands come to his sides, bunching his shirt in my hands. "I'll never forgive myself for not doing it sooner."

"Even if you did it sooner," I tell him, "he was the one who had to hit rock bottom."

"There are days when I hate him," he admits softly, "but then there are days, like tonight, when I think of the good times."

"You're a good man," I tell him.

"I don't know about that." He kisses my lips softly. "Because I wouldn't trade you and the girls for him." I see the anguish. "The girls are his, but you—" His voice is tight. "You're mine. I'm not sorry you're mine. I might be sorry about how it happened, but no way in fuck am I sorry for that. So I'm not sure I'm a good man."

"The girls, they're mine," I correct him, "and you have to know with the way they worship you that they think the world of you."

"I love you." Three words I've been saying to him silently every single time I look at him. Three words I say to him while I look at him right before he takes me in his arms to fall asleep. Three words I say every single time he slides into me. "I love the girls."

"I said it first," I counter quickly. "Every single time you hang up the phone, I tell you I love you." His smirk makes me smile.

"I don't think that counts." He steps closer to me. "Now, is that all you got?"

"I don't know what you mean."

"This last secret," he says. "Is it all you've got?"

"It's a pretty big one." I gawk at him.

"So was mine," he counters, and he's not wrong. "You forgive me?"

"For what?" I jump back, his hands falling from my face.

"For not doing anything sooner. For not being the stand-up guy you think I am."

"I've forgiven Benji," I admit. "Tonight, here in the room, telling you my last secret I had held on to. Telling you I've let him go. I've forgiven him as much as I can."

"I love you," he says again, and I huff out.

"You can't say it again." I fold my arms over my chest. "You have to give me a chance to say it."

"Baby, I love you."

"Christopher," I hiss, "you have to give me a chance."

"You had two chances; you didn't say it. I'm not going to not say it." He takes my lips in a kiss. It's hard and wet, and by the end of it, I'm plastered to his front.

"I love you," I say breathlessly. "Ha, said it first."

"Before," he says, "you asked me if this is serious." I wrap my arms around his neck. "Just so you know." His hands grip my hips. "It's as serious as forever."

The gasp leaves my mouth. "I thought you would hate me for what I did and for keeping it from you," I admit.

"Oh, we're going to discuss you keeping this from me," he warns, "but we'll do that naked so I can smack that ass of yours." He bends now, his forehead to mine. "I love you, baby."

THIRTY

CHRISTOPHER

I'M RINSING OFF the dinner plates while Koda gives the girls their bath. My phone rings from the island where I put it when I came in, right next to my keys and wallet. Shaking the water off my hands before grabbing the dishrag, I walk over and see it's Dylan and he's FaceTiming me.

I press the green button and wait for his face to fill the screen. "Where are you?"

"Hello to you too." I ignore his question.

"Yeah, hello," he snaps. "Now answer my question, where are you?"

"I'm at Koda's," I say, and if he's calling me, I know that things in the family have been chattering. With my family, there is always chatter. Usually it's just light and did you hear, but if my big brother calls me and asks me where I am, it's because he heard something. He usually lets Alex deal with all the other little stuff.

"You're at Koda's?" He raises his eyebrows. "On a

school night?"

"Cut the shit," I tell him.

"I'm not the one who has to cut the shit." I can see the humor in his eyes. "I got a very interesting phone call from my darling sister today." I roll my eyes. "And she was just, you know, asking me how I was, and then imagine my surprise when I find out that you went away for your bye week?"

"I always go away for the bye week."

"Oh, I know, but you always tell us where you're going and then send us your stupid thirst trap photos of you running on the beach or in the water looking to the side."

I throw my head back and howl with laughter. "So you went to Turks?"

"I did."

"By yourself?"

"No, I went with Koda."

"Interesting." I shake my head.

"What do you want to know?"

"Everything."

"You are such a Nosy Nancy," I point out. "Koda and I are together." I don't know why I'm expecting to feel guilty about it, but for the first time, I don't.

"Explain. How are you together?"

"I'm at her house on a school night," I say. "My clothes are in her closet. My stuff is half here and half at my house."

"Does she have stuff at your house?" I tilt my head to the side to think about it.

"No." I look over my shoulder at the empty hallway. "She doesn't."

"You paying for her house?" he asks, and the pit of my stomach gets sour. "Oh my God, are you leeching off your girlfriend?"

"I am not leeching off anyone," I refute quickly. "The girls are here, and it's easier."

"You know if you move them into your house, it'll be easier."

"I'll think about it," I say just to appease him, and truth be told, I really am going to think about it because there is no way my woman will pay for our house.

"But seriously, you and Koda?" His tone turns serious.

"Yeah, me and Koda," I confirm, my chest getting full when I think of her, "and the girls."

"Obviously." He scoffs. "It's a package deal, everyone knows that."

I hear footsteps behind me and look over my shoulder, seeing the woman who has my whole fucking heart. I mean, not the whole time, the girls have it also, but she's got it in her hand. "Hey, my brother is on the phone giving me a hard time," I tell her, and her eyes go big in fear, and she stops. "He says I'm leeching off you."

"You aren't leeching off me." She shakes her head, and I motion with my head for her to come to me. She walks over, wringing her hands in front of her, something she does when she's nervous. "Why don't we spend time at my house?"

"Um," she says, "you've never really asked me over."

"Oh. My. God," Dylan chides. "What a dick."

I glare at the phone but then turn back to see Koda smiling. "Baby, you want to go to my house, let's go to my house."

"I don't want to go to your house, Christopher." She ignores my brother's snickering. "I want to be invited over to your house."

I shake my head. "Why are you shaking your head?"

"Because I thought you didn't want to come over to my house."

She folds her arms over her chest. "How? Have you ever asked me to go to your house, and I said no?" I swallow down. "Even after all that 'you won't kiss me in his house,' never once did you invite me over to your house to kiss me."

"Alex," my brother calls his wife, "get over here."

"I'm letting you go."

"No," Dylan says, "I'm invested in this conversation."

"No, you aren't. You're waiting to hear what she says so you can gossip with Michael."

He doesn't even try to deny it. "You should be focusing on Koda and not on me. Answer her question."

"I didn't really ask him a question," Koda says softly from beside me. "It was more like a statement."

"All I heard is you're a dick and you never invited her over to your home," Dylan goads, "and you are making her pay for you to live in her house." He shakes his head. "Dude, I'm never, ever going to let you live that down."

"Eventually, we're moving to my house anyway," I say to Dylan, and I think maybe I should have had this talk with Koda before my brother. "I mean, not now.

The girls just moved from their house to this house," I backpedal, "so I didn't want to step on toes, but—"

"Move to your house?" she asks.

"Well, yeah," I say, "this house has four bedrooms."

"You sleep in my bed."

"Oh my God, this guy didn't even buy the bed," Dylan groans. "Did we not teach you anything? Koda," he calls her name and she comes over. "On behalf of the Stone family, I want to apologize for him being this way." He shakes his head. "Dad is going to kill you." He turns his eyes on me.

"Can you, like, shut up?" I tell Dylan, who pretends to zip his mouth. "This house has four bedrooms. One of them is your office."

"Okay?"

"Baby, where are our kids going to go?" I ask. She steps back, and even Dylan hears the gasp out of her mouth because he mimics it.

"Our kids?"

"Well, yeah." I look at her. "I mean, not now, but like when we have them."

"Imagine she is pregnant right now and you just said that," Dylan pushes. "How is she going to feel?"

"She's not pregnant now," I tell him, then look over at Koda. "Are you pregnant?"

"Are you insane?" she shrieks in a whisper so as not to wake the girls.

"Yes," Dylan answers right away, "he is."

"I'm not pregnant."

"Yet," Dylan adds, and I smirk.

"Exactly," I agree, "and when we have our babies, where are they going to go?"

"You want me to have your babies?" she whispers, pointing at herself.

"Well, our babies," I correct. "I want you to have our babies."

"I bet the first one is a boy," Dylan says and even Koda smiles.

"How many babies do you want?"

"Whatever you do, don't fucking say eight," Dylan advises. "Cooper is going to be bald soon with all the kids he has."

"I don't want eight kids." She shakes her head.

"We already have two."

"You want to have six more?" She gawks at me.

"No, I'm good with two more, maybe three, if it's two boys and try for a girl and vice versa."

"That's how it starts, Koda," Dylan chimes in. "Don't fall for that. Erika started with Cooper's two girls, and now she has a minibus full."

"Would you shut up?" I tell Dylan.

"Hey, I'm talking to my sister-in-law," Dylan quips.

"Sister-in-law?" Koda questions, looking at the phone and then to me.

"Well, after you get married," Dylan says, "but it's close enough. He's living with you, mooching off your food. Does he even get groceries?"

"Goodbye," I say and hang up while he's laughing.

"We should talk." I look at her as her face fills with a panicked look.

"I would say," she agrees, while I walk to her and put my hands on her hips.

"Do you want to have dinner at my house tomorrow?" I smirk, and she pushes me away.

"No." She turns to walk away from me, but I grab the loop in her jeans, pulling her back to me.

"My brother is right." I wrap my arms around her waist.

"About what?"

"Me staying here and not paying." My hand is flat on her stomach. "First thing I need to do is get the girls to decorate their rooms." She doesn't say anything. "Then slowly we start leaving things there until it's all there."

"B-but," she stammers.

"You go in tomorrow, and we'll get rid of anything you don't like," I tell her. "Couch, bed, fridge, don't give a fuck. You don't like it, it's out."

"That's crazy. I've been to your house before." She turns in my arms. "It's perfect. A little bachelor but—"

"You come in and make it a home," I say. "It'll be our home."

"With our kids, apparently," she jokes.

"With our kids," I agree. "Also, you should know that after that phone call, my family will be coming down."

"What?"

"It's their way of getting to know you and the girls. Making sure we know if we need them, they are there."

"I've been around your family before." She chuckles. "I just haven't done it as, you know."

"The girl I love." The minute I say that, she almost

stomps her foot.

"Dammit, can you let me say it once?"

"No." I bend to kiss her lips. "I think we do a sleepover at my house this weekend."

"Okay." Her voice is soft as I start to walk her over to the couch, my mouth attacking her. "Have to make a list"—she fumbles with my shirt to get it off me—"of the places we have to do it in your hou—"

"Our house," I cut her off, "it's going to be our house. And I can tell you right now, there isn't a surface in there that won't be used." I fall on the couch. "Also, I already have my list."

THIRTY-ONE

DAKOTA

THE DOORBELL RINGS, and the girls spring out of their seats on the couch to run to the door. "Don't open that door," I tell them when they disappear into the hallway. I nervously look over at the clock and see they're early.

"Oh my God," I mumble. "Don't freak out." I take deep breaths as I walk toward the front door. Every single step feels like there is concrete in my shoes.

"It's Justin," Rain announces, "and Caroline."

My heart speeds up when I hear this. "Christopher," I hiss up the stairs, waiting for him to stick his head out of my bedroom, but he doesn't and the front door is opened.

"Hey," Justin says, stepping into the house and squatting down in front of the girls to give them hugs.

"Would you let us in?" Caroline pushes Justin out of the way a bit, stepping in from the cold, followed by Zoe and Viktor.

"Girls," I urge softly, "let them get in, please." They

walk back to me at the same time as Christopher decides to grace us with his presence.

"Hey, you guys are here," he says, jogging down the steps, his hair wet from his shower, and I want to inwardly cringe. Nothing says I just had sex with your son like him coming down with wet hair.

He walks past the girls, going to his parents first, giving his father a hug and then bending to kiss his mother's cheek. I've met them before, so I don't know why I'm so nervous about this. Oh, that's right, because now it's different. I'm not just his friend's wife. I'm now the woman he's with. I refuse to use the word girlfriend at this age. "Hi, honey," his mother says softly while she hugs him. "You look good." She smiles at him while he moves from her to Zoe, kissing her cheek and hugging her in the same way he did his mother.

"Hi," Zoe greets cheerfully, "look at you." She puts a hand on his cheek. "He's glowing."

"I'm not glowing," he jokes before hugging Viktor. "Hey." The two of them share a look before Viktor slaps his shoulder and squeezes.

"He's not glowing," Viktor says, "it's just the look of love."

He shakes his head and laughs. "I guess that might be it." He smiles at me and the girls, who are standing in front of me.

"I'm sorry." I finally get my words together. "Let me take your coats."

"I'm in love with this house," Zoe says, turning to see the window. "It's even more stunning than the pictures."

"Isn't it?" I say, walking to her as she hands me her jacket. Christopher takes it out of my hands.

"I got it, baby," he says, grabbing the jackets and placing them on the stairs. I look over, seeing his parents share a look when both of their eyes go up, then they try not to smile.

"It smells amazing," Caroline states when she catches me staring at her.

"We made lemon muffins," Luna shares, jumping up and down, "and I did the icing."

"Well, then, I'm sure they'll be amazing," Justin says, awkwardly standing at the front door, not sure where to go.

"Please come in." I shake my head. "I'm so sorry." I laugh nervously. "Welcome," I say to them with a huge smile.

"I want to see this kitchen," Zoe states. "From the picture, it looked out of this world." She walks into the house. "Oh, it's stunning."

"Isn't it?" I smile as I'm running my hand along the granite island.

"Come and see the couch," Luna says to Justin, taking his hand.

"I want to see the couch too," Viktor says. Rain smiles and grabs his hand, and they pull them into the family room.

"Would you like some wine or maybe a mimosa?" I'm about to say something else when I feel Christopher behind me, his hand gripping my hip.

"Baby." He bends down. "Relax." He kisses my neck

right in front of his parents.

All I can do is stare at him, the stare turning into a glare. "Christopher," Caroline says, "stop making her nervous."

"I'm not making her nervous." He points at himself. "You guys are all making her like this."

"Christopher," I hiss, then look at his mother. "I'm not nervous."

"Well, at least one of us isn't." Caroline laughs, pulling out a stool. "When I met Justin's family, I think I shook like a leaf." Caroline puts her hands on the counter in front of her, folding them together. "They were just—"

She looks over at Zoe, who also pulls out a stool. "We were a lot." The two of them laugh.

"It's silly since we know each other. We've known each other for years," I finally say, "but it's a different hat."

"That's a great way of putting it," Caroline says, the softness in her eyes helping me relax a bit.

The doorbell rings, and I look over at Christopher, who looks at me. "I'll get it," he says, rounding me and heading for the front door.

"Sorry, we weren't expecting anyone else." I look at them and hear voices and laughter from the front door before I see Matthew walk into the room, slapping his hands together. "Couldn't let you guys have all the fun." Max follows him into the room, shaking his head behind him.

He walks over to Caroline, kisses her cheek, and then hugs Zoe. "Heaven forbid we have something where you aren't invited to."

"Heaven forbid," Max repeats behind him. "You would have thought you guys were keeping state secrets when he found out."

Matthew just glares at them before walking behind the counter toward me. "Hey, Koda." He hugs me. "You look good. Glowing."

"Jesus," Christopher says, "what is with this glowing thing?"

"It's love," Allison says, coming to hug me. "Sorry to interrupt, but we made him promise we would say hello and then leave."

"Good luck with that," Karrie says, pulling up a stool next to Zoe. "I love this kitchen." She looks around. "This house is so cozy." She takes it all in.

Max makes his way over to me, giving me a side hug before leaving the kitchen with Matthew and heading to the family room with the girls. His voice gets animated when they don't come to him. "Where are my hugs and kisses?"

"How're you doing?" Christopher says when he finally stands beside me, putting his arm over my shoulders. "Is your hair on fire yet?"

"You know that feeling you get when you think you're going to throw up?" I look up at him, and he nods. "I'm like past that and grabbing a bucket to puke in." He throws his head back and laughs.

"Good thing you love me, then," he says, and I bite down on my lip. "I'm going to make sure the girls are okay." He bends to kiss my lips.

I watch him walk away from me into the living room with the guys. "Are you okay?" someone asks from beside me, and I didn't even notice that Caroline moved.

"Yeah, I'm fine," I assure her. "I just wanted to make a good impression."

"Good impression." She throws her head back and laughs, and I see that the other girls are not even noticing our conversation. "You're kidding, right?"

"I don't understand," I ask, furrowing my brow.

"Koda. You made a good impression the minute we met you."

"Yes," I say, "but that was—"

"Was that not you also?" She laughs when she asks the question. "You're the same person we met all those years ago, just with a different hat.

"You know, when I met Justin's family, I was living in a one-bedroom apartment in the worst neighborhood. I had drug dealers living right outside my door." I stare at her. "And then, they are them." She points with her hand at the group of people just lounging in my house.

Christopher sits on the floor next to Max, who is stretched out, pushing Matthew's shoulder, who is also sitting on the floor. "So you may not be the person you were all those years ago, but you're you." She smiles big. "And you love my son, so it's a good impression right off the bat."

"I do, you know," I confirm softly. "Which I'm sure many people will think is weird. Hell, I even fought it for the longest time. But he's him, and he's perfect, and he's kind, and he's just…"

"I know," she agrees, looking over at her husband. "He's exactly like his father, so I know what you mean."

"Are we going to eat or what?" Matthew shouts from the family room. "Should we go out or order in?"

"It's too cold to go out," Justin says. "We should just order food here and watch the game."

"We should do Chinese," Karrie suggests. "Dumplings."

"Whatever you want." Matthew looks at her with a smirk on his face.

"We should order sushi also," Allison adds. "Max, can we have sushi?"

"Anything, angel," he says, and his look is pure love.

"Oh," Caroline says, "we should order pizza also."

"That works," Justin agrees.

"The last time we were here, we had the best butter chicken," Zoe remembers, looking at Viktor.

"Dear God," I say under my breath, and Caroline looks at me. "I'm going to have leftovers for a month."

"Welcome to the family, Dakota." She squeezes my hand before she walks away while everyone places different orders on different phones.

EPILOGUE ONE

CHRISTOPHER

Four months later

"UNCLE CHRISSY," LUNA says, coming down the stairs as soon as I walk in the door, "Mom says I can't take five dolls with me on the vacation."

I scratch the back of my head. "First of all, hi." I walk to her and pick her up, kissing her cheek. "And second, five dolls is a lot for vacation," I tell her.

"But they are going to be sad," she says.

"What if we got a camera and put it in the room so you can talk to them from the vacation?" I ask, and her eyes light up. "That way, they won't be sad."

She squirms out of my arms. "Can we?" she asks like I just told her that Santa is going to come over for lunch tomorrow.

"We can." I nod at her. "Where is Mom?" I ask, and she points upstairs, so we walk up the stairs toward the bedroom.

"Mommy." Luna happily walks in front of me, going past the bed and to Koda's closet. "Uncle Chrissy said I could take one doll." She holds up a finger, and I lean against the doorjamb. I see Koda packing things in her suitcase, her head bent, the hair falling around her face. "And we will get a camera in the room to watch them." Koda's eyes come to mine, and I can tell this is going to be another discussion about me not giving in to everything that Luna wants. "And when I'm at the beach, I can watch them and talk to them."

She stands. "Is that so?" she asks, and Luna stands there with one foot on her other. "Well, go choose which one you're going to take."

"Okay." She turns and skips out of our bedroom. My eyes go to the frames she's added next to our bed. One is with Koda and me, her in front of me, my arms around her as we stare into the camera. It was taken the day my family came down to welcome her. The one beside it is of the four of us sitting in her family room right after we ate. The frames are in my bedroom or what is now called our bedroom. We started with dinner there a couple of times a week when I was in town and then had sleepovers. Slowly, but surely, they brought more and more things over. Her house is now being rented out by a rookie on the team who got traded and needed a house for him and his family.

"Really?" Koda looks at me. "A camera in her room?"

"Yeah, sort of like those baby cams." I walk in and around her suitcase, grabbing her hips and pulling her to me. "Hi, by the way."

She puts her hands on my chest, and I look down at her bare hands, knowing that my ring will be on her finger after this holiday. "Hi." She smiles as I lean down to kiss her.

"I guess I should thank you for not giving in and letting her bring five dolls."

"Well, if she hadn't told me you said no." I wrap my arms around her, pulling her to me. "I probably would have." She shakes her head, chuckling. "How was this afternoon?"

"Well." She walks away from me, my hands falling to my sides. "One, are we going to talk about the fact you left when you knew Eddie would be here?"

"Nothing to really discuss," I tell her as she raises her eyebrows. "Eddie was coming to see the girls." She crosses her arms over her chest. "And it wasn't my place."

"Do you not live in this house with us?" she asks, and I try not to roll my eyes. "This is your house; how could it not be your place?"

"You know what pisses me off?" I point a finger at her. "This is our house. Do I need to remind you again?" Her cheeks get pink as she thinks of the last time she called this my house. I waited for the kids to go to bed and then ate her out on the couch for an hour, never letting her come until she said what I wanted her to say.

"Christopher," she hisses out my name.

"It's the first time since he's been back from Florida. I thought it would be good for him to have time with the girls and not feel like I was breathing down his neck. I did it more for the girls than anyone else," I admit finally. "How was he to you?"

"He was fine. Cordial, the way I wanted it to be. He looks like he's aged ten years."

"Well, his son died," I point out, "and the way we found out he's been dealing with it for a while, the guilt will sometimes push you even lower than you think you are."

"I can't imagine." She takes a deep breath. "But that's Eddie's journey."

"It is." I watch her. "But whatever his journey is, it's going to be the girls' journey also."

"It will be part of their journey," she agrees. "A very, very small part of their journey, you know why?"

"No, but I'm sure you'll tell me."

"Because we are going to make sure the rest of their journeys are filled with so many things that it won't matter. It'll always be their journey that their dad died and there will always be memories of before Dad died and after Dad died. But there will be so many more journeys and memories after he died that they'll fill up all the gaps and all the holes. I know this because you'll make sure we do it together. Me and you." I'm about to tell her I love her when she holds up her hand. "And by the way, I love you." I laugh. "I said it first."

I can't help but shake my head. "Fine, you said it first today."

"To me that's called a win," she says. "Did you pack?"

"I'm packing tonight," I tell her, and she gasps.

"The flight is literally at seven o'clock tomorrow

morning."

"It'll take me ten minutes to pack. I need shorts, shirts, and a couple of pants."

"How insane will the next two weeks be?" she asks of my family's annual vacation.

"It's going to be over the top. The girls are going to be spoiled to no end. We are going to have crazy, wild vacation sex." I smile at her. "It's going to be fucking glorious."

"We still have the girls," she reminds me, "and I think there are two beds in one room."

"Never." I shake my head. "I got us a two-bedroom suite."

"Of course you did."

"The girls have two beds. We have one very big bed." I wink at her. "I made a list."

She throws her head back and laughs but grabs my T-shirt on the sides with both hands. "We are never going to get to the end of our list."

"Good," I tell her, grabbing her face. "That means we have a lot of dates in our future." I kiss her lips. "I love you, by the way."

Her forehead hits my chest. "Always has to one-up me."

"Keeps you on your toes, baby." I tip her chin up with my fingers and bend my head to kiss her. My tongue slides into her mouth, and she melts in my arms.

"I got it." Luna comes into the closet, and I pull back. "I'm going to bring this one." She holds up her white-and-pink bear.

"That's a good one," Koda praises, wrapping her arms around my waist. "You can pack that in your backpack."

"It doesn't fit," she tells her and looks away from her mother, who disconnects herself from me.

"What do you mean, it doesn't fit?" She puts her hands on her hips. "It was empty."

"I added things," she explains, twirling around in the closet, pretending she's dancing with her bear.

"What things?" she asks her. "Let me go and see." She walks out of the closet, taking Luna with her. "You." She turns and points at me. "Pack your stuff."

Luna smirks at me. "You're in trouble, mister." She smiles and then is ushered out of the bedroom.

The kids are so excited for the trip the next day that when my parents show up to take them out for ice cream, I give a sigh of relief. I quickly run upstairs to take a shower, walking out with a towel around my hips, and one in my hand as I towel off my hair, seeing the bed empty but my closet light on. "What are you doing?" I laugh, making my way over to the closet.

I stop at the entrance in my tracks when I see her wearing one of my T-shirts, my luggage open that I started earlier but then pivoted when the girls asked me to go for ice cream.

She turns to me, the black ring box in her hand, and tears running down her face. "Baby," I say, taking a step into the closet, my heart is about to come out of my chest for two reasons. One, she found the ring and hates it, or two, she doesn't want to actually marry me. I feel like I'm going to throw up.

She looks at me and then down at the ring. "I wasn't snooping," she whispers. "I just wanted to finish packing for you so we could go to bed."

"One, I don't care if you snoop in my clothes," I say softly. "I have nothing to hide from you."

"I know." She looks down at the box in her hand. "The last time I went through his jacket, I found—"

"Baby," I say, my heart breaking that this is the memory she has. "I love you," I tell her, my heart beating in my chest because I know what I'm doing. I mean, I don't know what I'm doing, but I'm doing it, and it's nothing like I had planned. "Are you happy?"

"You have no idea." She shakes her head and smiles through the tears. "I don't think I've ever been this happy before."

"Good, that means my job is done for the day."

"Christopher."

"Are you going to marry me?" I just blurt it out, and the shock on her face is right away. "I asked you a question."

"Um," she stutters, "um…"

"So you don't want to marry me?"

"Are you serious?" she whispers.

"Well, I planned on doing this on vacation with roses and champagne, but it seems nothing with us will ever be conventional." I walk to her. "I'm sorry that you found it while you were packing my bag." I grab the box from her and get down on my knee in the middle of my closet, with a towel around my waist and her in my T-shirt. "But this is where it's going to happen." She puts her hand to her mouth. "I know we didn't find each other the way normal fairy tales are written." She smiles. "But I don't give a shit because this is our story, and we get to write it."

"Yes," she says, and I stop talking, "you asked me before if I was going to marry you." She walks to me, holding my face in her hands and bending down to kiss my lips. "I love you. You make me happy. You make the girls happy. You put us first every single time. With you, I never have to doubt my worth. With you, I never have to doubt if you love me. With you, I feel like I could take on the world."

"You could have taken on the world before me, baby, because you're that warrior."

"See, right there is another reason I'm going to marry you." She kisses my lips. "Now, can we go to bed?"

"Oh, yeah," I agree, getting up and tugging her around her waist, "but I want to make love to you with my ring on you and nothing else."

"Ohh." She looks at me. "I think I have a list of what I want to do with my hand with your ring on it." It's me who laughs as I put her back down and open the black box, showing her the oval ring with an extra band on the top and bottom. "The top band is for Rain, the bottom is for Luna," I tell her, and she gasps when I put it on her finger. "It's the three of you."

"Christopher." She looks down at the ring. "It's the most beautiful ring I've ever seen." She looks at me. "And that you included the girls." She shakes her head. "How did I get so lucky?"

I grab her face. "No, the question is how did I get so lucky?" I'm dragging her to bed when my phone starts ringing on the bedside table. "Ignore it," I say, getting into bed with her. The phone rings again and again.

"You should maybe answer that," she says, and I huff, turning and grabbing the phone. "It's Dylan."

"This better be fucking good," I hiss into the phone.

"Have you checked your texts?" he asks.

"No, I've been busy," I tell him, looking back at Koda, who is admiring her ring. "Why?"

He laughs. "Stone is losing his mind." He can't stop laughing. I don't know what I'm expecting him to say, but it's not what comes next. "Zoey just sent a picture of her and Nash at their wedding last night."

EPILOGUE TWO

Dakoda

One year later

"HAVE YOU PACKED your suit?" I stick my head out of my closet to look at Christopher, who is lying on the bed.

He looks up from the phone in his hand and nods. "Yeah, baby, I packed that and my shoes."

"It's going to be on the beach. Are we wearing shoes?" I look at him, panic rushing in when I put my hand to my forehead. "I thought on the beach we would be barefoot." I turn to look in my closet, seeing if there are shoes in there I can use since we leave in the morning and there is no time to shop. We're going on the family vacation, and since all the family will be there, we decided to get married on the beach. My parents are also flying out with us. Everyone is so excited about it.

"That's even better," he says, "I'll take the shoes out."

"Well, what about everyone else? Are they wearing

shoes?" I rush back into my closet, seeing two pairs of white shoes. "I mean, I had the dress altered in bare feet," I say, my voice cracking, "so it's not even going to look good."

"Hey." His arms wrap around me from the back. "You need to relax. You are going to make yourself sick again." He kisses my neck. "This whole month as soon as you talk about the wedding, you throw up. If I didn't know how much you loved me, I would think that would be a sign."

"It's not a sign," I say softly, turning in his arms. "Actually—" I stop when Rain rushes into the room.

"Christopher," she calls his name like the house is on fire. He lets me go quickly to rush to her. "Grandpa Justin said I could practice with the big kids at his hockey camp."

"Did he?" Christopher says to her as the two of them walk out of the room together. "That's going to be cool. You're going to show those boys a thing or two." Rain has excelled in hockey and was one of the top scorers on her team last year, and she played a level up. She's also in all sorts of different skating classes throughout the week. Power skating, stickhandling, three-on-three, figure skating, which she fucking hated, but apparently, it made her skate faster. Christopher took her to every one when he was home and not on the road. It was the sweetest thing to see the two of them leave together. Luna liked skating but she wasn't a diehard like Rain, so she stuck to learning how to skate on the weekends. "Baby." Christopher comes back into the room. "Aren't you coming with us?"

"I have to pack," I tell him. "I don't want to forget any—" I rush to the bathroom when I feel it happening. "Oh no, not again." I make it to the toilet with a second to spare before my dinner sits at the bottom of the bowl.

"Baby." Christopher turns on the faucet at the sink and hands me a glass of water. "I'm canceling the wedding," he declares. "I don't give a shit; we can get married in a fucking lawyer's office with no one there." I look over at him, grabbing the glass of water and rinsing out my mouth while he grabs a white washcloth, wetting it and then coming over to squat beside me. "This is fucking stupid."

"What is going on in here?" I look over his shoulder at Justin and Caroline, who rush in. "Is she sick again?"

"It's this wedding." Christopher gets up, throwing his hands up. "All this stress, we are canceling the fucking wedding." He puts his hands on his hips and I see Caroline's eyes go big while Justin agrees with him.

"We can get you guys married tomorrow." Justin pulls out his phone. "With no one there."

"That's what we need." Christopher points at him. "You'll take the kids with you and say, I don't know, we forgot something."

"Your passport is expired," Justin offers, and Caroline just looks at him.

"His passport?" She shakes her head. "He travels with his team for hockey to Canada. You think he's not going to know that his passport is expired?"

"Good point," Christopher says, "we can say I

misplaced it, and I'm going to find it."

"Oh, yeah," Justin agrees, "we need a marriage license, which you have, and then we need a judge to sign off on it, I think. Let me look up eloping."

"No one is eloping," Caroline says. "We've barely recovered from Zoey last year."

"I'm not eloping," I finally say. "We're going to get married in front of our families."

"Not if you keep getting sick," Christopher counters. "It's been over a month now, and it's every single time you talk about the wedding."

"It's not every single time I talk about the wedding," I snap. "It's usually after I eat or in the morning." I look up at the ceiling, blinking away the tears. "Can we not discuss this?"

"Yeah, we aren't," Christopher says. "It's a done deal."

"So you don't want to marry me?" I try to turn it on him, and now I can see Justin's head tilt to the side and his eyebrows pinch together, and Caroline folds her arms over her chest. "If you don't want to marry me, you should just say you don't want to marry me and get it over with."

"What?" Christopher whispers.

"You seem not to want to marry me, so fine, call off the wedding." I walk toward the bathroom door. Caroline moves over to Justin's side, pushing him out of the way to give me space to walk out. "I'll tell the girls the wedding is canceled, and you don't want to marry me." I blink away the tears. I know in my heart he wants to marry me, but I've been a hormonal mess for over a month. I fan my face to stop the tears. "Girls!" I shout for them.

"Are you crazy?" Christopher shouts from behind me. "Don't you dare tell them that."

"Why? It's the truth. You've been so focused on canceling the wedding that maybe it's you who doesn't want to get married." I look at him as the girls come into the room. "So this is your way out, to blame it on me."

"Have you—" He looks at the girls. "Can you take the girls out of the room?" He looks over at his father, who looks like he's seen a ghost, and Caroline, who is trying not to laugh.

"Oh no," I say, "no way, mister, you asked for it now."

"Say sorry," Justin says under his breath. "Just say sorry."

"I'm sorry." Christopher takes his father's advice.

"No." I shake my head. "After everything that I've been worried about. The logistics of the wedding. Making sure my dress was perfect so you would think I was the most beautiful bride. To getting the girls to have the same dress as me, but still their own style. To dealing with Matthew not to go overboard for the wedding reception. To making sure everything was perfect with Sofia. To counting down the days until I get to marry you. You tell me to call off the wedding."

"It's making you sick," he says, his voice cracking.

"Good God, it's not making me sick. I'm sick for another reason."

"Idiot," Caroline mumbles under her breath.

"I had this whole thing planned out." I throw my

hands in the air. "I was going to tell you on our wedding night."

"Oh my God," Justin says, putting his hand to his mouth, finally getting it.

"I'm pregnant," I finally hiss out, watching Christopher's face.

"What?" he asks, turning his head to the side a bit. "What did you say?"

"I said I'm pregnant." I put my hands on my stomach, and the girls gasp. "I'm going to have a baby," I finally tell him the secret I've been keeping for over a month. "I thought it was just the stress of the wedding planning, but then I would get nauseated and I couldn't smell certain foods. I took a test, just to cross pregnancy off the list. Turns out I couldn't scratch that off the list because I was with a baby."

"You have a baby in your belly?" Luna comes over to put her hand on my stomach. "Is it a boy or a girl?"

"We don't know yet." I look down at her.

"You're having a baby?" Rain asks softly, coming to me. I look at her face and worry that I should have pulled her aside. She might be only seven, but it feels like she's grown up a lot the past year.

"Yeah." I nod, then she looks over at Christopher.

"You are going to be the baby's dad?" I don't know if she's asking Christopher or telling him. "Are you still going to take me to hockey and do things with me?"

"Oh my," Caroline says.

"What do you mean?" Christopher asks. "Of course I'm going to do things with you. Why would you think

I wouldn't?"

"Because you're going to have a girl of your own," she states, and my mouth just opens, never expecting this.

Christopher is in front of her in two steps, which makes up the whole length of the room. "Rain, first of all, you are my girls," he reassures her. "You'll always be my first girl."

"Am I your girl?" Luna asks him when she gets to his side.

"You are my girl." He nods, then turns to look at Rain. "No matter how many babies your mom and I have, you two are *my* girls." He puts emphasis on the my.

"Is the baby going to call you Daddy?" Rain asks.

"Um, yeah," he replies, smiling, then looking up at me, tears in his eyes, "or Dad."

"Do I have to call you Dad?" Rain asks almost in a whisper as she looks down at her feet.

"No." Christopher shakes his head, taking her hands in his. "Of course not."

"Can I call you Dad?" she whispers, and I see a tear falling down her cheek.

He puts his finger under her chin and lifts her head up to see in her eyes. "Do you want to call me Dad?" he asks.

"You do stuff like a dad," she says. "You take me to school and pick me up. You give me a bath and tuck me in. You take me to hockey." I can't help the tears falling down my face. "So you're like a dad."

"Well, I do all that because I love you," he says,

wiping her tears off her cheeks.

"So I can call you Dad?" she asks, twisting her hands in front of her.

"Yeah," he says, pulling her into his arms as she lays her head on his shoulder.

"Do I call him Dad too?" Luna asks, looking at me and then at Christopher. "I can call him Dad too, right?"

"Of course you can," he says, opening his arms for her to go into them. He kisses both their heads. "You can call me whatever you want to call me. If you want to call me Dad, call me Dad. If you want to call me Uncle Christopher, you can call me Uncle Christopher."

"I want to call you Dad," Rain declares, pushing away from his shoulder. "Everyone at hockey thinks you're my dad," she shares, shocking us. "When we are on the ice, they say Rain's dad is the coolest."

"Well, I am," he deadpans, and I roll my eyes.

"Second coolest," Justin interjects, and I look at them, seeing Caroline in his arms, wiping her own tears away. "I was first coolest."

"You're the coolest grandpa," Luna corrects, "not dad. That's Uncle Chrissy." She gasps, "Oh no, I forgot." Christopher laughs so she doesn't feel bad. "That's okay." She looks at him. "Right, it's okay?"

"It's okay," he agrees with her. "Now how about you two take Grandma and Grandpa downstairs so we can have ice cream to celebrate."

Caroline claps her hands together. "We should have ice cream waffle cones," she suggests, and the girls' eyes light up, "with sprinkles."

"I'm assuming the wedding isn't canceled?" Justin says, slapping Christopher's arm and then squeezing it.

"I'm going to go brush my teeth." I walk around them, going to the bathroom while they usher the kids downstairs. He walks into the bathroom, leaning his hip against the counter.

"We need to talk." He folds his arms over his chest. I spit out the toothpaste before I rinse my mouth out. Only after I'm done does he pull me to him. "Number fucking one," he starts, "you are always beautiful. It doesn't matter what you wear, you always take my breath away, and number fucking two, how could you keep this from me?"

"I didn't want to keep it from you. I just thought it would be something special. Like, congrats, you're married and now stuck with me for life and I'm giving you a child." I put my hands on his chest. "Like a two-for-one special."

"You make me happy; the girls make me happy." I smile, thinking to myself that I can't believe I've been as lucky as I have been to find him in my life. "You having my baby." He shakes his head. "I have to tell you, there are no words that can describe what that does to me."

"I'm having our child," I correct him.

"My baby," he jokes, "I put him in there."

"I'm carrying him," I inform him.

"Yes, but you wouldn't be carrying him if I didn't put him there."

"Do you not want to put anything in there again?" I ask, and he laughs.

"I want to put it in you right now," he admits, "but my parents are downstairs, and you have that glow on your face after I fuck you, so that's a no."

"I wore that glow for two weeks last year on vacation. Several times a day," I remind him.

"Yes, but everyone was so focused on Zoey fucking up that they didn't notice your glow."

"Good to know," I say. "Now kiss me so we can go down and eat ice cream."

He leans down and kisses my lips. "I'll kiss you every day of my whole life," he declares right before he kisses me again, "in this life and in the next." My breath catches. "I'll find you no matter what life we're in." He kisses me again. "Because I can't live without you. There is no life I want to live in that doesn't have you in it." I get on my tippy-toes. "We may not have known at the beginning, but I think deep down I always knew"—he smiles—"that I was meant for you, baby."

Made in the USA
Columbia, SC
03 May 2025